Also By Laura Lukasavage

DARK INHERITANCE

Moonlight Secret

Moonlight Changes

STANDALONE

See You On The Other Side

Dark Inheritance

~Book Three~

Moonlight Legacy

Laura Lukasavage

First published in 2021 by Amazon

Copyright Laura Lukasavage

ISNB : 978-1-7366905-7-4

First Edition

Website:

https://lauralukasavageauthor.mailchimpsites.com/

Cover Design, Editing and Proofreading by Star River

Author Services

You can find them on Instagram at

@star_river_author_services

Dedication

For all those out there experiencing a loss who feel life is too hard to keep going. I'm here to tell you there's nothing you can't do or overcome in this world if you put your mind to it. Have faith and push for your own happiness and never forget where you come from or those who love you.

For all those who supported and helped me along in my dream. To my little sister Christina and my grandmother Rose, who helped me along the way to having my dreams become a reality.

Awake

LOGAN

My face feels unbearably warm and dry. All except one spot. The throbbing mess that is my forehead is overly moist in nature. Too moist. Making one thought take over my mind. *Am I bleeding?*

The pulse vibrating beneath my skin isn't only adding to my discomfort and confusion. It's making any attempt at opening my eyes very painful. Angering the throbbing monster that hides just beneath the surface. Increasing its intensity with every attempt to pry my eyes open.

Forgetting my eyes and the angry demon occupying my head, I try to focus on the rest of my body. *Everything feels intact.* I do a quick check, counting out fingers and limbs. All present. While taking mental inventory, I notice the dirt beneath my hands as it creeps up under my nails.

How did I end up on the ground?

I attempt to open my eyes once more, but they seem to be glued shut. Fighting past the increased throbbing as I continue the struggle to pry them apart, I try to recall the events that led to me ending up here.

Disoriented.

Alone.

Bloody.

How long have I been sitting here?

Pushing my legs out from under me, I can't remember ever feeling this stiff. My mind locates something. It's replaying a conversation with Angela. *What were we talking about?* I push past the pain trying to uncover the memory. A few seconds pass, and then I remember. Angela and I were talking about Amberly and me.

Amberly.

My eyes come unglued as they fly open, and the bright light hits them, bringing tears to the surface. I open and close them a few times before they adjust to the new view. Looking at my surroundings, my chest tightens at my findings. For as far as I can see, bodies cover every inch of the hard, dirt-covered forest floor. Blood stains the earth all around me. I jump to my feet so fast that I have to steady myself on a boulder nearby.

My legs are limp noodles, leaving me unsteady and unbalanced. Wobbling like a new toddler trying to take its first steps. Head spinning out of control, I raise my hand to it and quickly pull it away. The touch sends a painful shock running through my head. When I bring my hand down to inspect it, it's crimson in color.

That warm, wet feeling was blood.

Stabilizing myself, I test my legs, placing one in front of the other, slowly at first. Once they feel sturdy enough, I make my way around the motionless bodies at my feet, inspecting each one as I go. Looking only long enough to make sure it's not someone I know. Relief washes over me when I notice that so far, they are all from the opposite team. However, it's quickly replaced when I feel a tug at my heart.

Death is never something to take lightly. These people all had families just like we do, and now they will never get to see them again. All because they listened to some crazy psycho who decided he wanted to run the world. And for what?

I find myself asking why he couldn't just be happy with the power he already has. He's one of the strongest beings on the earth. Why does he feel the need to be the one to control it? I suddenly feel anger replace the sadness. This man came here to take Amberly from us, and for the first time, I find myself wondering if he succeeded.

My memory starts to flood back to me as I remember Amberly on the ground covered in blood and Aidan hovering over her. *He must have knocked me out.* I continue to look around frantically, needing to find someone. Anyone. I need to know what took place once I was out of commission. I need to know that she's ok. That everyone is.

I pass more bodies on my way, and this time I see many of the guards' from home, their bodies lifeless on the earth floor. Among them lay many of the pack. I close my eyes. I can't let myself feel their loss, not now. It's not time. I need to find her parents, Troy, Angela, and Amara.

Did he take Amara too?

I enter the cave, hearing nothing. It's so quiet, too quiet. I move deeper at a slow pace, unsure of what I will find. My body is tense, ready for an attack from any direction. I'm ten feet deep when I hear someone running. They are coming in my direction and fast. I stand my ground, ready for anything. It's too dark to make anything out past a few feet in front of me. Before I notice anyone approaching, someone tackles me to the ground. Just as I'm ready to throw them off of me, a familiar voice reaches my ears.

"Logan. Oh, my God. I thought you were dead." Angela's voice is on the edge of tears.

I've never found her voice as comforting as it is right now.

"Angela."

She gets off me slowly, moving to sit on the floor in the open spot next to where I'm now lying. She's close enough that I can see the tears running down her face, and I have to stop myself from reaching over to wipe them off her cheeks.

Brushing them away herself, she stands slowly then turns to offer me her hand. "Come on. Everyone will want to see you."

I take it and stand up. Not releasing her hand, I ask, "Everyone?"

She doesn't face me when she speaks. "Yes. Everyone is in the common room."

"You mean everyone who's still alive." I pause and look back in the direction of the exit. "I saw all the bodies. What happened? I don't remember much, I'm afraid."

She turns back in my direction but looks at the ground. "A lot. We can talk once everyone knows you're ok."

"Angela. Please."

The hesitation radiating off her is overwhelming. I immediately know something isn't right. "Everything happened so fast. One minute we were all sitting around talking, waiting, and next, they came from every direction. We couldn't even sense them coming."

I lower my voice, making my tone as gentle as I can. "Has that ever happened before?"

She shakes her head. "No. Especially when we are trying to find someone."

"I don't remember much, myself. I remember Julian looking at me, and I knew it was time to take Amberly and run, so we did. She fought me like crazy, but finally, I got her behind the cave, and then," I pause, trying to recall the events as they unfolded. "Then the next thing I knew, I went flying."

"Like I said, they surprised us all."

"After that, I remember waking up under some branches with Amara and Troy, and I went looking for Amberly."

Excitement is plain in her tone. "Did you find her?"

"Yes."

"I don't like the way you said that."

Sighing, my body hunches forward. "I remember her being stabbed and Aidan being there. I think he's the one who knocked me out the second time."

"That's what I was afraid of." Her words are so low I have to strain to hear them. "But wait. Did you say she was stabbed?"

Trying to pull the memory to the front of my mind makes my head throb in protest. "I'm not sure, but I think so."

Tugging on my hand, she says, "We need to tell Aaron."

I hold her in place. "I looked," I pause, not sure if I want to hear the answer to my question. "I looked around, but I didn't see Troy."

For the first time, through the darkness, I think I see a smile on her face. "He's fine. He's in the cave waiting for you. He's been a little," her smile widens, "tense."

"I can't say I blame him. We've never really been around this much violence before."

"That's not what I meant."

Confused, I ask. "Ok, then what do you mean?"

Her smile falters. "He's been tense because no one could find you. We thought you were dead."

I flash her a reassuring grin. "It's only been a few hours, so he didn't have that much time to worry."

"Logan. It's been almost two days."

If it wasn't so dark in here, I think my reaction would have scared her, so I'm grateful for it for the first time. "Two days!"

She nods her head. I can hear the sadness in her voice as she pulls my hand to follow her once more. "Please, can we join the others now? I promise I'll fill in all the blanks when we get there. Everyone's worried long enough, don't you think?"

I nod.

Two days. How could I have been knocked out for that long?

I glance at Angela through the darkness, and everything inside is screaming. *Something more is going on.* I feel a strong tug at my heart, hoping and praying it has nothing to do with Amberly. Angela hadn't mentioned anyone other than Troy. I'm elated that he's fine. Losing him would be like losing a limb and a brother. Irreplicable. So, I'm happy he made it through this nightmare. But what about everyone else?

✳✳✳

TROY

I can't stop pacing no matter how hard I want to. I feel like it's the only thing I've been doing since everyone re-entered the cave. My thoughts run wild with what could have happened to Logan and Amberly. Of course, my brain jumps to the worst possible outcome.

They're dead.

Gone.

You'll never see them again.

My mind is running rampant with these thoughts, but that's not the worst of it. I see them. Dead, bloody. I watch as they die in front of my eyes repeatedly while I do nothing to stop it. Nightmares. That's how I've spent the last two nights, but now these pictures are taking over my waking thoughts.

"Troy, will you please sit down?" I've never heard Amara try to sound gentle, and honestly, it's making me feel more uneasy.

I wish I could sit still, if for no other reason than to make Amara and the others feel a little less tense. However, the harder I try to reel myself in, the worse I seem to get. I mean, how are you supposed to stay calm when the two people who mean the most to you in this world just vanished?

Poof.

Gone.

Without any explanation.

They're either dead, or Vladimir's army took them, and either way, it's not a good situation. It had taken everyone in the pack to hold me back from going after the warriors to check for myself. However, my magic is no match against that many wolves, so I was forced to sit back and put my feet up.

Figuratively speaking, of course.

The thought that they are lost to me forever is gut-wrenching. The two people who knew me best in this world. Showed that they loved me despite who I am. I know I'm a handful, and my jokes are horrible, but they never cared. They always laughed and built me up. We never missed a day together. Well, that was until Amberly took off on her little wolf ride. Then everything changed.

Anger boils in the pit of my stomach.

No.

Don't do that.

It's not her fault for wanting to understand what she felt was missing in her life. To fill that void. I can't blame her for that. No matter what the cost is to us in the end.

Amara's soft tone pulls my thoughts back on track. "I get it, believe me. But Angela should be back anytime now."

"Not like she will have any new news," I mumble in frustration.

This is taking too long. We need to try something else. Anything else I need to know they are alright before I go mad.

"You don't know that."

I turn my back to her. "We've all had our turn of looking."

"It doesn't mean we didn't miss a spot. They could still be out there."

My mind takes over once more, envisioning the worst-case scenario. I'm afraid of what I'll turn into if the worst becomes my reality. Who will I become without them?

"What if there's nothing to be found?" I whisper.

She stands up, walks over to my side, and places a hand on my shoulder. "Don't think like that. I promise you we will find them."

I glance up at her and find myself grateful that she didn't go missing too. It hasn't been easy coming to this new village. I've always felt out of place here, but when Amara decided to stay, I was more than happy about it. Since then, she's made me feel more comfortable, almost like I could belong here too.

Two outsiders. The thought brings a small grin to my face.

She's a lone wolf. *What are they called again? Beta? No, that was Angela and Julian's position.* The thought of Julian sends chills over my body. They had found him shortly after the fight ended. I've never seen a look like that on Aaron's face before that night. He looked lost, defeated. Losing one of his Betas couldn't have been easy. I know when we find Amberly, it's going to destroy her.

Ok, enough. Think, distract yourself. What was it called? A Delta? No, that was someone already in the pack but at the bottom. Amara is an outsider. She comes from a different pack, a different world.

Now, I remember. She's called a Disperser. From what I heard among the group, that was normal in Aaron's pack. Angela and Julian, *ugh, get back on track.* They were both found and rescued by Aaron. So, Amara becoming part of the pack is already setting into motion, and I couldn't be happier for her. I want her to find a nice home again and to stop being afraid. She deserves that. We all do.

I'm just about to thank her for everything she's done since we returned to the cave when I see Angela re-entering the room out of the corner of my eye, and moments later, he comes into view.

"Logan."

Amara looks at me before she turns around. Following me with her eyes as I make my way across the room and to their side.

Filling In Some Of The Blanks

ANGELA

Troy reaches our side in a few short strides and, without warning, throws his arms up and around Logan, who smiles and hugs him back. Looking at them, I can't suppress my smile. *At least I did one thing right today.*

Moments later, Amara reaches our side. "Thank God."

Smirking, I say, "I found him just as he was entering the cave."

Looking at them, she asks me. "Where was he?"

My eyes scan over Logan's dirt and blood-covered clothes. "I don't know."

Amara moves closer to me as she whispers. "Did you tell him?"

Glancing at the ground, I mumble. "No."

"I think he will take it better coming from you than someone else."

"I agree."

The smile on Logan's face reaches his eyes as he pats Troy on the back playfully. "I just don't know how I'm going to tell him."

The boys end their conversation and walk over to us.

Troy flashes me a big goofy grin, and I have to stifle a laugh. "Thanks for finally finding him. I was just starting to worry."

"I didn't find him. He found me."

"He did say you bumped into each other in the cave, I forgot."

I smile widely. "So sadly, I can't take the credit for returning him to you."

We all look around at each other and laugh for the first time in days.

Logan ends our laughter, asking. "So, where is everyone else?"

Amara and I peek at each other. I know we can't keep avoiding telling him, but I'm going to for as long as I can. "Amberly's parents are in their room. They wanted," I pause, thinking of the right words to use, "some downtime before we all meet in the dining area in a few hours."

"To do what?"

Troy's words break through the silence. "To strategize."

Logan stares at him confused, "Meaning?"

Troy releases a sigh, "A lot happened while you were missing, man."

"Well, sorry my being unconscious was such an inconvenience."

From the look Troy is giving me, I know it's my turn to speak. "That's not what he meant, Logan."

"Then what?" He pauses, looking from Troy to Amara before bringing his attention back to me. "Will someone please tell me what's going on? And where are Amberly and Julian?"

I can barely hold back the tears at the sound of their names. Knowing my voice will only betray me, I turn away from them. I hear Logan walking towards me. Turning slightly, I see Troy puts his hand out to stop him in his place as he shakes his head back and forth.

Logan removes Troy's hand from his body and grabs me lightly by the wrist. "Angela?"

I don't turn around.

I can't.

Amara chokes out the words that I couldn't. "Logan, Julian is dead." Not releasing my wrist, he turns around to look in her direction, "and we can't find Amberly anywhere."

***

AARON

Removing my hand from Jocelyn's shoulder, I take a seat on the bed next to her. It's been two days since the fight ended, and we all returned to the cave to nurse our injuries. It wasn't until hours had passed that I realized Amberly wasn't in the cave with everyone else. We looked high and low for her for over a day. It was then that we realized she was nowhere to be found, which could only mean one thing.

She was taken.

Or dead, according to some people's opinions. Troy has been as nervous as a horse with a snake on its tail, making everyone else around here more uncomfortable than they already are. I can't say I blame him, though. I've been feeling it myself but being the pack leader comes with certain responsibilities and obligations. I can't allow myself to let my feelings bubble to the surface. I need to be here for the pack, for my family.

However, the blame still lingers and with it the truth. Somewhere amid all the craziness, we had lost track of our daughter. We didn't realize until way too late that someone had taken her from our home. Much too late to go after her. So, we did the only thing we could.

Regroup.

Heal.

Recharge.

And now it's time to plan.

"Jocelyn."

She looks at me through puffy, red eyes. For the last two days, the only time she stopped crying was when sleep would overtake her. It took all my strength to keep her from running into the woods to find Amberly the moment we realized she was nowhere in the cave.

"It's time," I whisper.

She takes in a fast, deep breath as she nods her head. I put my head in my hands, needing a moment to collect myself. Taking in a deep breath of my own, I stand and offer her my hand. She looks at it hesitantly before reaching out and putting hers in mine.

I've never seen her so defeated. We can't lose hope. I know our little girl is alive out there somewhere, and I intend to do everything I can to find her and bring her back home where she belongs.

✳✳✳

SERENITY

Aayda's voice pulls me back to reality. "How are you feeling?"

I open my eyes slowly. "I'm fine. Please, don't worry about me. There are more important things."

Anger flares on her face and in her voice. "There is nothing more important than our family."

With great sadness, I reply, "I know how you feel." I turn to Johnathan, "but right now, the most important thing is to find Amberly before it's too late."

Johnathan walks over to where we are sitting. "I couldn't agree with you more. But we can worry about her and you at the same time."

"There is nothing you can do for me, and you both know that."

Aayda places a hand on mine. "That doesn't mean we are going to stop trying."

"And I wouldn't expect anything less. But you know how you can help me."

With sad eyes, she turns to Johnathan. "We don't even know if she's still alive."

Closing my eyes, I whisper to no one in particular. "I do. She's alive." I open my eyes and look past them, "I can feel it."

A spark lit Aayda's eyes. "Then there's still hope."

I stumble over my next words, knowing it's going to hurt them more than me. "Yes. For her. She is our people's only hope. But you need to know there is nothing that can be done for me."

Her pained face returned to me. "But Amberly. She has your power. Can't she heal you?"

I shake my head and look at Johnathan sadly as he answers for me. "No. The main drawback of a healers' powers is no one can heal them once they can no longer heal themselves."

Aayda drops to her knees at my side, and I feel the sadness radiating from her in waves. Through her sobs, she says. "There has to be something. We can't just give up."

I place my hand on her cheek. "You have to. It's time. We need to focus on finding Amberly and bringing her home. She is the only hope our future has."

"She's only a child. I don't see her being able to do what you're hoping she can. I understand your need for her to be everything you think she is, but I think it's time to let that go. A child of eighteen cannot win the battle and war ahead and sure as hell can't lead and unite the forest."

"Aayda, how can you be so blind?"

"I'm not. I'm realistic. Even after all the weeks of training, she didn't last long, and she ended up being taken. What does that tell you?"

I close my eyes and release a tension-filled sigh. "She is still young. I remember a time when we all were." I look at them both. "How quickly you seem to forget."

Johnathan smiles. "Serenity is right. It wasn't until we were in our twenties that we can honestly say we mastered our powers. As for Amberly, she only just turned eighteen, and she's not like us. We have our powers, but she's all of us combined." He looks down at Aayda. "She needs time to grow into them just like we did. And she needs guidance."

Aayda closes her eyes, and I can see in her body language that she doesn't feel the same way we do. "Even if you're both right. She's gone. She's been gone for days." Opening her eyes, she continues. "Who's to say she hasn't already been turned? She may be alive like you believe, but if she's turned, none of it matters either way."

Johnathan's eyes hold a world of worry as he says. "Let us pray that that is not the case."

***

AMARA

After I blurted out what Logan was begging to hear, everyone went silent. Not a word has been spoken in what feels like hours. However, I'm pretty sure we've only been sitting here in silence for a matter of minutes.

Standing here looking around at each one of their despair-ridden faces, I can only imagine what's going through each of their minds. I haven't known them long, and I didn't grow up with them, so I can't feel the loss as hard as they are, but I still feel it.

Amberly saved my life in more ways than just the obvious. She gave me a home again, friends, and a reason to live. I didn't realize what I had shut out of my life until Amberly entered it. I was so closed off from people and the world around me. I was living in fear. Afraid to let anyone in. Afraid to lose someone all over again.

That fear consumed me for a very long time. But Amberly and everyone here made me realize I couldn't go on living like I was and that it was ok to need people. Her loss is affecting me more than I let on, and so is Julian's. I may not have known him as well as I know everyone else, but the way Amberly and the others would talk about him, I'm sad to know that I'll never get that chance. I mean, yeah, there was that one kiss that no one will speak about, but after that night, I didn't share many words with him.

The thought of Julian makes my heart ache. Not for me, no, but for Amberly. I know she's alive out there somewhere. I can feel it. And I know that when she returns, it will be to a world that no longer has the man she loves in it. I don't wish that upon anyone. I don't know how she will overcome that loss when she returns.

Logan's angry words pull me back from my thoughts. "What do you mean she's nowhere to be found?"

Angela's voice is full of sorrow as she answers him. "Our best guess is they took her back to Vladimir, which means there's still hope. If he wanted her dead, I think they would have killed her here with the rest of us."

He replies through bared teeth. "And how do we know they didn't kill her and take her body back as proof that the job was done right this time?"

Angela and Troy look at each other with sadness and despair echoing in their eyes, but they say nothing.

Logan screams. "See, you don't know. What if I'm right? What if she's dead, and we're sitting here doing nothing?"

Silence falls in the open air around us once more. Everyone's afraid to speak a word. For me, it's because at this moment I don't know what to say. There is nothing to make this better or change our current situation. I believe everyone else is staying silent in fear that the next words out of their mouths will only make Logan angrier.

My gaze lands on Troy, who has his eyes closed. His mouth is spread in a thin line as his brows meet in the middle of his face. I visibly see beads of sweat forming on his forehead.

He's concentrating hard on something.

But what?

I feel like I'm looking at Troy for the very first time. He is rather handsome. His shoulder-length, sandy blonde hair curls in just the right way. I can picture myself running my long fingers through it. *I always did like a man with longer hair*, I laugh to myself.

Troy's eyes fly open, and for a moment, I thought he heard me laugh but then I see it. In his eyes. A new light.

Whatever he was trying to do, he achieved it.

With a slight grin on his face, Troy walks over to Logan, slowly speaking in a low voice. "Focus, Logan. Think about her and focus on her energy." He pauses and waits as Logan reluctantly closes his eyes and takes in a long breath. We sit there for a few minutes before Troy asks, "Do you sense it?"

Logan's eyes fly open. "Yes."

Troy smiles. "So, do I. She's still alive, and we are going to find her."

Understanding Aidan

AMBERLY

I bludgeoned my screams into submission, not wanting to let them out, not wanting to show them my discomfort. But now I'm running out of strength, running on E, and the pain is getting so intense. Before I can stop it, my mouth opens and releases an ear-piercing scream. My head throbs, feeling like a sledgehammer is banging against it.

Something is trying to get in. *No someone.* I open my eyes a fraction of an inch, and there he is.

Aidan.

Everything comes rushing back. His power, him coming to the cave. He's trying to enter my mind, and I can't let him.

My eyes scan around the room, trying to find anything to focus on. *I can't let him in. I will not break.* My eyes pass by something the color of fire. I redirect them, moving backward until I find her.

Sage.

She's standing in the far corner chained up to a pipe that runs along the wall. I push the pain down as hard as I can, and I charge past Aidan heading in Sage's direction. I can feel the anger boiling over with each step I take. I make it a few short strides past him before I feel arms wrap around my midsection.

"Now's not the time." Aidan's tone is neutral.

"Let me go." I elbow him in the stomach, but his grip doesn't loosen, "That bitch killed Julian."

"And you'll have your pound of flesh but not now."

"Get your hands off me," I say as I try to wiggle free.

He lifts his hands above his head and takes a step back. "As you wish."

I turn my back to him, looking over my shoulder. "And don't bother trying to get in my head. It won't work."

"I wasn't trying for the reasons you're thinking."

I turn back towards him, crossing my arms over my chest in a defiant manner. "And what am I thinking since you know me so well?"

His grin sends chills down my spine. "You're thinking I'm trying to get in to control you. As the girl, Amara, I'm sure has mentioned that's one of my powers."

I nod, refusing to say anything that will give him intel on my family and friends that I pray are still alive.

"I don't wish to control you, Amberly."

"Then what is it you want from me? Why did you come to my village and kill all those people, and why did you bring me here?"

He takes a slow step towards me. "That's what I want to show you if you let me."

"I don't know you, and I sure as hell don't trust you. So, why in the world would I ever let you in my head?"

I see sorrow hiding deep in his eyes, and it makes me involuntarily suck in a breath. "Because it's the only way I can make sense of everything for you and the only way you'll believe that what I'm going to tell you is true and not manipulated."

Whatever he's selling, I ain't buying. However, I'm not stupid either. I know I'm not getting out of here, not like this. The only thing I know for sure is I need to get home, back to my family. Whatever I need to say to make that happen, I will.

Reluctantly I say. "I'll make you a deal."

Intrigued, he replies. "I'm listening."

"You give me your word that you won't try to control me if I let you in?"

He nods.

"Ok, then you can show me whatever it is, under one condition."

"Name it."

I look over to where Sage is watching us intently. "She's mine when we're done."

He glances at her before quickly turning his gaze back to me with a grin that reaches his eyes. "Deal."

AIDAN

I reach out to her mind with mine, hoping she will open it to me like she said she would. This is the only way I feel I can share the truth with her and have her believe it. She doesn't know me. Why would she trust me? The only thing she knows for sure is I came to her home and attacked her. Then there's what I'm sure Amara has told her of her time here and with me. Plenty of fun moments to share. More like nightmares. The things I've done, *don't go there. Now isn't the time. Focus on the task at hand.* Yes, the here and now. Only this moment matters.

Amberly only knows me as the enemy. Therefore why would she ever listen to me, let alone trust me? No, this is the only way. I need to show her. Make her see, make her understand this is the best and safest place for her. That I did the right thing by coming to get her. I need to show her inside. Deep inside. Past the murderer, the abandoned and abused child. I need her to see my past, what got me here. I need to show her how I know what I'm saying is the truth.

I think about all the important parts to show her, things that will make her understand me. Things that will show her that the words I'm going to say are the truth.

She's my sister.

I pull the earliest memory I think will help and move it to the front of my mind. I see Vladimir's shape inside a blur and yank it forward as I lower my shields to show her the memory.

"Someone said something to me today," I mumble.

"What was that boy? Speak up." The annoyance, clear in his voice.

"Someone told me that I don't belong here. That I'm not your son."

His grin turns sinister in nature. "Of course, you're not."

My heart stops. "But you told me."

He cuts me off with a vicious laugh. "You think a boy like you could have ever been from my blood?"

"I."

I'm frozen, fighting back the tears. Who would tell an eight-year-old boy that they weren't their father in such a cold-hearted way? I know he's never been nice, but my whole life, he's told me I'm his son, and I will be his right-hand man one day. To take over his plan of a better world. And now, out of nowhere, he's telling me it's all been a lie. Eight years of my life, thinking this man was my father, and he's not.

"Cat got your tongue, boy?"

Biting back the tears, I stick my chin out. "No."

"Well, then what do you need to say? Spit it out."

"You told me I was your son. That you were my father."

An evil chuckle rumbles through his chest. "You live under my roof. I feed you, clothe you and give you purpose. I'm the only parent you have."

"But where did I come from? Where are my parents?"

"Don't concern yourself with such things."

Anger boils in my chest, and I have to stop myself from screaming at him. "I have a right to know."

"You should know better than to talk to me that way." He moves closer.

I drop my eyes to the ground. "I'm only saying."

"No more of this. I don't want to hear about this again. Do you understand?"

Defeated, I nod.

Ending the memory, I push it to the back of my mind and pull forth another.

"Get up." He says through bared teeth.

I'm on the ground looking up at him. I taste the blood in my mouth, turn away, and spit it two the ground. "I need a minute."

"No warrior of mine asks for a break."

"I'm not a warrior. I'm a twelve-year-old kid."

In a flash, he has me by the shirt and hauls me to my feet. "You are not a child. You are a warrior. You are not weak. Do you hear me?"

Through bared teeth, I reply. "Yes, sir."

"Good." His smile reaches his eyes as he lowers me to the ground and turns his back to me. "Now, let's go again."

Quickly he turns, and his hands fly up. I don't have time to react, let alone block his attack. I go sailing through the air once more. I hit the wall hard and crumble to the floor, but I do not get up this time.

I grab for another. This one is where I asked him about my parents again. Recalling the memory, I'm surprised that I made it anywhere with the conversation. Remembering the one we had when I was only eight years old, I wasn't expecting him to give me any answers. But answers I got that day.

"They left you for dead. I saved you and took you to raise as my own. Satisfied? Was it worth knowing?"

"They didn't want me?"

"No. But I did."

I look at him through tear-filled eyes. "Why?"

"I could sense the power in you, and I knew you would grow to be someone I would want on my side for my cause."

I looked at him, confused. "Your cause? You've mentioned it repeatedly, but you always leave out the details."

"One day, I will tell you about it, but that day is not today."

He starts to walk away, but I stop him with one last question. "Who were they?"

He turns. "Who?"

"My parents. What were their names? Who were they?"

With bitterness in his tone, he answers. "Your mother was from the witch village; her name was Jocelyn, and your father was from the wolf village, and his name was Aaron."

"Was?" I choke out the words, afraid of his answer.

"Yes. They no longer matter. They do not hold a place in your future, so they are no longer to be thought of or talked about. Do we have an understanding?"

All I can manage is a nod.

I end this memory and move on to the next. Pulling it to the front hard, needing to move on from the last. Feeling anger at him and my parents for treating a child the way they did. Vladimir, with his abuse, and my parents for discarding me like day-old meat.

Vladimir's training me once again.

Hard.

Intense.

Brutal.

"I need a break." I pant.

"Breaks are for the weak, and I didn't raise you to be weak."

He attacks again.

I deflect.

Energy almost extinguished.

"I need a minute," I beg.

"Your enemy will never give you a time out."

He lunges at me once more.

I move, barely in time. He smiles over his shoulder at me as his hands raise from his sides, and I see it too late. Fire shoots out and hits me in the chest, sending me flying across the room until my back hits the wall, and I crumble to the ground. I can hear him walking over to where I now lay. I look up at him from the ground to see him smiling down at me.

"You're weak."

"No, I only need a minute."

"Go train and come find me when you think you can take me on. I don't have time for this."

He walks away as defeat washes over me.

I leave this memory.

Share another with her. One I'm hoping will open her eyes and make her see the truth.

"She's alive." I hear Vladimir say angrily to someone.

I walk into the room. "Everything ok?"

He dismisses the other man.

"No."

I approach him slowly. "What is it?"

"A problem I didn't think I had."

"Maybe I can help?"

He looks at me with a devilish grin. "I don't think you're ready. Not for this."

I stand up straight. "I am, sir."

He approaches me as his smile widens. "You really think you're ready to kill your own sister?"

He walks past me as his words reach my ears. "Sister?"

"Yes. Did I not tell you that you had a sister?"

I look over my shoulder at him. "No, you kind of left that part out."

"Yes. Your parents had twins. You and her."

Anger starts to take hold. "Why did they keep her but not me?"

"That is a very good question. But not one I bothered to concern myself with."

"But I want to know."

"Why? It's the past. Nothing matters. They aren't a part of you anymore, remember. Stop letting them hold you back."

Annoyed, I nod my head in agreement. *"But you said you wanted her dead? Why?"*

"Because she will be the end of me." *He looks at me harshly,* *"and I don't think you're ready to follow through on what I need to be done."*

"You mean killing her?"

"There is no other choice."

Yes, there is. She's my sister. She didn't abandon me like our parents. She was a child just like me. Does she even know about me? I walk away, knowing there is nothing I can say to change his mind. Or is there?

I leave this memory and show her another of me alone, thinking, planning.

There has to be something I can do. I won't let him kill her. She's the only true family I have. My parents didn't want me, but maybe, just maybe, she will. I've never let myself need anyone, not since Vladimir told me the truth, but my sister. She's a different story. Someone untainted by the life I've lived all these years. Someone who may not have known about me and may need me as much as I need her. I will find a way around this. I will not lose her, not to this life. Not to him. I've lost enough at his hands already.

I move on to me in my astral form as I watch her. My sister. She's looking around the forest. This memory is from about a year ago. She's hiding in the forest playing some kind of game with her friends. I can sense that she feels uneasy like someone is watching her, and I wonder if it's me she's sensing. Time passes slowly, but then she finally sees the wolf, and when he talks to her, I can hear it in her mind as it echoes in my own. A power I never knew I even had.

I show her all the times I watched her. When she left home. The trip through the woods with the wolf when she nearly died after being mauled. I watched her in so many moments over the last year, I went unseen, but she didn't. I could see her heart almost like it mimicked mine. I always felt like something was missing, but I always thought that emptiness was my parents' absence, but now I know it was her. She is what I've been lacking. Seeing the goodness in her, I know there has to be some in me too.

I let her in, let her feel my emotions and thoughts in each memory. Begging her to know I mean her no harm. I drop my guard lower, showing her all my planning and why I brought her here. The real reason.

Then I feel a snap.

I open my eyes to find her panting, trying to catch her breath. Something breaks open inside of me, seeing her like this up close.

Without thinking, I walk to her side and put my arms around her reassuringly.

"Are you alright?"

She glances up at me with tear-filled eyes. "You knew all this time who we were to each other, and instead of coming to me, coming to us, you spied on me and then tore me from my home. No, I'm not alright."

I take a step back. "I never thought of it that way."

"Of course you didn't. Why would you?"

"I only wanted to get to know you. To find a way to."

She cuts me off. "You wanted to get to know me? Did you ever think I would have wanted the same?"

I feel her hurt as it becomes my own. *She's right. I wasn't thinking about her at all.*

The next words out of my mouth are ones I've never spoken before in my life. "I'm sorry. I didn't think it through."

"No kidding."

"If I could go back and do it differently, I would. But that's not one of our powers."

She's silent, and I find myself afraid to ask her the question occupying my mind.

"If I had approached you, what would you have said? Would you have wanted to know me?"

She's quiet for a moment. Pulling out of my embrace, she replies. "You're my brother. Of course, I would have wanted to know you. I would have had a million questions, but I would have wanted you in my life."

I feel the smile creeping up on my face, but the look on hers tells me to remove it before she notices. "What?"

"I don't blame you. Whatever happened, it wasn't your fault. You can't control who brought you up and the things they taught you or made you do."

I nod, not wanting to interrupt.

"But Aidan, I don't think you get what you've done."

I rub my jaw forcefully. "You think this is who I wanted to become. What I wanted to be?"

The desperation is clear in her eyes. "I'm not talking about that, Aidan."

"Oh, so you weren't talking about me being a killer?"

The word makes her flinch.

I say almost in a whisper, "I only wanted to meet you, get to know you in this way," I gesture to her with my hand, "instead of how I have been."

She looks away from me but stays silent.

Trying to hold back my anger, I ask, "How is what I did any different than what that wolf did? He watched you for many more years than I did."

I immediately regret my words as pain embeds itself in every line of her face. Walking back to her, I whisper, "I'm sorry. I didn't mean to hurt you. I just want you to understand."

Looking at me with tear-filled eyes, she says. "I can't."

"I know you felt it too. Like something was missing, and you never knew what it was. I felt the same thing. We were missing each other."

"Even if that's true, the way you did this isn't right. People are dead because of what you've done."

I look away from her for the first time. "No. That was Vladimir's doing. He wanted you all dead," my gaze returns to her, "if I didn't do what I did, all of you would have died instead of the few who did."

The waterworks start. An overflow in her eyes sends them trailing down her cheeks as she turns away. I reach out a hand to comfort her but then think better of it. "Amberly, I wanted, no, I needed to save you. Can't you understand that?"

"You think because you did it this way that I'm safe?" Her stare is hard, "if so, you're more naive than I thought."

"What are you talking about?"

"Vladimir will never let me live. So, all you've done is bring the cattle to the slaughter."

I shake my head. "No. He won't hurt you."

"You don't know that."

"Yes, I do."

Confusion and uncertainty spread through her features. "Why do you think that?"

"Because you're going to join our team. Then you will no longer be a threat to him."

She defiantly shakes her head. "I'll never do that."

I smile at her. "You won't have a choice."

"We always have a choice."

Turning my back to her, I reply, "You let me in your head, remember?"

"So?"

"Once I'm in, I can always get in." Turning around to look at her, the anger is clear in her stance, "If the only way to save you is to change you like I have done to many others before you, then I will do it."

"I thought that Vladimir was the one who put everyone under their mind control. It is, after all, his power. Amara did say you were behind some of it, but I just figured."

"Vladimir has me back up what he's already put in place."

She smiles at me cockily as her arms fold over her chest. "Well, he hasn't been in my head, so it looks like you're out of luck."

"I don't need him. If this is the only way to keep you safe, so be it."

She looks to the floor. "I'd rather die."

Fear spreads through my body at her words. "Don't say that. You don't mean it."

She glances at me with more anger than I've ever seen on another human. "I do mean it. I would rather be dead than some zombie form of who I really am."

I say the next words in a pleading tone, begging her to understand. "This is the only way."

The calmness to her voice is comforting and stops me in my tracks, "What if it wasn't? What if there was another way?"

"I'm all ears."

"What if you came home with me?"

Anger flares in my heart. "That's not a good idea."

"Vladimir lied to you, Aidan. My parents," she pauses and closes her eyes, "our parents." She opens them again, looking at me, "they never knew you even existed. They never would have abandoned you. Can't you see he took you, he lied to you because he knew without you on his side, he didn't stand a chance in coming up against us? He didn't have any hope of winning. He stole you from your family, Aidan."

Her words shatter me.

I'm falling.

The ground rises up to meet me.

I'm weak.

Her arms are the only things keeping me on my feet. I glance down at her, trying to make sense of her words.

Could it be true?

Could my parents really haven't known?

Did Vladimir take me from them?

I mean, why would she lie?

The voice in my head replies, *To go home.*

No, I know her better than I think she knows herself. She wouldn't lie, not if she knew going back would endanger anyone else she loves. She knows she wouldn't be able to take me down on her own. I'm stronger than her. I've had more time to train, and she knows that. She knows in saving herself, she would doom more of the people she loves. So, what she's telling me must be the truth.

What am I going to do?

I'm shaken to my core. Never in all these years did I think that would have been a possibility. I mean, why would I? There was no reason to ever think that Vladimir was the one lying. That he had taken me away from my family. Even if he had, why wouldn't they have found me by now? Did Vladimir lie to me about not having the mind-controlling power until I came around? What else could he be lying about?

I need to know the truth. The thought of returning to her home, the place where I caused so much damage, pain, and death, cripples me. But I need to know if what she's telling me is true. What happened? But more importantly, can I be forgiven?

I find my footing. Looking down at her, I whisper, "Thank you."

She nods.

I can't make out what she's feeling right now, but I know what I need to do. I know I'm going to regret it, but nothing else matters at this moment other than knowing the truth and making sure that, no matter what, my sister is safe. I look at her once more over my shoulder before I exit the room.

Strategy Time

AARON

"She's alive." Logan's words echo in my mind.

Angela's anticipation is clear in her voice. "We need to go after her."

Troy looks at Logan before saying. "I'm ready."

Amara smiles. "She would do it for any of us."

Still trying to process Logan's words, I look around at them in awe. These kids are warriors in every sense of the word. They would do anything for someone they love. Someone in their pack. I turn to Logan and whisper. "You're sure?"

He nods his head, and to further reassure me, he says, "As kids, we are taught how to sense each other's energy. Each person is different, so that's how you can tell them apart. A few minutes before you entered the room Troy reminded me," he pauses for a moment to look over at his friend and smile, "and I closed my eyes and focused harder than I ever have in my life. And I felt her."

"You felt her energy?"

He nods.

"But are you sure that means she's alive?"

"You can't sense someone's energy unless they are."

For the first time, I feel the weight on my heart lessen. "We need to tell Jocelyn."

"Let me. You stay here and talk over our next steps with the rest of the group. I want everyone to be ready to go when we get back. Time is critical right now." Logan says as he runs off.

Angela comes to stand next to me. "Logan's right. We need to move fast if we have any hope of getting to her before something happens."

I nod in both agreement and understanding.

Amara's worried voice reaches my ears. "It's already been too long. I know she's strong, but with how hurt she was, I don't know how long she can put up a fight against them entering her mind."

"What do you mean as hurt as she was?"

Amara looks at her comrades frantically. No one says a word, so she sighs before answering me, "Before I fell completely unconscious, she was going a few rounds with this crazy couple, and she took a few good hits." She pauses and looks over at Angela before continuing. Almost like she's unsure. "She hid us under some tree branches and leaves, but I came to for a short moment, must have been before Logan, and well, I saw –," she pauses again.

Worried she isn't going to continue, I ask, "You saw what?"

"The girl she was fighting. She had a knife, and she was coming up behind Amberly, and before I fell back into my unconscious state, I'm pretty sure she stabbed her."

I can barely keep myself erect. I wobble to the side, quickly straightening myself before anyone notices. At least I thought I did. I see Angela now standing next to me with her hand behind my back, ready to support me if I need it. I smile down at her to let her know I appreciate it.

Stabbed.

My daughter, stabbed.

What if Amara is right? Even if she did survive that attack, how will she be strong enough to keep herself alive or keep them from entering her mind and changing her forever?

I look at each one of them, stopping for a moment at each person. "We need to move. Fast."

✳✳✳

LOGAN

I run to Aaron's room on pure instinct. Every cell in my body buzzing under my skin. Julian's dead, and I don't know how I will make that ok for her, but right now, that isn't what I need to focus on. She's alive, right now, she's alive, and we need to get to her before she dies from either her wounds, or by Vladimir's hands, or worse, Aidan brainwashes her. I know Amberly would rather die than let them in her mind. She would never in a million years let up. One thing she's always fought for is keeping herself in control of her powers and who she is as a person. So, I know she would never let someone get into her mind and wipe it. For that fact alone, I know Vladimir will kill her.

I've seen how strong she has become these last few weeks, and even though I don't know Vladimir personally, I know he's strong. I can only hope we aren't too late.

Nervousness fights to make its way to the surface as I reach Aaron's door. I slow down, taking in a slow deep breath.

Release.

Lift my hand.

Knock.

Moments later, the door opens, and I'm greeted by a Jocelyn I've never seen before. She's always been so collected and together. To see her this way worries me. Her hair is a mess all around her, and her eyes are so red and puffy I can barely make out her eye color.

"Logan?"

"Aaron wanted me to come and get you. Well, that's a lie; I kind of ran off and told him I was coming to get you."

I can hear the concern in her voice. "Why? Is Amberly-"

Cutting her off, I say. "She's fine. She's alive."

Light creeps into her bloodshot eyes. "Are you sure?"

I nod. "I remembered the trick you taught us as kids. Well, Troy did."

She looks confused.

"The one where we can sense each other's energies."

Her eyes widen. "Oh my god, I can't believe I forgot about that."

"I didn't think about it myself. I was too consumed with worry, but for once, Troy calmed me down." I chuckle lightly.

"You sensed her?"

"Yes."

For the first time, I see a hint of a smile making its way onto her face. "She's alive."

I grin and nod.

"We need to go after her."

Taking a step forward, I say, "That's why I came to get you. Everyone is planning as we speak."

"We are going to go after her?"

"Yes. If I have anything to say about it. Even if I have to go alone. I'm going to bring her back."

Her smile starts to disappear. "But what if..."

"What?"

She pauses. "What if she's no longer Amberly?"

I shake my head. "She's too strong and stubborn to let them get in her head."

A stubborn look creeps into her facial features. "You're right. She always gave me a run for my money, so I'm sure she can manage to hold her own." I see the worry starting to take hold again. "At least for a little longer."

"I promise we will get there in time."

She releases a sigh. "But what if we don't? What if she couldn't hold on?"

"Then we will find a way to bring her back." She stays silent, so I place a reassuring hand on her shoulder. "I'm sure between Troy, me, you, and her father, one of us could get to her."

"But what if she doesn't want to be reached?"

I look at her in surprise.

"When I thought I lost her father, no one could help me in my grief."

"It's Amberly. Do you really think the loss of one person would make her not want to come home? Not want to live?"

"My daughter is more like me than she cares to admit."

"So, what are you saying?"

Her eyes grow sad once more. "I'm saying if we manage to get her back, herself or not, we are going to have our work cut out for us. She's going to need a lot of time to heal, and I'm afraid with everything going on in our world right now that she won't be able to get what she needs, and because of that, she won't be smart in one of the fights ahead." She looks down. "I'm afraid we will lose her either way."

No Longer Empty

AMBERLY

Julian.

He's the only thing that occupies my mind. Well, him and what Aidan showed me. He'd been watching me all this time. I can't help but be a little angry at that. I never knew what was missing from my life. I felt the empty space, and no matter how hard I tried to fill it, nothing worked. I never understood why. But he did. He knew about me, watched me from the shadows as I stayed in the dark, literally. Never knowing he was there. That I had a brother, and what I was missing was my twin.

Ok, he's only known for a year. I get it, but this last year my whole life changed. I was uprooted from everything I've ever known, and I really could have used him. I needed him more this past year than ever before, and he chose now to come to me. And don't even get me started on the way he did it.

The anger inside is boiling over and getting harder to control. I try to push it down, succeeding for now. The truth is, that emptiness I've felt all these years is finally gone. It's silent. Now I know why I felt so alone, so empty. Because I was missing half of me. I was missing him. My brother.

I have a brother.

But one thing I'm still having a hard time understanding is how my parents never knew about him. How could that have happened? I guess that's something we will figure out together. Aidan knows the truth now, that Vladimir lied to him, used him, and I pray that's enough to turn him around. I know if I can get Aidan to listen to me, we could go home together, and he could see he doesn't need Vladimir anymore. He can have everything he's ever wanted, ever felt like he lost. He could have a family.

I can't imagine what his life was like growing up with that monster. The little bit he let me see makes me understand him much more, and I find myself wondering how I would have turned out had the roles been reversed.

Thinking of Sage, I go back to that moment when she took him from me. *She killed Julian.* I want more than anything to get justice, make her pay for taking him from me, but then I would be just what Vladimir wants me to be.

I would be evil.

I would be a killer.

I would be everything I've fought to never become.

And I would be walking right into his hands.

A life for a life isn't the way. Julian wouldn't want me to avenge him, not if it meant losing myself. I close my eyes and see his face. I can feel the tears rolling down my cheeks as my eyes stay closed. The thought of returning home and not to him makes my heart ache. He is my home, and I feel I have no place left on this earth without him. I feel broken. I wasted all that time being mad at him, the time we could have had together if I would have stopped being so stubborn.

From the moment we met, I knew he was going to change my life forever. He first changed it by helping me learn the truth about who I was, who my father was. Then again, when he returned my father to me, bringing my family back together. Then he changed it most profoundly. He showed me what it was like to fall unbelievably, wholeheartedly, and madly in love with someone else. To care about them more than yourself. To feel the difference in his touch versus someone else's. To feel the strength inside me grow when I was around him. To experience what real love could be when it's with the right person.

My eyes fly open.

There's still hope.

I get to my feet, setting my destination. I need to find Aidan, and we need to leave. Together. I need to get home to the one person who can change my future forever.

Serenity.

***

AIDAN

Amberly's words continue playing on repeat in my mind. Over and over again with every step I take.

"Vladimir lied to you, Aidan. My parents, our parents, they never knew you even existed. They never would have abandoned you. Can't you see he took you, he lied to you because he knew without you on his side, he didn't stand a chance in coming up against us? He didn't have any hope of winning. He stole you from your family, Aidan."

I want to confront him about what she told me, but I know if I do, not only would he deny it, but he will kill her. He won't hesitate, and he will do it in front of me to make a point. So instead, I decide to run what my original plan had been by him. Not like I'm going to do it, but I would like to see his reaction.

I pop my head into the training room to find him alone.

"I was hoping I could talk to you."

He doesn't turn to face me. "What about?"

"My sister."

He sighs. "That again. When are you going to give it up? Learn that you're better off without such distractions."

Fury turns my vision red. "She's not a distraction. She's my family."

"Does your family," he puts a lot of feeling into the word, "know all the horrible things you've done?"

I remain silent.

He smiles sinisterly. "That would be a no."

"I plan on telling her."

His eyes catch mine. "Everything?"

I nod.

"You plan on telling your sister how you tortured half the people in this place? How could I hear their screams from everywhere in this place? You plan on telling her the countless people you butchered in the name of me and my cause."

Speechless, I nod again.

He chuckles sadistically. "She will never accept you as her brother."

The words run from my mouth before I can stop them. "You don't know a thing about her."

Amused, he says, "Then enlighten me."

Scrambling, I remember why I came here. "It won't matter either way. She will accept me. I can guarantee it."

"How do you plan on achieving that?"

"I'm going to do to her what I did to most of the others here."

"You want to mind wipe her?" He asks with a smile that reaches his eyes.

"Yes," I say confidently.

He places his hand on his chin, and I see the wheels turning in his mind. "That could work." He glares across the room at me, "but if it doesn't, you know what you must do. There is no other option."

I nod my head in agreement.

"Then go. Prepare. I want her on our side by tomorrow."

I take one step towards the door.

"If she isn't by tomorrow. I will do what needs to be done." He flashes me a devilish smile, "I can't wait any longer. I won't let one girl put an end to everything I put in motion over the years."

I turn away and exit the room. I've never seen him so excited. He believes that either way, he has won, but he couldn't be more wrong in his thinking. The only thing that matters to me now is

Amberly's safety. She's my sister. Since she's been around, I feel calm, and the empty space is gone. Full. I don't have this heavy weight on my shoulders anymore. She was my missing piece, and I don't want to go back to how it was without her.

If I have to choose between Vladimir and her, it will always be her. I know what I have to do. We have to leave tonight. It's the only way I know she will be safe.

I will take her home.

Back to the place where I won't be accepted.

A place she was happy in before she ever knew about me. *What if he's right?* I can't lose her, not now. *It doesn't matter. I need to put her first.* If taking her home, saving her life means she walks away from me, well, that is something I'll have to live with. I would rather she be alive and hate me than dead.

***

AIDAN

"We are leaving. Tonight."

Surprise is all I see on Amberly's face. "What?"

"I'm taking you home."

I can see the happiness in her eyes before it turns to fear right before me. "You have to come with me."

"I can't."

She grabs me by the shoulders. "If you don't, he will kill you."

I grin at her. "I won't go down without a hell of a fight."

"Aidan, no. Come with me."

"I already told you I'm taking you home."

"But then you plan on coming back here."

I turn away. *I can't go with her, not after what I've done.* Even if what she said was true and my parents never knew about me, they would never welcome me with open arms, not with everyone who has suffered at my hands.

Almost like she read my mind, she says, "They will forgive you."

"You couldn't know that."

"They're our parents. Trust me, I know."

"And what if they don't?"

She smiles at me for the first time. "I'll make them."

"I don't think it's a good idea, Amberly."

"It's better than you staying here and dying." She moves her hands from my shoulders and places them in my hands. "We just found each other. You wanted to get to know me, you did all this so that you could, and now you want to throw that all away?"

Her eyes are pleading with me as I whisper. "No."

She squeezes my hands. "I want the chance to get to know my brother. Please, don't take that from me. You've had the time to watch me, to know me, but I haven't."

I sigh. "I'll go with you."

Her smile widens before she pulls me in close.

A hug.

This is what it feels like?

She pulls back to look up at me, and a questioning look appears on her face. "What?"

"Nothing."

"When can we leave?"

"Once everyone is asleep."

"I can't wait for you to meet our parents."

And just like that, I'm a ball of nervous energy once more.

I've always wondered what they were like. Why would they give me up? How could they? But now, my thoughts are changing. If they never even knew I existed, how will they react to learning they have a son? How will they handle knowing *I'm* their son?

A killer.

I peer down at Amberly, unsure if she knows what we are getting ourselves into. I only hope once they all know the truth that they can somehow forgive me. For everything. I promised her I would go with her, give them a chance, us a chance. After all this time, we deserve it. And more than anything?

I need it.

Reminiscing

LOGAN

Amberly is the only thing that's been on my mind since I returned to the cave. I wonder if she knows that Julian is dead. I couldn't imagine living in a world that she wasn't in, so I can only imagine how she will manage. Her heart is broken. I can sense that much. I've been trying to get a read on her since I focused on her energy earlier. By what I'm getting off of her now, I would think she does know about Julian.

I'm finding it hard to tell the difference between my thoughts and feelings and hers. We've been in each other's lives for so long I often found it hard to separate them. However, one thing is certain. The heartache I'm feeling now is definitely hers.

I want to bring her home, need to, but I know in doing so it will only bring her more pain, and the knowledge of that kills me. I would give anything to see her happy and safe. To protect her from worry, loss, and the battles ahead of us. *Why can't we just be what we are?*

Teenagers.

This isn't something any of us should have to deal with. Loss is something everyone goes through at some point in life but not this early. It shouldn't be this early. In the last year, we have been through more than most people go through in a lifetime. Who would have thought a year ago that this is where we would end up? Our biggest care in the world was not getting caught sneaking out of the village and now. Now, look at us. We have never been so separated. We've always been so in sync with each other that we would finish each other's sentences and now. Now we have to make time to even talk to each other. We have to plan things out, and we have to train every day just to stay alive.

This isn't a life anyone should have, and now it seems to be ours. I live for the time when we can go back to how we were. We will never get our innocence back, and that's ok, but I miss the simple things. Knocking on her door early in the morning to take a walk around the village. Getting Troy and Amberly together to go gather things from the gardens for food that day.

Laughing.

Singing.

Playing around.

Making up our own games.

Being a part of each other.

Being one.

I miss those days, and I would do anything to have them back again.

✳✳✳

AARON

I peek down at Jocelyn to see she's still asleep. I'm not looking forward to the conversation we will be having once she wakes up. I know she will argue with me until she wins, like always. However, there's no doubt in my mind that I'm right. She needs to stay here while I go find Amberly and bring her home. I can't worry about her and our daughter at the same time. When I made it back to the room and saw Logan and her talking, I could see a new light in her features. One that I haven't seen since the night before the battle. There was no doubt in my mind that he had told her our daughter was still alive and that we were going to get her. At that moment, I saw pure determination in her eyes, and I knew she planned on coming with the rest of us. I would have expected nothing less. I know no one could stop me from going, so I know I won't be able to stop her, but still, I need to try.

The thought of losing Amberly is hard enough, and it's something I can't let myself think too much about. But taking Jocelyn with me when a fight will more than likely break out, I can't do it. I couldn't lose them both. Not again. Losing my family once nearly killed me, and I think a second time would.

"You have your intense thinking face on." She says in a sleepy voice.

I glance at her and smile. "You know me too well."

Smiling back, and replies. "What's going on in that head of yours?"

"Nothing you're going to like."

Her smile vanishes as she sits up in bed. "Tell me."

I look at her sadly. "I need to go alone."

"Not going to happen." She flashes me her stubborn face for effect.

I sigh. "I was afraid you were going to say that."

"You should know me well enough to know there is no chance in hell I'm staying behind."

"I know."

"Then why even say it?"

"Because I had to, at least once."

She places her hand on mine. "We are going to get our daughter back, and we are all going to come back home. Together."

"I know."

"Say it like you mean it."

I grin. "I know we are."

"That's better." She relaxes and places her head back on her pillow. "We have waited too long to find each other again, and I won't let it be taken away from us. Not now, not ever." She glances in my direction. "We are strongest together, and together we will survive whatever comes our way."

"I know, you're right."

Her smile widens, reaching her eyes. "As always."

I laugh. "I wouldn't go that far."

Her eyes open once more. "Oh, wouldn't you?"

"Sorry, but no."

"Well, you might as well admit it now because you watch and see. We will bring her home, and we will be together again, mark my words. And together, we will defeat Vladimir."

"I have no doubt in that, my love."

"Good."

We share a smile, and then I lean over to kiss her on the forehead before taking my place at her side on the bed. I hold her hand as I drift back off to sleep, knowing that tomorrow we will see our daughter again.

Returning Home

AIDAN

"It's time to go."

Amberly nods.

It's a little after 2 a.m., and I have no doubt that everyone in the camp is sleeping. Vladimir expects Amberly to be under my control by sunrise, so we have to leave now. I need to get her home, get her safe. Well, safer than she is here anyway. At least there, she has more people to look out for her than just me.

"Aidan?"

I stop turning around to look at her. "Yes?"

"How far are we from home?"

I know that wasn't what she was going to ask, but I don't push the subject. "Not far."

"Oh." The worry is clear in her voice.

"I know what you're thinking." I smile weakly.

She looks at me but says nothing.

"We are close, but I know Vladimir. Once he sees we are gone, he won't come charging in after us."

"Why not?"

"Because he's too smart for that."

Looking away from me, I see a small grin of her own creep onto her face. She's confident and cocky. We are definitely related. I laugh internally. "You mean he knows he can't beat us." She pauses to glance up at me, "at least not us together."

"Something like that. He will take some time to regroup before he comes after us."

"So, if we're smart, we should take the fight to him. Come after him before he has the chance to come after us."

I look at her in awe. "Well, yes."

"Then let's get going. We have some training to do."

I suppress a laugh. "Someone's a little too eager."

Her smile fades. "To get home, yes." She looks down at her feet, placing one in front of the other. "But to train. Not so much." I can see the sadness hidden in her eyes. "And going home might also mean returning to a place that only reminds me of what I lost."

I hesitate, unsure if I should say it. "You mean, Julian."

She nods.

"I'm sorry. I never meant to bring you any kind of pain. I wanted to get in, get you, and get out."

"I know."

I look at her, surprised. "Do you?"

"Yes. I could sense it in your mind. I know you would never intentionally hurt me."

I shift my focus to my feet, not wanting to see the hurt in her eyes anymore. "If I could change it. If I could bring him back for you, I would."

Her hand touches mine lightly. "I know."

I look over to find her smiling at me. I smile back as she says. "But there might still be hope."

"What do you mean?"

"Serenity. She's back at the cave."

It takes me a minute but then I remember her power. "She's the healer, right?"

"Yes."

I smile. "And you're hoping that she can heal him if she hasn't already."

Her smile grows till her eyes become slits. "No. I'm hoping she will teach me how to do it."

✳✳✳

AMBERLY

The distance between Vladimir's village and the cave wasn't far at all. We did run almost the whole way, though. Aidan told me on the journey that it had only been two days since the battle ended. The night we left was the third. The journey took us about a day and a half to get back home. Meaning my family has been worried about me for almost five whole days, and I can't imagine what's going through their minds.

We didn't talk too much along the way; running kind of makes it hard to hold a real conversation. The trip wasn't an easy one by any means. There were a lot of hills, and I found myself almost falling every couple of steps. If it hadn't been for Aidan, I would have been covered in dirt and bruises by the time we made it home. I also don't know when it happened, but my body healed itself of my knife wound somewhere along the way. Thankfully. I know I never would have been able to make this trip if I was still injured. My limbs are on fire, and my lungs are burning, but I refuse to stop. Scanning the forest, I begin to notice my surroundings. I turn to Aidan and smile.

"I know where we are. We aren't far now."

Aidan smiles at me for a moment before he returns his gaze to the ground, and his smile disappears.

I stop turning in his direction. "What is it? What's wrong?"

"Maybe I should wait here."

"Don't be ridiculous." I reach out my hand to him.

"They might not understand."

"Like I told you, I'll make them understand."

He smiles lightly at me. "I don't doubt that, but maybe you should go ahead of me. This way, you can explain. People don't generally do well with surprises."

I grab his hand. "This is a good surprise, I promise." I smile at him playfully, "Plus, I won't let anyone hurt you."

"I'm not worried about me." He replies with a sinister grin.

I laugh as I pull him along after me. This is what it feels like to have a brother. I've been missing out.

***

LOGAN

"Everyone ready to go?"

I look around, noting all of them nodding their heads. It's been almost five days since the fight, and for me, that's too long. We should have left the day I made it back to the cave. Looking around the room, I notice two important people are missing.

"Wait. Where are Amberly's parents?" I ask no one in particular.

Angela walks up next to me. "They said they would meet us outside."

I nod my head in understanding. To my surprise, Angela takes my hand in hers and pulls us forward. This seems to be happening a lot lately. I stare down at her, confused. *When did we cross over into touching territory?* She pulls me along to the exit of the cave. When we make it outside, I turn around to make sure the others are still following us. Part of me wishes they weren't right behind us because I feel like Angela and I need to talk about this. I would be lying if I said I didn't feel something changing between us, something I definitely didn't expect. But also, something I don't mind at all. Part of me feels like maybe this is happening too soon and too fast, but then again, all the best things seem to start that way. Out of the blue when you least expect them.

A few steps into the woods and I take notice of Aaron and Jocelyn. They are engaged in what seems to be a heavy conversation.

"Is that?" I look over at Angela to see her straining her eyes. "Oh, my God, it's Amberly."

I turn my attention to where she's looking until my eyes find her. My heart leaps in my chest with excitement until my eyes come to rest on another person standing next to her. She's not alone.

"Who's that with her?" Angela asks.

Amara answers in a whisper. "It's Aidan."

We all turn to look at her, but Angela is the one who speaks. "What? Are you sure?"

She nods.

Angela looks back in Amberly's direction. "But why would he be with her?"

Amara replies in such a low voice that I have to strain to hear her. "Maybe he got in her head. Maybe they came to finish us off."

"Alone? That makes no sense. No matter how strong they both are, they know they aren't a match for all of us." I say while trying to cloud my worry.

Why did he come with her? Amberly's not stupid. She wouldn't bring him with her unless she had no choice. Maybe it's an ambush. My eyes rack across the landscape, checking every direction. There's no one. They are the only ones.

It doesn't make sense.

✳✳✳

AMBERLY

I see my parents standing in the distance, looking at each other. They haven't noticed me yet. I turn to Aidan and smile, but he doesn't return it. He looks on edge. I take his hand in mine, trying to reassure him as I pull him forward with me. As we move closer, I see people emerge from the cave. I focus using my wolf vision like my father taught me until they come into view.

"Logan," I whisper.

Out of the corner of my eye, I see Aidan looking at me. I want to run to my parents and friends, but I know I can't leave his side. I can feel how nervous he's getting with each passing moment, and I promised him things would be ok. I made him come this far with me, and I won't have it be for nothing. I will make them listen, make them understand. I flash him a reassuring smile and press us forward.

As we move closer, I see Logan and the others run towards my parents. When they reach their side, they point in our direction. I need to know what they are saying for Aidan's sake, so I use my wolf senses. My ears close the distance between us, making out whispers at first. I push a little harder until their words become clearer. They come in a rush as I try to make sense of who's who.

After a short moment, the outside noises disappear, and all that's left is their conversation.

"It's Amberly," Logan says as he points in our direction.

My parents turn and smile as my mother starts forward, but Logan grabs at her. "It's not safe."

She turns to him with a questioning look. "What are you talking about?"

"Amara thinks there's a good chance she's not in control of herself. She thinks they got in her head."

My father takes a step forward. "Who's that with her?"

"That's what I mean. It's Aidan." Logan answers.

My father places a protective arm in front of my mother and the others. "All of you get inside."

Angela steps forward. "I'm staying with you."

"No. If what Amara says is true, it's not safe. Get everyone inside and wait for me. Gather the pack just in case Amara is right."

I look over at Aidan as everyone, but my father reluctantly re-enters the cave.

"What's going on?" Aidan asks.

"It's ok."

He looks at our father, and I can tell his uneasiness is growing. We walk forward until we are standing within twenty feet of our father. His stance tells me he's ready for anything. I turn back to Aidan.

"Wait here for a minute, ok."

Without hesitation, he nods his head in agreement.

I move forward slowly.

Very slowly.

"Dad."

I can see the uncertainty in his eyes.

"It's me. I promise I'm myself."

He stares at me, not saying a word.

"Dad. It's me."

He looks me over slowly. Taking it all in. *He's trying to read me. The way only a wolf can.* A wolf can sense danger from smell alone. It's a musk that predators give off. At least that's what I've been told. Who knows how true it is. I know I haven't been able to figure it out yet. He looks me over for what feels like hours before I see the realization on his face as a smile creeps onto his face as he steps forward and takes me in his arms.

"We've been so worried." He mumbles into my hair.

"I know I'm sorry. How's mom?"

"A wreck."

I pull back,- looking up at him. "Then we better keep this short."

He smiles at me before his gaze rests on Aidan. "But first, tell me, what is he doing here?"

I look over my shoulder and flash a reassuring smile at my brother. "He saved my life."

"What?"

"And there's something else."

He takes a step back to get a better look at him.

"It's going to be hard to believe. Vladimir was more tactical about his plans than we thought."

"Amberly." His tone is final. Telling me to spit it out.

"Turns out I have a brother."

He looks down at me, puzzled. "Your mother had another child?"

I choose my next words very carefully. "You both did."

Confusion embeds in his features.

"Turns out Vladimir stole him. I'm still a little blurry on the details myself."

"It's a lie." He says through bared teeth. "He's trying to trick you. It's part of Vladimir's end game, I'm sure."

I take my father's hand. "He's telling the truth, dad. He showed me, shared his memories with me." I look over at Aidan. "I can feel it inside of me. I know it's the truth."

"What do you mean?"

"My whole life, I felt something was missing. I always thought it was you." I look up at him, "but then when I found you, that void was still there."

Sadness creeps into his expression.

"I was so happy when I found you, but I couldn't understand why I still felt like something was missing. But when I saw Aidan for the first time, something clicked. Something about him felt familiar. I couldn't make sense of it. How did I recognize someone I had never met before? Then when he told me I was his sister, it all made sense. For the first time in my life, I feel whole."

His gaze returns to Aidan. "But it's not possible. I would have sensed him when I sensed you."

"Vladimir did something to hide him from all of us. That's the only thing I can think of."

"It's. It's impossible." His gaze intensifies, bewildered. "I have a son?"

I smile softly as I nod. "Yes."

"Why didn't he come over with you?"

"I wanted to talk to you first. He's afraid of how everyone will react considering what happened here a few days ago."

Without hesitation, he says, "I would like to meet him."

"Before you do, there's something I think I should mention."

His look tells me to continue.

"The things Aidan showed me, they were," I pause, looking for the right word, "dark."

His eyes go distant.

"He's very broken."

"What did he show you?"

"Vladimir. Training him. He was ruthless. Aidan was only a boy, and the things he did to him. The things he made him do."

Standing up straight, anger takes over his features, "He's home now. There's nothing we can't fix. As long as we are together."

"Now you sound like mom." I smile.

"Well, she is a wise woman."

"Sometimes." I giggle.

"Don't let her hear you say that." His laugh makes his shoulders vibrate.

The seriousness returns to my tone. "Just tread lightly. I think it's going to take him some time."

"If he's anything like you, he will be just fine." His smile widens, reaching his eyes. "I will make sure the others don't bother him."

"Thanks, dad. I promised him if he came back with me, things would be ok."

"We will do our best to keep that promise then. There is nothing that can't be forgiven. There is good in his heart. We only need to remind him of it."

Smiling, I gesture to Aidan, telling him to come over. He hesitates for a few seconds before making his way slowly over to us.

"Aidan, this is Aaron, our father."

Aidan looks down at me in surprise and then back up at Aaron.

"Amberly told me what happened. I don't know what to say." The sadness is clear on his face, and I see a hint of uncertainty in his eyes. "But I want you to know your mother, and I knew nothing about you. If we had, nothing would have stopped us from coming to find you." His features turn serious before he continues. "Nothing."

Aidan looks at the ground but doesn't respond. My father looks over at me, unsure of how to proceed. Then he lifts his hand and places it on his son's shoulder. "You're safe now, you're home, and that's all that matters. The rest," he smiles, "The rest we can fill in later."

I feel Aidan relax for the first time.

Aaron looks over at me. "Let's go join the others. We have much to talk about."

Finding Serenity

ANGELA

"If her mind has been wiped, what can we do? How do we get her back?" I ask Logan.

There is only sadness in the features of his face. "I don't know. If I know her as well as I think I do, she won't want to come back."

"Logan, don't say that."

He looks down at me sadly. "I mean, could you blame her?"

I think about Julian for the first time in nearly five days. I couldn't let myself think of him before now. It hurts too much. I don't know how Amberly is going to deal when I can barely do it myself. I look up at Logan to find my features mimic his own. "No, I don't, but we will be here to help her get through it."

"I don't think that will be enough."

"It has to be." Looking away, I say in a whisper so that no one hears me, "I can't lose Amberly too." But by the change in his facial features, I'm pretty sure he heard me.

I can't think about losing Amberly after everything. Knowing she was out there somewhere and alive was the only thing that got me through these last few days. Well, that and Logan. I can see now why Amberly always talked so highly of him. She really does have good taste in friends and men. I catch myself staring at him at the same moment he does. Blood rushes to my cheeks as I quickly look in the other direction.

Pulling me from my thoughts, Amara asks, "What do you think is going on out there?"

"Hopefully, nothing," I reply.

"I think if it was good news, Aaron would have come back in by now," Troy says without looking at us.

The anger is clear in my voice when I reply. "Will everyone stop thinking negatively, please!"

They all look at me in surprise, and suddenly, I'm aware of my outburst. I turn my attention to my feet as I whisper, "I'm sorry."

"Don't apologize. Everyone is on edge right now." Logan says as he places a hand on my shoulder.

"Hey, guys, I think he's coming back inside," Troy says.

We look over at the entrance and see Aaron, a few steps behind him is Amberly and behind her is Aidan. When everyone sees him, they go stiff. I look at Aaron and see no worry in his eyes or in his expression. Instead, I see something that looks like happiness and hope. I turn to the others.

"It's ok, you guys. Relax."

"Are you crazy? Why is he letting that psychopath into the cave?" Amara asks.

"I don't know, but right now, it doesn't matter. Amberly is here, she's ok, and Aaron sees no danger. You need to learn to trust your alpha. He will fill us in when the time is right. Until then, trust that there is a reason he is here." I glance over at her. "Aaron and the rest of the pack won't let anything happen to you."

The terror is clear in her eyes, and I'm a little worried about her doing something reckless because of that fear. I know I need to get to the bottom of what's going on and fast. We don't need anything going wrong. We all need answers. Amberly is home, and we need to focus on that. I start to make my way over to Aaron when Logan stops me.

"Where are you going?" He asks.

"To get some answers."

"Not without me."

I smile at him and reach out my hand. He looks down and takes it without a moment's hesitation, and we walk over to Aaron together. The others stay back, no doubt leaving us to get the answers we all want and need. Reaching them, I can't stop myself before I throw my arms around Amberly immediately.

"Thank God you're ok," I say in a sob.

She hugs me back nice and tight. "Same. I was worried about everyone."

I pull back and look past her to the man in question. "So, you want to fill us in?"

She and Aaron both look at Aidan and then back to us. Aaron is the one who speaks. "Aidan will be staying with us now."

Aidan's body tenses, and I feel how nervous he is but none of that matters. Why would Aaron let him stay here after everything that happened, everything that he did? I know Aaron, and I know he must have a very good reason for something that seems so reckless and not thought out.

Amberly looks at me, no doubt seeing the questions in my eyes. "He saved my life. I wouldn't have made it out of there if it wasn't for him."

For the first time, Logan speaks with anger clear in his tone. "You wouldn't have been there in the first place if it wasn't for him. And everyone wouldn't be dead either."

I see the pain in Amberly's eyes for the first time, and I feel anger towards Logan for putting it there.

"I'm sorry." Logan places his hands over his eyes and rubs at them feverishly as he releases a long sigh. "It's been a long couple of days." He removes his hand and places it back at his side, turning to look at Amberly. "I didn't mean it."

"Yes, you did. But I understand." She walks over to him slowly and places her hand in his. "You've always trusted me, so that's all I'm asking of you now. Please. The rest I can fill you in on later."

I can see the sadness that lingers in both their eyes as all of us watch them. Then Amberly turns to me. "Where is Serenity?"

Surprised it takes me a moment to answer her. "She's in her room with Johnathan and Aayda."

Turning to Aidan and her father, she asks, "Can you keep him company until I get back?"

Aaron nods and places a hand on Aidan's shoulder before ushering him away from us.

Amberly turns her attention back to me. "I need to get to her right away."

"Ok. I can take you. We moved some rooms around since you were last here."

"I'm coming too," Logan says as he follows behind us.

"Angela?"

I turn around to look at her, "Yes."

"Where did you put his body?"

Knowing right away what she's asking, I lower my head. "We put him with everyone else. We haven't had the heart to bury anyone. Not yet, at least."

"Good."

Her one word takes me by surprise but not as much as the smile that follows.

What is she up to?

***

AMBERLY

"How are you feeling?" I ask Serenity.

She's getting weaker and paler as the days pass; I barely recognize her. She's becoming a shell of herself. *Her wound must have been worse than she led me to believe.* Suddenly I feel bad for coming here to ask her for her help, especially knowing there's nothing I can do for her.

Smiling at me, she says. "I've had better days." Turning her attention to Johnathan and Aayda, "but we feel better now that you're home."

"Thanks to Aidan. I never would have gotten out of there if it wasn't for him."

Johnathan smiles. "I was happy to hear he returned with you." He looks around the room. "We all were."

"You were?"

Aayda speaks for the first time. "Yes. We," she pauses almost as if she's unsure if she should continue. She looks over at Johnathan, who smiles at her and then continues for her.

"There were things I couldn't tell you before because things had to unfold the way they were meant to, and we didn't want to intervene."

"Ok," I reply, still very confused.

"We know Aidan is your twin." Serenity says with a smile.

I look at her, and I'm sure my surprise is all over my face. "You all knew?"

"Yes." Aayda answers.

Johnathan walks over to me. "I'm sorry if you feel like we hid something from you, but you had to find out the truth on your own. This was something we couldn't meddle in. I hope you can understand."

I can only manage a nod.

"But that is a conversation for later. You came here for a reason, did you not?" Serenity asks.

I smile at her. "Yes. And I know it's late, and you're not feeling well, but time is really of the essence."

She nods her head. "I know what you've come to ask me."

"You do?"

I can tell she's holding back a laugh. "Yes."

I let out a breath, afraid to ask. "Please, tell me it can be done."

I see the sadness as it enters her eyes for the first time since I entered the room. "It is a long shot. I will not lie to you."

Johnathan moves forward. "What are you two talking about?"

Serenity turns to him. "She wishes to bring back the boy."

Johnathan's gaze falls on me. "Serenity is too weak to be healing anyone, let alone bring anyone back from the dead. I'm sorry, but the answer is no. She may not be willing to say no to you, but I'm sorry I must."

"She wasn't asking me to do it." Serenity lays a hand on Jonathan's arm.

He glances at me. Worry clear in his eyes. "You can't."

"I'm sorry if you don't agree, but you can't tell me what to do."

Anger is infused in his tone. "How can you be so careless and naive? Do you not see what that power has done to *her,* and now you wish to share in her fate? You're signing your own death warrant. You only just turned eighteen. This power takes something from you every time you use it, as I'm sure Serenity has already told you. And yet, you still wish to use it. He wouldn't want you to. Not for him."

Serenity tugs on his sleeve. "Johnathan, you of all people should understand why she wants to try, but more than that, why she needs to."

Aayda walks over and places a hand on his shoulder. "They are stronger together, my love. You know this better than anyone." She turns in my direction. "She needs to at least try." Looking back at Johnathan. "She will never forgive herself if she doesn't at least do that much. Don't try to take that from her."

I see the battle going on within him before he turns away and says in a whisper. "Do it if you must, but I will not be part of it. If Serenity wishes to show you what to do, so be it." He walks over to the door and stops. Looking over his shoulder at me, he continues. "I do hope it works for your sake. But moving forward, you cannot use this power so recklessly." He glances at Serenity, "I hope you can make her understand that." Then he exits the room.

Aayda looks back at us apologetically and then follows him.

Serenity pulls my attention back to the current situation when she asks. "Are you sure you're ready for this?"

"Not at all. But like she said, I have to try. I'll never forgive myself if I don't do this. I'll always look back and wonder what if I had tried."

"I understand. But Johnathan is right. You can't always run to this power to fix things. It isn't a crutch. And sometimes you need to say goodbye to those you love."

I look to the door. "I understand."

"Do you?"

"I look at you, and I see how much you have changed in the last few days, and it makes it very clear for me. I know I need to be careful with this power. But just like you, I also know it's not that easy to let someone you love go when you know you have the power to bring them back."

Serenity's expression turns sad. "I do understand. More than you know. But like Johnathan said, this time around, we need to learn from the flaws of this power."

"I know."

"You can't heal everyone. In the battles ahead if someone dies," she closes her eyes, and I swear she knows something she isn't telling me, "If you bring this boy back and he only dies again in the next battle," she opens her eyes, "you can't just keep healing him. Do you understand what I'm saying?"

Annoyance is rising from the pit of my stomach. I understand where everyone is coming from, but how often do they need to tell me the same thing and hear my same reply? I look at Serenity's frailty, and I know she means well. I can only imagine the pain she is in right now, and I know this isn't a fate she wants me to share. How can I blame her for that?

I can't.

"I do."

For the first time, she starts to relax, and I'm glad I can finally make her see that I do understand the severity of using this power too much. But at the same time, if something happens to someone, I love I can't promise that I won't fall back on this power.

"But."

She looks at me like she knows what I'm about to say.

"I can't promise you if something happens to him or someone else in the fight ahead that I won't step in."

She closes her eyes, lets out a sigh before smiling at me. "I understand. But you also need to know there is a balance." I can see there is more she wants to say but doesn't.

"What do you mean?"

"Death is a part of life."

I nod my head. "I understand that."

"I know you do, but sometimes it is someone's time, and you need to let them go."

"But what if I'm not strong enough to do that?"

She smiles. "One day you will be. Maybe not right now, but with time you will come to understand the importance of letting people go."

There is definitely a hidden message in her words. Ignoring it, I let out a sad sigh saying the only obvious thing she is talking about at this moment. "You mean you."

Surprise takes over her features. "Yes. I'm worried they aren't there yet."

"You mean Jonathan and Aayda."

She nods and looks at me with a very serious expression. "I need you to do something for me."

"Anything."

She closes her eyes. "When I'm gone, I need you to help them. Make them understand. Let them know I was ready, and I'm at peace."

"I will do what I can."

"Thank you."

"It's the least I can do."

I know there's something more to this conversation. Something else she isn't telling me. Is someone else going to die? Will I bring him back only to lose him all over again? What isn't she saying? I want to ask her these questions and so many others, but I know now isn't the time. It's already been days since the fight, and if this is going to work, doing it sooner rather than later is the smartest move.

Serenity straightens herself like she's found a new source of energy. "Now, let's go see about bringing your boy back."

I smile at her as every cell in my body comes alive.

I ignore the pit in my stomach.

I'm about to see Julian. His lifeless body.

I really hope I can handle what I'm about to do. I need this to work for all the obvious reasons and more. I need him. I can't win this war without him. Knowing that I won't have him here with me when it's over, that thought cripples me. I don't care about winning if, in the end, I'm without him anyway. I would still put everything I have into the fight to protect everyone else I love, but I wouldn't care if, at the end of it all, I made it or not.

I saw firsthand what being without the person you love can do to you. My mother was a shell of the person she is now. I don't want to become that person. I won't.

This has to work.

The Kiss

ANGELA

"Logan."

He keeps walking. "I don't want to talk right now, Angela."

I run, closing the distance between us. "Why are you being like that?"

"Like what?"

"She's home, she's safe, and you're still angry. I don't understand."

He sighs. "I'm sorry I don't seem happier." He finally stops, turning to look at me. "Please, tell me, how am I supposed to feel right now? How am I supposed to be acting?" Blood rushes to his cheeks showing his anger at the situation we are now in. "She brought him with her. The man who knocked me out, the same man who took her away from us in the first place. The very same person who may not have killed Julian himself but is still responsible for his death. I'm sorry, but I can't understand it, and I sure as hell don't trust him."

I place a reassuring hand on his shoulder. "I understand your uneasiness, but you know her better than anyone. She always has a reason for the things she does. And like she said, he did save her life."

He closes his eyes. "Yes, and I'm grateful," he opens them and looks down at me, "but that doesn't forgive everything he's done, and she shouldn't be so naive to just let him walk in here like she has."

"You think it's part of Vladimir's plan?"

Looking forward again, he answers. "Honestly, it could be."

He takes off again, and I follow. "I don't think Amberly would be that easily deceived. Don't you think you should be giving her more credit?"

"I don't know about that. She tends to fall for the pretty boy act a lot lately."

I stop walking as his words hit me. He faces me, realizing I'm no longer next to him. "I'm sorry, I didn't mean."

I put a hand up. "You've said enough."

I start to walk off, and he grabs my wrist lightly. "Please, I didn't mean it like that."

"I know you weren't fond of Julian, and I understand why but he was my brother, my best friend, and his loss has affected me more than I let anyone see. And for you to say something so carelessly."

He trails his pointer finger along my cheek, wiping at the tears that escaped without my knowledge. "I'm sorry. It was stupid. I haven't slept the last few nights. I know that's no excuse, and I'm not trying to make one, I promise. I just don't want you to think of me as someone careless like that."

I see the worry forming in his eyes. "I know you're a good guy, Logan. If I thought otherwise, I wouldn't waste my time with you. And despite what you know and think of Julian, he was a good man too. But none of this changes the fact that Julian's death has affected me, and it has affected Amberly. If you care for her the way I think you do, that should be enough for you to be sympathetic to the situation. If not for my sake, then for hers."

"I care about your feelings too, not just hers."

I find myself at a loss for words. We sit there in silence for a while, and even then, I can only manage to get out one.

"Logan."

"Yes."

Don't go there. "You need to be more understanding. You should talk to Amberly. Don't jump to conclusions on why he's here. Ask her."

"You're right."

I grin. "I know."

"Cocky today, aren't we?"

I shake my head. "Nope, not enough."

I can tell he's thinking hard about something. Before I get the chance to ask him what's wrong, he leans over and, to my surprise, kisses me. Our lips touch for a moment as his hands cup my face, and I taste the salt from my tears. And as fast as his lips were there, they are gone again. When I open my eyes, so is he.

$$***$$

SERENITY

"Are you sure about this?" I ask Amberly one last time.

"I've never been surer of anything in my life."

"Just remember there's a chance it won't work. A lot of time has passed. His soul could have moved on by now."

She nods her head in a determined fashion. "I know."

"Amberly. I don't want to see you more hurt than you already are. You need to prepare yourself for the possibility that he won't come back. Because there is a higher chance that he won't."

Amberly stops walking and looks at the ground. I can tell she is hurting, a hurt that I still carry with me after all these years. I know how this kind of loss can affect someone, and I wish I could take it from her.

"I know there is a chance he won't come back." She looks up at me. "But I need to have hope that we will be luckier than those odds." She releases a long sigh. "I need to have faith that what we have runs deeper than death. We've been through too much in such a short time for it not to." She begins walking again, but this time it's at a much slower pace. "I need to believe that we didn't meet by chance and that our short time together wasn't meant to be that, that it's meant to turn into something great. I know I probably sound crazy and like a lovesick teenager, but it's the only thing keeping me going right now. Thinking that I might be able to see him again, kiss him again, hold his hand one more time."

Now it's my turn to sigh. "I understand."

She stops abruptly. "You do?"

I nod my head and smile at her. "Yes. I once felt a love like you and Julian have."

"What happened?"

I stop and close my eyes. Trying to picture his face. The way his light caramel hair would rest just above his hazel-colored eyes. "He was taken from me way before his time." I open my eyes sadly and look at her. "Vladimir killed him."

"I'm so sorry."

"It was a long time ago."

I see the sadness grow in her eyes for me, and it only makes the pain hurt more. "If you don't mind me asking, why didn't you heal him?"

"It was before I knew how to use that part of my powers. By the time I knew how to do it, it was too late." I turn to look at her, "That is why I don't want to give you false hope because I don't know how long after someone has passed that we will still be able to bring them back. I also don't know how much it's going to take from you. Your energy, your life force."

"I understand."

I look back in the direction of our destination. "Good. I want you to know what you're getting yourself into and the risk."

"I do."

I glance over at her. "And you're willing to pay the price at any cost?"

She nods her head and says forcefully. "Yes."

I look forward and smile. "I knew that would be your answer."

"How do you know me so well and know what I would say or do when we've barely known each other?"

"You remind me a lot of myself."

She looks surprised. "I do?"

I laugh. "Yes. Why does that surprise you?"

"Because you're so different from Johnathan and Aayda. I don't know how to word it, but I respect you more. I know that might sound weird. But you're different from them. I can see it, feel it."

"That is because we are one and the same."

She smiles at me.

"Johnathan and Aayda have always had each other, and that has made them standoffish if that makes any sense."

She nods. "It does."

"They aren't like you and your friends. Even when you couple up, you still stand by each other; include each other."

"But they seem to be that way with you."

"I think that's because we lost the others. When that happened, the three of us got away, and it's been only us ever since. Because of that, we've gotten closer."

"You weren't always close?"

My smile reaches my eyes. "We were teenagers. Young. We didn't have time for anything other than the person we were with. Not until they were no longer there."

We round the corner, and Angela comes into view. Amberly notices her just as quickly and turns to me with an apologetic smile as she walks over to her.

As I watch them talk, I close my eyes and take a seat. I'm more exhausted than I care to admit and way more than I let on. Talking about Fredrick with Amberly was hard for me. I haven't mentioned him out loud in hundreds of years. For the first time, I find myself more than ready for the pain to end. I know I will be with him soon, and that makes my heart ache less. I know it will be hard for Aayda and Johnathan to let me go, but like I was telling Amberly, sometimes it's better to let someone go. Sometimes it's their time, and sometimes, like me, they are ready to go home.

$$***$$

ANGELA

"What am I doing?" I ask myself.

"There you are."

I turn around to see Amberly walking down the hall towards me, blood rushing to my cheeks. I turn around, hoping Amberly was talking to someone else. I know I need to tell her what happened and to try to make sense of it, but at the same time, I know right now is not the time to do that.

"Hey."

I turn around slowly. "Hey, what's going on?"

She looks over her shoulder, and I follow her gaze till I see Serenity. "We are going out to the woods."

"What for?"

"I'm going to try to bring Julian back."

My heart skips a beat. "You're what?"

"I asked Serenity to show me how."

"Are you out of your mind?"

Hurt mixed with confusion takes over her features. "I thought you of all people would understand."

I sigh. "Of course I do, but."

"But nothing."

"I should have put it together earlier when you asked me about his body." I pause, looking at her in concern. "You're going to try then?"

She nods.

"Just promise me you thought this through."

"I have."

I sigh. "I mean, really thought it through."

She's starting to get mad; I can tell from the way she is looking at me. "I have, Angela."

"I'm sorry. I just want to make sure you know what you're doing. I've heard Johnathan talk about your power, and I'm just worried."

She shrugs it off. "Don't be. I promise I've thought this through a lot."

"And what if it doesn't work? Are you prepared for that?"

I can see the sadness creeping up on her face, and I feel bad for asking. "Yes."

"What if it kills you, Amberly?"

She smiles. "It won't."

"You don't know that."

She looks down at her hands like something's missing. "Yes, I do. It's hard to explain, but I can feel it." She turns around to look back at Serenity again. "Serenity is strong, but I feel like I'm stronger." She faces me. "I don't think it will affect me like it has her."

"But you don't know that for sure."

"You're right; I don't. But I have to believe I was given this power for a reason. Why be able to heal people but not use it?"

"It's one thing to use. It's another to abuse."

Hurt fills her eyes. "What is that supposed to mean?"

"Never mind."

"No. What did you mean by that?"

I breathe in slowly. "All I'm saying is when someone is hurt, maybe it's ok to heal them. They aren't dead, and you aren't upsetting the balance. However, when someone is dead, and you bring them back, the balance is broken. It will find a way to restore itself."

"Do you not want him back?"

Her words cripple me. "Of course, I do."

"Then why are you fighting me on this?"

I close my eyes. "I don't know, Amberly." I open them. "Serenity was given the same power and did what you're planning to do now, and look at her."

"I have."

My anger is starting to boil over inside of me. "And you still want to walk down this path?"

She looks at me sadly. "It's Julian."

"I know. I would give anything."

She stops me short. "Then let me do this."

"He wouldn't want me to. If he knew it would cost you something, no matter how small, he would beg me not to let you do it."

"You're not letting me. It's my choice."

"You're right."

She nods in defiance. "I'm going to get him back." Turning her back to me, she takes a few steps toward Serenity before stopping to look over her shoulder in my direction. "I'm bringing him back for the both of us."

Pain fills my heart. Pain of his loss. But something more takes hold. Disappointment. I know I could stop her, but do I really want to? *No, you don't.* I'm selfish. I want my brother back just as badly as she does, and part of me doesn't care what it costs.

One thing is clear and one thing alone.

I'm a horrible person.

Making Questionable

Decisions

ANGELA

Once Amberly and Serenity disappear from my view, I start thinking. Thinking about life and where I am and where I've been. We've all overcome so much to be where we are today, but most of us have nothing to show for it. No one to share this life and its burdens with.

Aaron was lucky enough to get Jocelyn back, but Amberly lost Julian, and I pray she can get him back, for both our sakes. Losing him has opened my eyes and heart in more ways than I knew were possible. The thought that I might have him back is something I can't entertain, not until it becomes a reality.

You should have stopped her.

I know, and if anything happens to her because of this, I will never forgive myself. When Julian died, I felt like my soul went with him. I don't feel like myself. Yelling at people, not caring if Amberly does something that risks her life, and then there's Logan.

I knew I was starting to feel things for Logan, but I always shut them down. Mainly because of Amberly. I don't want to be one of those friends that get with the guys they have been with. After all, there is such a thing as girl code. But I'm also coming to realize you can't control who you have feelings for. If we could, I think we would do it a lot more. The other reason I kept my distance was that I've been closed off, and I've chosen to be that way for longer than I can remember.

I think everyone puts up a wall around themselves. We're human. It's a defense mechanism, and it's normal. However, once Logan kissed me, everything went out the window. I don't want to hurt Amberly, and I don't want to lose her as a friend, but I also don't want to let this pass me by. I feel like what Logan and I have is something stronger than what I've had with anyone in the past. He makes it harder to turn away, harder to not reach out for his hand, and I know there has to be a reason for that.

I never wanted it to happen, but somewhere along the way, it did, and I can't change it, and even if I could, I don't think I would want to. Kissing Logan felt right, different. We may not be as close as he and Amberly are, but I do consider him one of my best friends, and we get along so well that I don't see any way it wouldn't work out. But that doesn't mean I can't get hurt.

I decide to stop letting my worries get in the way of what I know in my heart I want. I smile and set the course in a new direction. The last place I saw Logan.

LOGAN

Angela's eyes catch mine from across the room, and my heart stops. *What should I say to her?* I kissed her. I REALLY KISSED HER. What came over me? I mean, I like her. There's no denying that, but how could I just go and kiss her like that? We've become such good friends in the short time we've known each other, and I don't want to mess that up. What if I already did? What if, by kissing her, I destroyed whatever relationship we did have? I'm sure she hates me. I would hate me. She has more than enough on her plate right now, and she doesn't need some lug like me coming in and acting like a dumb teenager. Letting the hormones take over all his actions.

I glance back in her direction to see she's only a few steps away.

"Angela, I," she silences me with her hand.

She quickens her stride, closing the distance between us so fast that my eyes barely catch the movement. *Brace yourself. She's going to hit you, and it's going to hurt.* I close my eyes, waiting for the pain to come. After all, I deserve whatever she gives me. I was an ass for the things I said and an even bigger ass for kissing her the way I did. I stand as still as possible, anticipating her slap as nervousness builds in my stomach. I'm just about to open my eyes, but then I feel her arms go around my neck and pull me downward. I open them as our lips touch. Staring down at her for a brief moment before I fall into the kiss. I lift my arms and throw them around her back, pulling her closer.

AIDAN

As Aaron shows me around the cave, people lock eyes on me and take a defensive stance. It happens every time I enter the room. That is until Aaron introduces me, then most of them relax, a little at least. He doesn't tell them I'm his son. Of course, why would he? Just like everyone else in this cave, I'm on guard, readying myself for anything.

I can't blame anyone for their actions. I'm the reason their people are dead and that most of the ones still alive are beaten badly. I may not have inflicted the pain with my own hands, but I did bring the fight to them.

"Jocelyn."

Anything but this.

I'm not ready for this.

"Aaron, there you are." Smiling as she approaches us.

"I'm sorry I had to take a little detour." He replies to her while looking over at me.

The worry is radiating off her when she asks him. "How is she? How is our daughter?"

He smiles down at her reassuringly, "She's fine."

I can see the relief as it washes over her, and she smiles. "Where is she? I want to see her."

I find myself wondering if she could come to care for me the way she does my sister. She's had eighteen years with her, to grow and to come to love her. But for me, she knows nothing about me, other than I've been working for Vladimir and that I'm a killer. How could a mother ever be proud of her child if he was a murderer?

She's going to hate you. My inner voice whispers.

You should leave.

Maybe I should.

"I'm not too sure. I think she went to look for Serenity."

Confusion takes the place of her smile. "What for?"

"Again, I'm not too sure. But there is someone I would like you to meet. Maybe we can go to the room and talk." He gestures towards me with his hand.

Suddenly I feel very uneasy. I've never been this on edge or nervous around anyone. What if she doesn't believe it, or worse if she wants nothing to do with me? I can't say I would blame her. I don't like myself most of the time, so why should I expect her to? I can't change my past; all I can do is make amends for all the wrong I have done and take responsibility for my actions. But I fear without my family, I won't be able to. I need them more than I would care to admit. Being around Amberly woke something in me, the good part of me that I pushed down all my life. She brings it out in me, and without her, I'm afraid it would disappear again. Return to the darkness, never to be seen again. I don't want that. I want to be good, be better. I never asked for this life. It was chosen for me.

A dark thought crosses my mind.

What if she tells Amberly she can't be around me? What if she makes me leave? All these questions plague my mind as I look at them.

She glances in my direction. "Why would we need to go to the room?"

"Just trust me. This is a conversation we need to have in private." Aaron replies.

Jocelyn groans in annoyance. "Fine. But after, I'm going to find our daughter. She's going to need her mother, now more than ever."

"She's stronger than I think you give her credit for."

"Strength has nothing to do with it. Losing the love of your life," She looks at my father sadly, "can bring the strongest person to their knees. We should know that better than anyone."

"That we do."

I notice tears shining in her eyes. "I don't want that for her. There must be something we can do. Anything."

"If there was, I would have already done it."

My parents look at each other sadly before my father walks over to her and takes her hand in his, bringing it to his lips. The way they look at each other makes me envious. I've never had anyone look at me the way they do. But then again, I've been living with Vladimir and his band of crazies. How could anyone ever look at me like that? I'm a killer. I'm nothing.

Aaron pulls her in for an embrace as his words break me from my dark thoughts. Silencing them, for now at least. "We will figure it out."

"I hope so. I don't think she will make it through this."

"You did."

She leans her head back to get a better look at him. "I was also older than she is now, and I had a village to care for and a child growing inside of me. I had no choice but to bury the grief of my loss."

"Yes, but I do believe that together we will help her through this. Julian," his voice breaks as he says his name, "his loss is hard on a lot of people. Our daughter will find a way through her grief. She will love again. She is young and strong. There is nothing she can't overcome. We only need to remind her of that."

"I think you're giving her too much credit."

"And I think you aren't giving her enough." He grins down at her.

"Hmm, would you look at that?"

His smile fades, unsure. "What?"

"It appears for once you could be right."

His smile returns in a giddy fashion. "Well, what do you know?"

She taps him on the chest playfully. "Don't let it go to your head. Remember, I'm the one who's always right."

He chuckles lightly while placing a kiss on her forehead. "Yes, my love."

Placing her head back on his chest, she mumbles. "I guess let's go get this conversation over with."

"The way you talk to me, woman. You know the right words to bring me to my knees." He says in a playful tone.

"I was simply saying."

He cuts her off in a happy tone. "I know what you were saying."

"Why are you picking on me?" She smiles up at him.

"Because I went eighteen long years without being able to. I have a lot of time to make up for."

She rolls her eyes at his stupidity. "Boy, I'm in trouble now."

"Yes, you are Miss Grayson."

Her smile lessens, and I can tell from her expression she's about to get very serious. "I was thinking."

"Yes."

"Remember all those years ago, before we thought we lost each other?"

He places a hand on her cheek in a loving gesture. "How could I ever forget?"

I'm gonna puke.

Placing her hand on his, she closes her eyes but only for a moment. "I was thinking about changing my name."

"Really? To what?"

Wow, my father is a moron.

"Really?" She giggles.

Confusion is clear in his tone. "What?"

Before I can stop myself, the words come flying out of my mouth. "She means she wants to take your name."

They both look at me with wide eyes before turning to one another.

Aaron speaks first. "Really?"

Her laugh shakes her small frame. "You need to find another word."

"I'm sorry. I'm just."

She cuts him off again. "Surprised."

"I don't think that's the word for it."

"Just think about it."

Releasing her, he takes her hands in his. "I don't have to think about it."

"Oh." She says in a discouraged tone.

"I want you to marry me, Jocelyn. I always have. That's never changed."

Excitement exudes off of her. "It's settled then."

"Yes. We will."

They speak at the same time. Aaron saying, "get married tonight." Jocelyn, "get married once things settle down."

Aaron smiles down at her. "I was thinking more like right away. We already have a reason to celebrate now that our daughter is home safe. So why wait? I think we've waited long enough. Don't you?"

No words come from her. Instead, she throws her arms around his neck, pulling him down for a kiss. Passersby stop in their tracks to look at them with googly eyes. *Suckers.* Everyone here is so cheery.

This is going to be harder than I thought.

They pull away from each other, foreheads touching as they look each other in the eyes, grinning from ear to ear. Then applause erupts through the room, and I can't stop myself from rolling my eyes.

Like a teenager, Aaron puts his hands in the air nodding his head in a douche baggish fashion before addressing their audience. "Thank you, thank you. We're here all night."

Jocelyn's cheeks flush as she grabs for his arms, making him lower them. "Let's go."

My parents start to walk in the direction of what I would guess is their room, and Aaron looks back over his shoulder at me to let me know to follow them. I've never in my life felt weak, or uneasy and being here with them, I'm feeling all kinds of things that are new to me. Many I don't care for, but some, some aren't too bad.

Watching their very public display of affection did make me want to vomit in my mouth, but it's also something I've dreamt about. Seeing a couple being truly happy and in love with one another. I wanted to believe the world could be a good place, but I never got the chance to see or experience any of it. Not until now.

Suddenly I find myself thinking about Amberly and wondering where she is and how she's doing.

Meeting My Mother

AIDAN

"Our son. How is that possible?" A puzzled look takes over Jocelyn's features as she looks over at me.

"I'm a little lost on how myself but Amberly's sure it's the truth, and I believe her."

She walks over to me slowly.

"Jocelyn," Aaron calls to her almost in a whisper.

Before I have time to react, she places her hand on my cheek.

"Jocelyn, don't!" I hear Aaron yell as he runs in our direction.

The skin of her hand becomes very warm, and moments after it connects with mine, the heat starts to spread through my whole body. I feel weak, and everything starts to go black. I feel her hand

leave my cheek as I drop to my knees. I blink frantically, trying to shake off the tired feeling taking hold of me.

"What did you do to me?" I ask her.

I look up to see her smiling down at me, "I did what I had to. I stripped some of your energy."

Hurt, I ask, "Why?"

"Because all I know about you for sure is that you're dangerous."

I shake my head back and forth, trying to clear the cobwebs. "I didn't come here to hurt anyone."

"You can say that, but it doesn't make it true."

I reach my hands out in front of me, offering them to her. "Read me then. I have nothing to hide. I know that's one of your powers."

She looks down at me hesitantly.

"Please, do it."

Jocelyn looks around the room like she's thinking about her next move. She glances over at Aaron, who looks more surprised than she does.

"I only came here because Amberly asked me to. I didn't want to come."

She looks at me accusingly. "Why come only because she asked?"

"Because I wanted to get to know my sister," I pause and look at Aaron, "and she wanted to get to know me."

"So, you tricked her."

I shake my head, starting to get dizzy again. "No. I told her," I look at Aaron once more, "told everyone the truth. If you don't believe me, I can't say I blame you, but I am telling you the truth."

"Maybe. Or maybe it's your truth."

I look at her, confused. "What do you mean?"

"Vladimir told you, you were our son; doesn't mean he wasn't lying."

Aaron takes a step towards us. "It wasn't a lie, Jocelyn."

She turns to him, looking furious. "You can't know that for sure." She turns back to me, "we don't know what powers he has; he could be tricking you."

"Everything I did, I did to save Amberly. That's all I cared about. I thought bringing her back with me would save her," I look at the ground feeling defeated, lost, and unsure of anything, "but once I realized it didn't make a difference, and he would kill her anyway, I got her out of there." I look back at them. "She begged me to return with her, and against my better judgment, I did."

They look at each other, unsure.

"Please, just read me this way. You know for sure what I'm telling you is the truth, and we can move past this unpleasant exchange."

Jocelyn looks down at me with hostility. I place my hands behind me so she knows I'm no threat. Her hand reaches out once more. It takes a lot of effort not to move away, knowing the pain that is coming. Her hand connects with my skin, and I feel a sharp sting as I suck in a deep breath.

"Jocelyn." I hear Aaron pleading with her.

"No, let her. I'm fine," I say to him.

Aaron doesn't move from his position, but I can tell from the look on his face he's not happy about it. I focus on the woman hovering over me as I concentrate on bringing down my walls and letting her completely in. We sit in this place for a long time. Aaron takes a seat sometime during the interrogation.

I pry my eyes open with some effort to look up at the woman hammering away inside my mind. Even with her eyes closed, I can see the tears finding their way down her cheeks. Seconds later, her eyes fly open, and she releases me as she falls back into Aaron's arms, sobbing.

"Aaron."

"It's alright. I'm here." He says while rubbing her back in a calming motion.

Her sobs shake her body viciously, and I find myself wondering which memories she stumbled upon in my damaged dark mind.

"What did you see?"

In a broken voice, she says, "It was horrible."

"Tell me."

"Vladimir, what he did to him." Her gaze lands on me, "he's had such a hard life."

She gets up slowly as Aaron uses his arms to steady her. They make their way over to my side then Jocelyn kneels down beside me, resting her hand gently on my cheek.

"My poor boy. I'm so sorry, I had to be sure. I shouldn't have done that. I didn't know." The tears in her eyes stream down her face in a panic. "I'm so sorry we weren't there for you."

My words come out in a jumbled mess. "You believe me?"

She nods her head and smiles. "Yes. I saw enough to know you're telling the truth."

Aaron looks down at us and asks her, "But how is it possible? I should have been able to sense him when I sensed our daughter."

She turns to look up at him. "I'm not sure. But I intend to find out." Looking back at me. "Does Amberly know everything?"

"Yes. I showed her like we just did. I told her she was my sister. I needed her to know why I did the things I did, and I knew if I showed her, she would understand. I knew she would believe me."

She places her hand on mine, trying to comfort me. "I understand, and I thank you for trying to protect her."

"She's my sister. I will always protect her."

Aaron smiles. "As you should."

I lower my gaze. "I'm sorry for my actions. I didn't realize what I was doing. I thought it was the only way."

"You don't need to apologize. You were only doing what you were taught to believe was right. No one can blame you for that."

She looks back at Aaron again. "They have us to blame. We should have known something wasn't right. We should have sensed you. We should have been there."

The pain on their faces takes me by surprise. Amberly told me they didn't know. That Vladimir took me, and they would have wanted me, but how could I believe that? But now, seeing them like this, I know it's true. If they had known, they would have done anything to get to me.

They would have loved me.

My life wouldn't have been filled with beatings, being torn down and told I would never be good enough. I never would have turned into this version of myself. If they were my parents from the start, my life would have been full of love and happiness. Of things, I don't understand. Things I can't express yet. I wouldn't have become the one thing I hate most about myself. The one thing I can never remove from my past.

The thing that makes me tainted.

I'm a murderer, and that will never change. No matter how much I want it to, no matter how much they love me, or we all wish things had been different. This one fact will forever be embedded into my DNA.

You are a murderer.

Cold-blooded.

Unforgiving.

Merciless.

No one could ever truly love you. You're kidding yourself.

My inner demon is resilient. But he's right. Like Vladimir said, I'm good for one thing. Bringing pain to everyone around me.

✳✳✳

AMBERLY

"Ok, what now?" I ask Serenity.

Looking down at Julian's lifeless body is one of the hardest things I've ever put myself through. Seeing him and the others dead in my dream wasn't real. It was something I worked so hard to prevent from happening. But really losing him was something I never let myself imagine.

Losing anyone would break me but in a different way. Everyone I love has a different part of my heart and soul. They affect me in different ways, and so their passing would take a different toll.

Losing Julian feels like I've lost my way, path, and future, and I don't know which way is up without him. The thought of this not working isn't something I can give power to. It has to work. Because I don't know what I'm going to do if it doesn't.

"Place your hands anywhere on his body." Serenity's voice comes to me from far away.

I do as she says.

"Now, close your eyes."

I do.

"I want you to focus all of your energy and all your love for him at once."

I try to focus like she asks.

"Are you doing it?"

I manage a nod.

"Once you feel it in your chest, I want you to move that energy only to your hands."

I feel the weight of it building inside my chest like she said, but I know it's not all there yet. I need more time.

"Once you have it in your hands, I want you to send it to your fingertips."

It's getting harder and harder to breathe.

Focus, Amberly. You can do this. You need to do this.

"Once you do. I want you to think of all that love and energy flowing from you into Julian, and I want you to picture all his wounds healing and him opening his eyes."

I take in a slow deep breath.

I hold it.

Concentrate.

I exhale.

I feel everything I have reaching my chest, and I push it to my hands in one movement. I take in another breath.

Hold it.

Concentrate.

I exhale.

I move the energy to my fingertips like she said. I think of Julian's touch, his smile, his kiss, the electricity that courses through me as his skin touches mine.

You will come back to me.

I focus all of my love for him, everything I have, and I let it go, let it pass through my fingers, and I feel it as it leaves me and transfers to his body.

And....

I feel heavy.

Weak.

Serenity's hands are the only thing holding me in place. I open my eyes and look down at Julian. I think about him healing and opening his eyes like she said. I think about him smiling up at me.

"How long does this normally take?"

There's sadness in Serenity's voice when she answers. "We should know within a few minutes."

I look up at her for the first time and wish I hadn't. I can see it on her face now. I turn my attention back to Julian and raise his hand to my lips and hold it there.

I'm not ready to let him go, not yet.

I can see it clearly now. Our future, one we build together for many years to come. There's nothing I long for more. I've never wanted something as much as I want him. It's more than want. It's a need. I can't imagine going through the rest of my life, growing old, laughing, loving, without him there with me every step of the way.

I look back at Serenity, and I know there's no mistaking what I'm seeing on her face even as she smiles down at me.

She doesn't think this is going to work.

She doesn't think he's going to wake up.

I look back down at Julian as I feel the tears roll down my cheeks and off my face as they land on his body below me.

∗∗∗

SERENITY

Her energy is building. I can sense it. A few moments pass, and then I see the essence of her strength as she's moving it through her body. I see it as it transfers from her into the boy. But I still feel the same. He still feels the same. I look down at her, hoping to give her whatever strength I have left in me. I reach out, trying to steady her as I look on at Julian's motionless body.

He's still lifeless.

His heart is still silent.

I can feel it.

As she looks up at me, I try to make my smile believable. *It didn't work.* It's a matter of minutes now before she realizes it too. I don't know how to shield her from this. Losing someone you love is hard enough, but losing your partner, the one person you're meant to share every moment of the rest of your life with. The one person who is supposed to be by your side through every laugh and every smile. Every cut, bruise, and tear. The one who's supposed to be there through all the ups and downs. To lose that person is a fate worse than death.

We all want that in our lives. We search the world until we find it. We need that other half to make our lives feel whole, and without it, we are only a fraction of ourselves.

I look down at her once more. What will she do now? I don't know if she's strong enough to handle this kind of loss. But we need to make sure she does. We need her here to fight. Without her, we will lose, and the world is lost.

"How long does this normally take?" She asks in a weak voice.

I can't hide the sadness in mine when I reply. "We should know within a few minutes."

I already know the truth, but that won't stop me from trying to spare her this for a few more minutes. Anything I can do to protect her, I will.

She glances up at me for a moment before looking back at the boy. She grabs his hand in haste and lifts it to her lips. Not speaking a word to me.

She knows.

We sit in silence for a few more minutes before she turns to me once more before tears begin to stream down her cheeks. I never had any children of my own, but I took to Amberly in an unknown way since we arrived here. Now I know she's the closest thing I've ever had to a daughter, and I would do anything to protect her.

There's only one person I know she will listen to. One person, she can fall into with her whole heart in a moment like this. This person would do anything for her in return, and she needs him more than ever.

With nothing else to be done, I reach out with my mind to Aayda.

Aidan

Aayda

"It's taking too long; we should go find them," Johnathan says as he continues to pace the room and make me more nervous than I already am.

Serenity should be here in the room with us, resting. She's not strong enough to be out doing what she's doing. I know it's important to teach Amberly everything we know, but she should have done it from here. From the safety of her bed. It makes me sad to think our time with her is limited. We've been together so long, the three of us, that the thought of one of us not being here anymore, it's more than I can stomach.

The girl has become important to her. Not in the same way she is to John and me. I can see it in her eyes, hear it in her voice. She looks at the child as if she could be hers. Out of all of us, Serenity is the one who always wanted children, and I think she would have been the best at it. She has the maternal instinct, the softness needed to be a good mother. I never had that, and I always questioned if the time ever did come, would I be ok at the job?

Part of me is happy I never had to find out, but on the other hand, I wonder what it would have been like to have little feet running amok around our home. Having a small person with a mixture of John and my features.

No. Serenity is the one who lost out. I always thought she should have been a mom, but this life we were given wouldn't allow it.

Vladimir and his crusade wouldn't allow for it.

I couldn't imagine taking a child with us as we ran for our lives, always in hiding. That wouldn't have been a life for any child. It sure as hell wasn't one for us.

A voice in my head pulls me away from my thoughts.

"Aayda?" The urgency in John's voice tells me my reaction startled him.

Once her voice is gone, I smile at him. "It's alright. It was Serenity."

He stands, his body tense. "Is she ok?"

"She's fine, but she needs me to do something and fast."

"What is it?"

I look over at him sadly. The thought of ever losing him, it's something I could never let enter my mind and to know that Amberly will be without her John saddens me on a level I don't understand. "She needs us to find Aidan and bring him to Amberly immediately."

"Why?"

"She fears he's the only one who can ground Amberly now."

He looks at me, and understanding becomes plain on his face as all his features go from ones of worry to ones of sadness. "It didn't work then."

"I'm afraid not. And it's a matter of minutes before Amberly realizes it herself."

He grabs me by the hand. "Then let us go."

LOGAN

Kissing Angela is different than kissing Amberly. I know that's not what I should be thinking about right now, but I promise there's a reason. With Amberly, she was the only girl I ever really had feelings for, so our kisses were intense. With Angela, they feel soft and comforting. I feel a calm with her that I never had with Amberly. And for the first time, I find myself wondering if Amberly and I were ever really meant to be more than friends in the first place. What I feel right now with Angela, Amberly, and I didn't hold a candle to.

There's something about her I can't figure out, but this feels right. It feels like I'm where I belong. I always found myself on edge with Amberly, but it doesn't feel forced or thought out with Angela. It just happens.

That's how it's supposed to be, right?

I place my hand on the lower part of her back and pull her all the way to me as my other hand gets lost in her hair. Breathing her and this moment in as our lips crash together like we've been separated for years.

I'm pulled from the ecstasy of the moment when she pulls out of my embrace and away from me so fast, I almost get whiplash.

She throws her hand over her mouth. "I shouldn't have done that."

I find myself panting trying as I try to catch my breath. "Why not?"

She looks around the room frantically. "What if someone had seen us?"

Surprised, I say. "Why would that have mattered? Are you embarrassed to be seen with me?"

She closes her eyes and folds her arms over her chest like she's trying to protect herself from something I don't see. "No. It's not that."

"Then what?"

She looks at me sadly. "Amberly."

Before I can say a word, she turns and walks away. Leaving me with nothing by my thoughts and the memory of what just took place.

***

JOCELYN

"We've lost so much time," I say to them sadly.

Aaron takes my hand in his. "All that means is we have more to catch up on." He looks over at our son. "Right?"

Aidan nods.

"I'm so sorry, Aidan."

"Please, stop apologizing. It's not like you knew about me."

I look at him sadly. "What did Vladimir tell you?"

He looks at me, confused. "What do you mean?"

"I mean, how did he say he found you?"

I can see anger taking place in his eyes. "He told me you threw me away like an old pair of gloves," he looks over at us and smiles, "but it wasn't true, so I can't blame you for something you knew nothing about."

Annoyed and angry, I come up with an idea. "I want to try something if you'll let me?"

He nods.

"I think I might be able to figure out how he hid you from us. I can go into your mind and access the moment it happened."

Aaron moves in his seat, and I can tell he's eager, and so is Aidan from the look on his face.

"When can we do it?" He asks.

"Tomorrow. I've put you through enough for today." I smile at him forgivingly.

"You were only doing what any sane, smart person would do in your situation."

"Thank you for being understanding about it, but I should have listened before I jumped to such drastic measures."

"Yeah. You should have." Aaron says with a smile.

We all look at each other and start laughing.

"This is nice," I say to no one in particular.

Aidan surprises me when he says. "Yeah, it is."

"I would like to get to know you better," I say.

A small smile takes place on Aidan's face. "I would like that." He looks at Aaron. "I would like to get to know both of you." His smile disappears. "Even after Vladimir said you didn't want me, I still wondered what you were like and what it would have been like being with you."

I place a hand on his. "Well, now you don't need to wonder."

We smile at each other, and my heart feels full. Both my children are here, and they are safe. That's all that matters.

Aidan's words pull me back to this moment. "So, earlier." He says shyly.

"Yes?" I ask, not sure what he's talking about.

"I overheard you and Aaron, remember?"

Aaron moves forward. "What are you talking about, son?"

"When you said you were going to get married tonight."

My cheeks flush as I forget he was there for the moment Aaron and I shared. A moment that should have taken place in the privacy of our own room.

"I think we have too much going on right now."

Disappointment is clear in his eyes. "Don't let me stop you."

"It's not that. There is a lot to process, and I still need to check on Amberly and see how she is after everything."

"So, you're not getting married?" He asks.

"Not tonight," Aaron says sadly. He reaches over and takes me by the hand, "but very soon. We don't plan on wasting any more time."

∗∗∗

AIDAN

There's a knock on the door, and then Johnathan and Aayda enter the room.

Aaron addresses them first. "What is it? Serenity? Is she ok?"

Aayda smiles at Aaron. "She is doing as well as can be expected in her condition but thank you for your concern." She turns to look in my direction, and I take an involuntary step back. "We've come for the boy."

Aaron looks between us before coming to take his place in front of me, and if I didn't know any better, he looks like he's in a protective stance. "Why?"

Aayda's smile expands across her face. "We mean him no harm. Serenity needs the boy. She thinks he is the only one who can help Amberly."

At the sound of my sister's name, I think of her and…

Now I can feel it.

The emptiness.

The ache in her heart.

The uncertainty.

I look at Aayda. "It's Julian."

She nods her head.

Aaron looks at me, and then Jocelyn whispers. "What about Julian? What's going on?"

Aayda replies. "Amberly asked for Serenity's help to try to bring him back."

Jocelyn's mouth drops. "She what?"

Aaron's tone omits his anger. "What is she thinking?"

Jocelyn looks at him. "She's not. That's the problem. I told you she wouldn't be able to handle losing him. I just didn't think she would go to this extreme."

"So, I guess you're happy then?" I ask.

They both look at me. "About what?"

"That it didn't work."

I see the shock and hurt in their eyes when she says. "Why would you think that?"

"Because if it did work, then she would have lost part of herself." I look at Aayda, "isn't that how their power works?"

She nods.

I continue, "I've only known you a short while, but I'm fast at picking up people's personalities. I know you don't want her hurting, but you would prefer that over the alternative. She might have walked away fine, but there's really no way to know for sure. So, maybe it not working was for the best."

The sadness in Jocelyn's voice is obvious. "No. Julian will be missed. He had his whole life ahead of him, and he made Amberly happy. That's all we want for her. However, if bringing him back, anyone back, would cause her damage to herself, then no. Call me selfish, but I wouldn't want her to use her powers. Not if the cost was part of herself, and I know Julian would feel the same way."

She turns away, finding her place on the bed as Aaron touches my shoulder, reassuring me, and then moves to her side. He places the same hand on her shoulder, trying to comfort her, and then she looks over at me. "I don't know how she's going to make it through this."

I walk over to her side and kneel down in front of her. "I'll be there to help her put herself back together. I promise."

She looks me in the eyes. "Maybe I should go with you. She's going to need me."

Aayda speaks. "No. Only your son. She needs him."

"But she needs me too. I've lived through similar pain."

Aayda looks back and forth between Aaron and Jocelyn. "I know you have, and I know you wish to be there for her now, but she doesn't need you. Not yet."

"But I'm her mother."

"And I wish I could tell you that would be enough, but right now, we can't take a chance that she goes off the deep end. She needs her brother, her twin. If anyone can reach her, it's going to be him."

Jocelyn looks down at her hands like she's unsure what they are there for.

Aayda smiles at her. "Right now, she needs someone who can feel her pain as their own. Your pain is gone now that you are reunited with your lost love. You won't share what she's feeling." She turns to look at me. "He will. They are twins. I'm sure he can feel her pain already."

As if that was a cue, I feel a pain in my heart. I stand up fast and look down at my parents once more. "I need to go. Now!"

Parents.

The word sounds weird to me, even in my head. Something I never thought I would have, and now I do. So many things are changing, I hope I can keep up. The thing that matters most is getting to my sister. Her pain is so strong.

I head for the door, stopping to look back at them one more time. "I will be back with my sister. I promise she will be ok."

My father nods, and I walk out the door.

Loss

DEAN

"Amberly's back. Does she know about Julian yet?" I ask Amara.

She looks at me as sadness spreads across her face. "Yes."

"Oh, man." I lift my hand to play with the hair on the back of my neck. "How is she doing?"

"As well as can be expected, I guess."

I lower my hand to my side. "Maybe we should all get together and do something tonight. To distract her."

She looks up at me for the first time. "I think that would be a good idea. After what she's trying, I think she will need it."

She starts to walk away, but I stop her with my question. "What is she trying?"

She turns around to look at me. "To bring Julian back to life."

"What! She can do that?"

"Apparently, that's one of her powers."

"Where did you hear this?"

"Everyone is talking about it. Apparently, one of the pack was outside of Johnathan's room when Amberly went there to ask for Serenity's help to heal him."

I look at her, unsure. "You think it will work?"

She looks at her feet as she kicks a small pebble with her shoe. "Honestly, I don't know. Bringing someone back from the dead. I've never heard of it being done before."

"Well, I hope she can do it."

Amara looks up at me with a look I can't describe. "I hope she can't."

Shocked, I ask. "Why would you say that?"

"Because as much as it sucks and as much as it hurts. Death is a part of life. There is a balance, and if she starts messing with it, one of two things could happen."

She pauses, so I ask. "Which are?"

"Well, one could be that it throws things off in our world. Meaning, he was supposed to die but because he didn't, the future we were meant to live is changed, which can make things worse for us. The second is a life for a life. A debt will be owed, and all debts are paid. One way or the other."

***

JOHNATHAN

"I really thought it was going to work," I say to no one in particular.

"So did I," Aayda says as she places her hand on my shoulder.

I sigh, placing my hand on hers. "We needed him alive."

"There is more to life than fighting my love."

Looking up into her loving eyes, I reply. "Yes, I know. It would have been good to have him here for the fight ahead, but that isn't what I meant."

She sits down next to me. "Then what did you mean?"

"Amberly. She needs him. He grounds her while at the same time makes her more alive." I turn in her direction. "I worry what she will become without him."

"She is strong."

"Yes. Stronger than she knows. But I fear this will give Vladimir the edge he's been waiting for."

I hear the worry in her voice. "What do you mean?"

"Losing someone you love changes you."

"Yes."

I look over at her. "It can let darkness into your heart if you let it."

She shakes her head. "No. Amberly, won't be that easily influenced."

"I don't know, my love. We see the darkness is possible. Aidan shows us that much. And the journals."

She cuts me off. "You and Serenity have believed in that girl since the beginning. Don't stop now."

"I have faith in her. I do. However, life has taught me a lot, and now without him here to anchor her and in his place." I sigh. "In his place is someone darker and connected to her in more ways than Julian ever could have been. It causes me to have doubt."

"But he's open to the light now. We've seen it."

I nod. "Yes. But the darkness will always be there. And they are twins. What one has, the other can inherit."

"Well, then we will have to just stick around and make sure she stays in the light."

I look at her sadly. "I wish it was something to be fixed that easily."

"I'm not naïve. I know it won't be easy."

"If she's closed off, there's nothing we can do to change that or the outcome. Not without the boy."

She looks at the door. "Let us hope then that her brother will be enough to ground her like Serenity thinks." She looks over at me. "And let us pray harder that he will not return to the darkness, leading her down the path alongside him. We can't afford to lose these battles ahead."

I look at the door. "I know."

✳✳✳

JOCELYN

"I need to go find Amberly. It's been too long."

Aaron looks at me sadly. "It's only been twenty minutes. You need to trust our son. He will bring her to us when she is ready."

I look over at him, and it's hard to hide my excitement when I say. "Our son. We have a son."

His smile reaches his eyes. "Yes."

I look away from him. "I'm still having a hard time wrapping my head around it."

"You're not the only one."

Smiling, I say. "You always wanted a son."

He looks nervous. "I."

"Don't think I forgot about all our late-night conversations."

He laughs. "I know you better than that. You never forget anything. Especially the things I would like you to forget."

I turn away, embarrassed.

I can sense the worry in his voice when she says. "But."

I look over at him. "What?"

"I would be lying if I didn't say I was worried."

My smile disappears. "I know. Me too. Vladimir had a hold over him for eighteen years. And from what I saw, he did a lot of damage."

"How can we correct eighteen years of hate and darkness?" Sadness lingers in his eyes, "And murder. How do we erase all of that? How do we forget what he's done?"

I look down at my hands. "Maybe we start by not forgetting. He needs to remember and learn and own his mistakes." I peer up at him. "But most of all, he needs to know we love him, and we will love him no matter what his past was. We're his parents, Aaron. We need to be there for him now more than ever."

He nods. "You're right."

"Aren't I always?"

He smiles. "Hey, I'm right sometimes."

I scoff. "Yeah. Rarely."

Our futures aren't going to be easy. The days ahead are going to be hard. Amberly will need us more than ever to help her pick up the pieces and put them back together again. Then, while dealing with a shattered daughter, we need to work on our son who I feel is still full of darkness. We need to get him to see he belongs here and that he can walk away from the last eighteen years of his life and still live in love and happiness surrounded by his family. Then there's the fight that I know is coming our way. Vladimir won't just let Aidan walk away, and he knows to turn the world into his version of utopia, he needs to get rid of my daughter. We have many battles ahead of us, and none are going to be easy.

I look over at Aaron and smile.

As long as we have each other, there's nothing we can't overcome.

Together.

We can do anything.

***

AAYDA

"Serenity is in no condition for the battle coming our way," I say to Johnathan.

"I agree."

"What are we going to do? I can't lose her, John, not yet."

He looks at me, and I find his eyes mimic mine, and I know he's just as worried when he says, "I know."

I lean into his arms as they encircle me, and I feel they are the only thing stopping me from falling into pieces. Our whole lives have been running and battles. When will it end? When can we live in peace and just be together?

"We can't leave. You know that, don't you?" His words feel far away.

"Yes. I would never suggest it. They need us, especially now with Amberly only a fraction of herself."

I sit up, and he places his hand on top of mine. "We need to help them train more. The next battle won't be as easy as the last, and I fear without much guidance, none of them will walk away from what's coming next."

"We need them to win. If they don't."

He looks at me sadly. "I know." He turns his attention to the doorway. "If Amberly and the others don't come together and get through this, the world is doomed." He looks back at me. "There will be no one to stop the other seven, and the world as we know it will be covered in darkness."

The words fight their way to the surface until they win and fly from my mouth. "They are closer than we thought."

Surprise takes over his features. "What do you mean?"

"The other seven. I've been sensing them a lot more lately."

I see the worry forming in his eyes as he says. "I have too."

"Why didn't you say anything?"

He turns away before answering. "What good would it have done? It won't change anything. They show up a week or a month from now. Either way, they are still coming, and either way, we know what the outcome is going to be."

I suck in a slow breath. "There's still a chance."

"It's getting smaller and smaller."

Looking at the door, I exhale. "As long as we keep them on the right path, they could win. I've never known you to be so negative."

"The boy is still a wild card. He worries me. I'm not trying to be negative. It's simply what I've been feeling."

"I know he's a wild card, but with her guidance, I see him coming to our side."

"With Amberly's help? You mean the girl who's broken and shattered? She can't even help herself right now."

I sigh. "True. But the only thing I know for sure is he wants her safe, he cares for her, and those feelings will make him leave the dark in his past."

"We can only hope." He looks at me, "how long do you think we have?"

"Until Vladimir comes. Days until the final battle. If I had to guess, less than two weeks. I don't know, maybe three. Yes, three at most for sure."

His gaze falls to the floor. "That's what I've been feeling as well."

Inconsolable

AMBERLY

"I don't understand. He should be waking up." I turn to Serenity, who continues to look down at me. "Why isn't he waking up?" I ask her frantically.

She looks at the ground and lowers her voice. "Amberly. I told you there was a very strong chance it wouldn't work."

I don't let her finish. "No. No. He's going to wake up." I shake her hand off my shoulder and pick Julian up in my arms. "He's going to be fine." I move the strands of hair out of his face. "He's going to open his eyes and smile at me. I can feel it."

He's going to come back to me. I can't do this without him.

I knew from the look on her face earlier that it hadn't worked. I can't accept it. I won't. For us to come this far only to lose one another doesn't seem right. We've overcome and been through so much together. We can get through this.

I remember the day he found me in the woods. How afraid I was to see a wolf his size but hearing him in my thoughts created a new life for me. I trusted him, trusted my gut, and left everything and everyone I ever knew to get answers. He saved me from that wolf on our journey, and during the fight, it was like we became one. I had never felt something like that before. Then we made it through me almost dying, not once but three times by my current calculations. We got through my feelings for Logan and him kissing Amara, and we even got past my father and the pack rules. If we could overcome all of that, then there has to be a way now.

"Too much time has passed, sweetheart. I'm so sorry."

I shake my head. "No. You're wrong. You'll see he's going to wake up. Just give it some more time."

"Too much time has passed already. If it was going to work, he would have woken up by now."

"No!"

I can't let her words in. She's wrong. It's going to work. It has to. I can feel it in my bones. He's going to wake up. He can't leave me here. I need him.

"Amberly. Please, let me take you inside now."

I only shake my head, letting her know I'm not moving.

"It's cold out here. You're going to get sick."

"I don't care. I'm not going to leave his side."

She exhales a slow breath. "It's time to let go, honey."

"I can't."

Slowly she places her hand on my shoulder. "You need to. It's time to grieve and move on."

"How can you even say that?"

"I don't mean it to sound harsh, but you can't lose yourself in this. It isn't what he would want for you."

I look down at Julian's still lifeless body, and even though I know, she doesn't know him. I know she's right. He wouldn't want me to be sad or to dwell, but it's not that easy. What if it were me who died? How would he have gone on after that? I know he wouldn't give up on me. He would believe there was a way. He wouldn't give up until he tried every possible avenue to get me back. I have to do the same. We finally made our way back to each other and overcame everything in our way. It can't end like this. We deserve our happily ever after.

"Amberly." His voice comes from far away.

I turn around to see Aidan running down the hill towards us.

✳ ✳ ✳

VLADIMIR

"I'm sorry, sir, I can't find them anywhere."

I bare my teeth. "It's because they aren't here." I turn around with anger at its purest form on my face, "Who was on watch last night? I want them brought to me immediately."

"Yes, sir."

He exits the room, and I'm alone once again.

In the darkness.

Just like I like it.

Aidan thinks he can escape me? He is sadly mistaken.

I will find him. I will kill his sister, and I will make him watch me do it. He needs to learn there are consequences to actions. After everything I've done for that boy, how dare he defy me. I don't think he understands what I'm handing over to him. My legacy, my utopia. His family can't give him what I am offering. If he stands with them, only death will come. What legacy could they hope to give him? They are tainted and impure. The world needs to be rid of his family's kind. I was making an exception, letting him live. Some say I'm soft when it comes to him, and maybe I am. After eighteen

years of molding him into the perfect weapon, he's the closest thing I've had to a family or a son.

That doesn't matter now. I won't let one child destroy what I have worked centuries on building. If he stands against me, stands with them, then death is what he's chosen.

"Here you go, sir."

He shoves the night watcher to the ground, and I smile down at him.

Time for my fun.

Time to learn about consequences.

✳✳✳

AMBERLY

"I don't understand. It should have worked." My words sound hoarse as I peer up at Aidan. "Maybe I should rest and try again in the morning. I'm just tired. Maybe I didn't have enough energy to pull it off." I look at my feet. "Yes, that's it."

"Amberly."

I look back up at him, afraid of what I might find there. I haven't known him very long, but I feel connected with him like we are one and the same. Maybe it's the twin thing. I feel like he's always been around, always been with me, and I have a sneaky suspicion he knows me better than I know myself and that alone scares me.

"I think you know that's not the problem."

I turn away.

"Julian's gone. You need to let that in. You need to grieve."

I pull away from him and fall to my knees. He kneels down next to me, moving the hair from my tear-soaked face. "I'm sorry. I'm new to this. I don't mean to hurt you, but you need to let it in, deal and move on. We don't have time to wallow in these things, not yet."

I stare at him, barely able to make out his shape through the tears that now fill my eyes. "How can you be so closed off?"

He looks hurt by my words. "I don't mean to be." He leans back. "I'm trying. I really am." He closes his eyes. "When you're brought up the way I was, love and friendship are considered a weakness," he looks at me, and I can see the pain in his eyes. "If it were you lying there, I don't know what I would do or how I would react. Like he is your weakness, you're mine. My only weakness."

I take in a short, surprised breath.

He smiles at me lightly. "And Vladimir knows it. He will be coming for us, for you, and I won't let anything happen to you." He turns to look deeper into the forest behind us. "I need you at the top of your game, not what you are now." He looks back at me. "I need you strong. You won't last five minutes against anyone the way you are now."

"I know that."

"I need you to care that you won't."

I turn my attention to my hands as they take in a fistful of dirt. "I can't. Because I don't care."

He sucks in a short breath before saying. "Amberly, this isn't the end of your life. Losing Julian isn't the end of you. You will love another."

I look up at him angrily. "I don't want to love another. Don't you understand?" Looking into his eyes, I can see he's not like everyone else. Something is missing. I remember his earlier words before continuing, "I don't think you can."

I can see my words hurt him. "Yes. I'm not like you. Maybe in time, I'll understand, but right now, all I care about is keeping you alive."

"Even when that's not what I want."

"Especially then." He smiles down at me as he stands up and offers me his hand. "He wouldn't want you to give up."

I look at him as I place my hand in his. "How do you know what he would and wouldn't want?"

"Because if he loved you, he wouldn't want you to share in his fate. He would want you to live and to keep living," He smiles at me as he pulls me to my feet, "I know because it's what I would want for you."

$$***$$

AIDAN

As I watch her sleep, I wish I could understand what she's feeling. I can see and feel how much pain she is in, and it hurts me knowing I can't do anything to help her. I can't even talk to her about it because I don't understand it myself. Tonight was horrible. I said all the wrong things. The harder I tried, the worse it got. I find myself wishing for the first time that I could trade places with someone else. I want to understand. I need to. It's one thing to feel it because she's feeling it, but it's another to understand it.

I know if we were to trade places, I would feel like she is now. If it was her, if I had lost her tonight, I would have been the inconsolable one. But still, I can't seem to wrap my head around her emotions. Mine would be for the loss of my sister, my twin, someone I'm connected to. Her loss is for a boy. I can't seem to get my head around it, but I know her pain is something real and strong because I can feel it. I only wish I could understand, could be there for her the way I need and want to be.

It's hard to really be there for someone you care about when you can't understand what they are going through. I've never loved anyone before. I don't even know if what I feel towards her is love or not. Other than anger, fear, and pleasure, I haven't experienced emotions. How am I to know what I'm feeling now if I've never felt it before? I know I care for her and would do anything for her. Protect her, keep her from harm and hurt no matter the cost to me.

Is that what love is?

Being here only reminds me more of how different and damaged I am. I'm a hollow shell, and I find myself wondering if it's too late for me. Can I truly learn a new way and live my life differently? Can I be forgiven? Will I be able to forgive myself?

As I look down at my sister, I find myself truly afraid. Afraid she will see me for what I really am and see that there's no hope for me. Once she sees that side of me, I'm afraid she will give up, leave, and walk away. Leaving me only to return to the darkness.

I wouldn't blame her for turning away from me. I don't even like me. This person I've become isn't who I wanted to be. Now that I have her, I want to be a man that would make her proud to call me brother. I want her to see me as I want to be.

A good man.

A caring man and brother.

The little voice inside my head whispers in a sinister voice, *She's going to leave you. She's going to walk away.*

She won't.

Oh, but she will.

I need her. If I hope to change who I am, be a better man, and atoning for my mistakes, I need her. She's the only thing in eighteen years that has made me want to be better, want to change. Without her, I'll revert back to what I was. A monster in its purest form.

I think of my father, my real father. A leader. He's a good man, I can tell by the way he is with my mother. He's loving, understanding. Genuine. I want to be that man. The version of myself I would have become if they had raised me. Not what Vladimir turned me into. Amberly is the key, and without her, I would be nothing more than what I've been the last eighteen long years.

Nothing more than a murderer, hands forever stained with the blood of innocence.

I will not become that man again.

The man alone in the dark thirsty for the next battle, for death.

I will not let it in.

The hunger for carnage. The bloodthirsty man Vladimir turned me into, the man he always wanted me to be.

I will not let him win.

✳✳✳

JULIAN

Desperate for air.

I open my mouth, waiting for it to come.

Nothing.

My lungs, burning.

My mouth, dry.

Eyes glued shut.

Pain everywhere.

Where am I? The last thing I remember.

Amberly.

She was hurt.

I move my hands to my chest.

Or was it me that was hurt?

Confusion taking hold. Trying to think hurts. I feel like my mind is fighting to catch up to every thought. Nothing is working right. My thoughts, my actions feel distorted. They don't feel like my own.

What happened to me?

I need air.

I try again.

Nothing.

I need air now!

I focus.

I breathe in hard.

Air enters my lungs.

I feel them expand.

I choke.

I cough.

I ache.

I need to open my eyes, I need to get up, I need water, I need....

I need to find Amberly.

Planning

AIDAN

I wake up from a deep sleep and turn my attention to the clock sitting on the nightstand next to me. Almost midnight. *Why am I so hungry?* I look over to find Amberly still fast asleep. I cover her shoulders with the blanket and exit the room.

As I try to remember the way to the dining room, my stomach releases a loud growl. I can't remember the last time I was this hungry. The cave is so big, and Aaron showed me around so fast that I can't remember which tunnel to take.

I turn the corner and smack foreheads with someone.

I look down to see the girl called Angela, now nursing her forehead. She looks up at me and smiles. "Sorry, I wasn't watching where I was going."

"I can see that." She looks surprised. "But I wasn't either."

"Where were you off to?"

I hesitate for a moment before I answer her. "I was getting kind of hungry."

"I can show you where the dining hall is."

I lift my hand to shrug her off. "You don't need to bother yourself with that. I'm sure I'll stumble across it sooner or later."

"No, bother at all." She turns around, looking over her shoulder at me, "follow me."

I glance around, noticing no one else is in sight, and figure she is my best option. But part of me still wonders why she would help me out at all. Why is she being so nice to me?

She looks back at me before asking. "Where were you coming from?"

"I. I was with my sister."

Sadness fills her eyes. "Oh, how is she doing? I heard," her voice cracks, "heard it didn't work."

I glance down at my feet. "As good as can be expected, I guess. She really thought it was going to work."

"I think we all did."

"Maybe it's good that it didn't."

She slows her pace. "Why would you say that?"

I shrug. "From what I heard, bringing someone back takes a huge toll on the person doing it. I worry about her, and if it did work, what would happen the next time someone died? She would keep bringing them back. Until she couldn't anymore. Call me selfish, but I choose my sister's well-being over anyone else. Including myself."

She stares at me in surprise before turning around.

I lower my voice when I ask, "Did you know him?"

She nods. "He was like a brother to me."

Now that's something I can relate to. "I'm sorry. That kind of loss can't be easy."

She smiles at me lightly. "Thank you." She lifts her hand to gesture to the room in front of her. "Here we are."

My eyes open wider in surprise. "Wow, it's bigger than I remembered."

She laughs. "Yeah, we get that a lot. Do you need me to show you around?"

"No, I'm ok. Thank you for your help."

She smiles, turning to walk away. "No problem."

I call after her. "Angela."

She stops. "Yeah."

"I'm sorry again for your loss."

She nods her head at me in thanks and exits the room leaving me alone to ransack the kitchen.

***

VLADIMIR

"I want everyone ready to leave in two days' time."

My new second in command walks over to me. "Sir, are you sure that's a good idea?"

"Are you questioning a direct order?"

I can smell his fear, and I grin.

Fear is good.

"No, sir. I only want to make sure we are ready for the fight. We don't want to fail you, and now without Aidan."

Anger erupts. "I don't want to hear that name."

"Yes. Sir."

I look down at him. "As for the traitor. Don't worry, I will deal with him."

"Sir."

"I'm strong enough to take him on."

Uncertainty is clear in his eyes, no matter how hard he is trying to hide it. "I don't doubt that sir. But now with him and Amberly and everyone else they have. I don't feel we are ready as a whole to take them on. Not yet. We need time. I don't want us to lose this battle for you and your dream for the new world."

"Thank you for caring, but I know what I'm doing."

He turns his attention to his feet. "As you say, sir. I will ready the troops."

"Good."

As he leaves me, only the thought of ending their species once and for all occupies my mind. They are like cockroaches. In my way, a nuisance, and even though you don't want it, they keep multiplying and are hard to kill.

But I will.

I will put an end to them once and for all.

And the first ones to go will be Aidan and his manipulative sister.

$$***$$

AMARA

"Hey, stranger," I say to Troy as he's in earshot.

Grinning, he replies. "Hey, yourself."

"I've been wondering where you got to."

"Was just around."

I smile. "Oh, yeah?"

"Yeah." His grin widens.

Things with Troy and I have gotten weird, to say the least. Since the battle ended, it's mainly been him and me while everyone else dealt with all the destruction and death around us. We were, after all, the only outsiders left. Logan was missing, and Amberly was taken. So, I guess it was pretty normal for us to come together since we knew each other better than anyone else in the cave.

For those two days, we searched for Logan together. During the hours of searching, we would talk a lot. About each other, stupid stuff and then some things that weren't so stupid. Somewhere along the way, between the searching and talking, there was a shift. Troy isn't really what I would call my type, so the way I feel took me by surprise. He's funny and a pain in the ass, sweet at the same time, and when things are tough, he is always there when you need him. He really is a good guy to have around. We were getting to know each other, and things started to shift before the battle, but these feelings became more concrete once the battle was over.

Hence the reason for the weirdness between us.

"Troy?"

"Yeah."

"You like me, right?"

He looks at me, surprised. "What's not to like?"

I sigh. "No, I mean you *like* me, right?"

"Oh." He tugs his long fingers through his hair. "I um."

"Really? You're choosing now to get choked up. You never shut up any other time. Like for real, it's an easy question and an even easier answer. It's one word, man. You can't get out one word? Yes or no. That's all you need to say."

Then his lips are crushing against mine.

Forceful but pleasant.

Calm but wild in nature.

He shut me up by kissing me.

Troy is kissing me.

Wow.

I've kissed my fair share of people, but when I say kissing him is mind-blowing, that's an understatement. I've never felt this kind of electricity before. It's intense, and all I want to do is keep kissing him. I don't want to stop. His lips on mine, his hands wrapped around me, this feeling it's creating just feels right.

And calming.

With everything we have going wrong in our lives right now, one nice thing can go a long way, but who would have thought this would have been the one right thing? I know I didn't.

***

TROY

I don't know how to answer her question. I mean, of course, I like her. What's not to like? She reminds me of myself, and I think that's cool as hell. She's outspoken, a jokester, and she's real. She's beautiful and smart too. Who wouldn't like her?

Her words bring me back to reality. "Really? You're choosing now to get choked up. You never shut up any other time. Like for real, it's an easy question and an even easier answer."

Oh, my God, I need to shut her up. Well, Logan did tell me the best way to shut a girl up. But I don't know if it will work on *this girl*.

She continues. "It's one word, man. You can't get out one word? Yes or no. That's all you need to say."

Ok. I'm chancing it.

I take a step forward and place my hand half on her cheek and half on her neck as I pull her closer to me, bending down until my lips touch hers. I wait for her to start hitting me, but it never happens. Instead, she starts to kiss me back.

Relief hits me.

Wait.

She's kissing me back.

With her, this feels different.

Intense.

I can feel her energy running through her body, almost like it's entering mine.

I've never felt this before. What does it mean?

I place a hand on her back and move her closer to me as the heat in her body increases and spreads to mine, intensifying.

What is this?

I wonder if she's feeling this too.

Her arms go around my waist and pull me even closer.

When Amara first came to the cave, everyone was unsure about her, especially after hearing Vladimir's name. But I felt something different when I looked at her. I saw myself. I could tell she was scared, alone, and blocked off. When she had told us she had decided to stick around, I almost couldn't hide my excitement.

I never really cared enough about girls. I mean, I would hook up with them, but that was it. I never had the time for anything else. Never cared to. Amberly was more than enough to deal with on an everyday basis. I didn't want to have another one to worry about every day. Logan and I would get overrun, and then what? No more of the guys chilling. It would be whatever the girls wanted and when they wanted it. But with Amara, things felt different from day one. I didn't want to keep away from her. Instead, I wanted her around.

I never saw her as losing my independence. I saw her as gaining something. Gaining a friend, a companion, and someone I could have around whenever Logan was off with Amberly. But now that that's ended, I feel a little guilty moving forward with Amara. But at the same time, this couldn't feel righter. It's surprising and scary because, in a way, we barely know each other, and it feels like no time has passed at all. But at the same time, it feels like this is where we were always meant to end up.

Almost, like maybe, I never cared too much about other women because I was waiting for her all along. She's different from any other girl I've ever known, minus Amberly. The two of them, in some ways, could be a guy the way they act and how independent they are. But for me, that's a turn-on. A woman who wants you but doesn't need you because she can take care of herself. What man wouldn't want that? That trait in a woman makes her more likable because she only adds to who you are.

More than knowing she doesn't need me but yet accepts me makes all the difference in a man's ego. It definitely makes me feel better about myself. She could have any man in this cave, and yet I kiss her, and she chooses to kiss me back.

Wait, she kissed Julian too.

I'm overthinking this.

I move away from my thoughts and allow myself to get lost in this moment with her. Our lips locked together like no one could sever them.

I definitely wouldn't want them to.

I feel like things are looking up like they will work out for the best for the first time. It's not only because I'm kissing her, and she's kissing me back. It's more like intuition. Us united makes me feel like nothing can stand in our way.

This Can't Be Happening

Not Again

JULIAN

I push open the door slowly.

It's dark.

I put one foot in front of the other.

Struggling.

Pain spreading.

Body shutting down.

I need water.

No, I need Amberly.

I try again.

I stumble.

I fall to my knees.

I look up.

There she is, asleep in her bed.

Amberly.

She's ok. Thank God she's ok. I need to get to her, need to touch and hold her. I need to know she's really ok that this isn't a dream. I fall forward and place my hands on the ground in front of me.

I can't move.

I can't stand.

I'll never make it to her side.

I look up at her once more.

Defeated.

I open my mouth.

Dry.

I choke out one word hoping it will be enough.

"Amberly."

AMBERLY

I wake up with tears still in my eyes. I wipe them away angrily. Aidan's right. I need to deal with this. *But how?* How can I do that?

How can I let him go when I'm still dreaming of him saying my name? How can I let go of someone I should have had forever? We didn't get enough time. This isn't supposed to happen. We are teenagers. We aren't meant to fight and die, not at this age. I shouldn't have to say goodbye, not yet. Not when we were only starting. I throw my hands over my eyes, and I can't stop the sobs that come next.

That's when I hear it again, almost as if it's a whisper.

"Amberly."

I look over at my door, and there, on the floor, is Julian.

It can't be. I have to be dreaming.

I need to wake up.

I want to wake up.

"Amberly. Please. I need you." The words crack as they come from his mouth.

I look at him again as he raises his head, and our eyes meet.

"Julian."

I jump out of my bed and run to his side, falling to my knees in front of him. I slowly place my hand on his dirt-covered cheek as my eyes fill with tears once again.

"It is you."

He smiles as he weakly raises his hand and places it on my tear-covered cheek, and I place my hand over his. I close my eyes as he leans over until our lips touch. That electricity I missed so much runs from my lips down to my toes, and I can't help letting a moan escape from between my lips. But it's short-lived as I feel his lips go slack, and his hand falls from my face as his body falls forward, and I catch him in my lap.

"Julian?" I shake him lightly, getting no response.

Panic takes hold.

I look down at him and whisper. "You're going to be ok."

I look to my door and yell the next words at the top of my lungs, praying someone will hear me. "Help! Somebody help me!"

* * *

ANGELA

"It's getting late. Maybe we should check in on her tomorrow." Logan says over his shoulder.

I look back at him and the others with an annoyed look on my face, so they know I mean business.

Troy laughs and says. "Or not."

I face forward again. "We are going to make sure she doesn't need anything, and then we can all go back to our beds for a restful night. Unlike Amberly, who probably won't get any sleep." I look back at them. "Everyone ok with that?"

Amara smiles and says. "Hey, you're the boss, and I, for one, would stay with her all night if she would let us."

I face forward once more. "Now that's what I like to hear."

Everyone giggles behind me, making me smile. Ever since Aidan told me what Amberly was trying to do didn't work, I've wanted to go and check in on her. I can only imagine how she is feeling right now. I know if it was me, I would want to be alone, so I know she does too, but at the same time, I would want to know I still had people here who cared about me. So that's just what she's going to get. She needs to know she's not alone in this, and we are still here. We love her, and we will help her get through this. No matter what it takes. After all, she would do the same for any of us.

I know it's very early or very late, depending on how you look at it. It's probably around 3 a.m. now, but we are all awake, so there is no time like the present.

"Help! Somebody help me!"

I turn around to everyone. "Did you hear that?"

Logan's eyes widen in pure concern. "Amberly."

Without another word, he pushes past everyone and runs down the hall in full sprint, leaving us running to catch up. `

***

LOGAN

I run down the hall as fast as I can, and I don't stop until I'm pushing open Amberly's door. I look down to see her on the ground. She isn't alone. She looks up at me with tears in her eyes.

"Logan. Please, help me."

I walk into the room, and when I make it next to her, I drop down on my knees. That's when I realize the person she is holding in her lap is Julian. I look at her in surprise. "How?"

She looks at me, confused, as she shakes her head. "I don't know. I thought it didn't work."

"What didn't work?"

Hurt is plain in her eyes when she looks at me. "I tried to bring him back tonight."

Anger mixed with worry boils inside my veins. "You did what?"

"I had to do something."

"Amberly, that was reckless."

Her eyes plead with me. "You would have done the same thing if it were Troy or me, and you know it."

I sigh, knowing she's right. "Fine, you got me. I'll let it go, for now. But you said you thought it didn't work, so how?"

She looks down at him. "I don't know." Looking me in the eyes, she continues, "I thought it didn't work. But then I woke up and thought I heard him say my name, so I thought I was still dreaming. But he said it again, and when I looked down there, he was." She looks back at Julian's unmoving body. "We have to help him."

Before I have the chance to say anything back to her, I hear the others approaching the doorway. I turn around to see Angela enter first as she stops dead, looking down at us.

"Jul-" she looks at me as she chokes on his name. "How?"

"I don't know. I just walked in," I turn my attention back to Amberly, "and he was here."

"But Aidan said it didn't work."

"That's what she thought." I look down at Julian. "But here he is."

"Can we please talk about this later? We need to get him help. Now!" Amberly almost screams the words at us.

I turn around to Angela as she's pushing past Troy and Amara as she yells. "Help her get him to Aaron's room. I'll let him know you're on your way."

I look at Troy. "Help me carry him."

He nods and moves past Amara and into the room. Without a word, he leans down and grabs one of Julian's arms carefully. I take the other as we slowly get him off the ground and start to exit the room. I turn around to the girls. "Meet us at Aaron's, ok?"

Amberly can only manage a nod when I turn my attention to Amara, she says. "I have her. Go."

Without another word, we head out the door and down the hall. When we are out of earshot, Troy whispers to me. "Dude, I don't think it's a good sign that he's this cold."

I look down at Julian, who's still unconscious, and his breathing is shallow and labored. *We need to move and fast.* I don't think Amberly will make it through this twice, and neither will Angela.

"We need to hurry," I say to Troy as I pick up the pace.

✳✳✳

AARON

"I want to go see Amberly first thing in the morning. I don't care what anyone has to say about it." Jocelyn says to me as she lays down on the bed.

"Yes, darling," I say sarcastically with a smile on my face.

"I'm serious."

"I know you are. I'm worried about her too. We will go together first thing, ok?"

She lowers her head to the pillow. "That's what I wanted to hear."

I smile at her as she closes her eyes. I take off my shirt and make my way across the room to the bedside. So many years I went without her, and every day was worse than the last. The ache always seemed to get bigger as the days passed, but the moment she walked back into my life, it was ripped from me. I don't know what I would do if I ever lost her again. To have this, her, here with me and know I get to go to sleep next to her every night and wake up to see her lying next to me every morning.

I can't even imagine how Amberly is going to get through this. I barely did it myself. How can we possibly help her move on? I never could, and neither could her mother. And if I know Amberly as well as I think I do, that's the first thing she will say to us. She will justify staying in her pain because she knows it's what we did for all those years. How can we tell her to do something we couldn't do ourselves? How can we help her when we couldn't help ourselves?

Having Jocelyn and my family back, it's everything, and I don't know what I would do if I ever lost it again.

Knock. Knock.

Bang. Bang.

I turn around to look at the door in complete disbelief. Who would be at my door at this hour and banging at that? No one ever does that. Jocelyn sits up in the bed before I turn my back to her. I'm steps from the door, and then it opens wide, almost hitting me in the face as Angela walks through it.

"Aaron." She chokes my name out.

She's panting hard. I walk over to her and put a hand on her shoulder. "Breathe. What's going on?"

"Amberly?" I hear Jocelyn say from behind me, and from how close she sounds she must have gotten out of bed. *So much for our relaxing night.*

"No, she's fine. It's Julian. He's alive."

"What?"

"Well, I don't know, really. When we walked in, he looked," she stops and looks up at me, "dead."

"Wait, I'm confused."

She closes her eyes. "We were going to check in on Amberly before we all called it a night, but before we got to her room, we heard her screaming for help, and when we got there, she was on the floor with him in her arms."

I turn away from her and collect my shirt from the foot of the bed and throw it over my head. "Where are they now?"

"Coming here. I told them I would go-ahead to let you know what was going on."

I take a seat on the edge of the bed and put my head in my hands.

Julian.

He's alive.

"Aaron."

I look up to see Angela standing over me. "Yes?"

"What if he's still dead and she?"

"Don't think like that."

She closes her eyes. "I don't know what else to think. He was dead. She tried to heal him over seven hours ago. Nothing happened. It wouldn't have taken that long." She opens her eyes and looks down at me. "Would it?"

"I don't think so. But then again, I don't really know how that power works."

She kneels in front of me and places her hands on mine. When I look at her, I can see the hurt and pleading in her eyes. "Aaron. We need to do whatever we can. I can't," she pauses and looks down at our hands. "I can't lose him. Not again." She looks up at me again, "I barely made it through it the first time."

I remove my hand and place it on top of hers. "I know. I barely did either."

Julian was the closest thing I had to a son before my son showed up on my doorstep. Losing him was harder for me than I let on. I'm the pack leader, the alpha, and I need to keep it together for that reason alone.

"Aaron." Logan's voice comes to us from the hall.

"Come in," I yell.

Logan and Troy walk in with Julian's arms over their shoulders. I must stop myself from sucking in a breath when I see him. Angela was right when she said he looks dead. I just hope looks are deceiving.

"Put him on the couch." I gesture to them.

They lay him down carefully and move out of my way. I look back at Jocelyn and then Angela as I pick up his ice-cold hand and place my finger over his wrist.

There's a pulse.

It's faint, but it's there.

I turn around to Angela and smile. "He's alive."

"Oh, thank God." She places a hand over her heart and closes her eyes.

"But it's faint."

Angela opens her eyes and looks over at me. "Well, he's been out there for what. Three days, now, right?"

I nod my head, trying to understand where she's going with this.

"So, he's had nothing to eat. Nothing to drink in almost four days."

I nod my head and mentally hit myself on the head for not putting it together myself. "He needs fluids."

Angela walks over to me. "I'll go to the kitchen and bring back whatever I can carry. We need to set up an IV drip. It's the fastest way to get it into his system."

"Ok, I'll get on that. You take those two with you and bring back all the fluid you can and something to eat for when he wakes."

They nod in my direction as they leave the room.

I look down at Julian's unconscious body and smile. Thank God it worked because I don't know how we would have gotten Amberly through it. I barely survived when I thought I lost my family, and every day, it ate away at me a little more, so I know from experience there would have been nothing I could have said to her to make her feel better or heal her. As for me, he's been like a son to me all these years. His loss was something I was ignoring because I couldn't think of a life without him in it. Around to annoy me and make me want to pull my hair out. I smile at the memories that start to flood my mind.

"Dad."

I turn around to see Amberly in the doorway, and she looks like a mess. Tears covering every inch of her face, and the rest of her is covered in dirt, I'm guessing from Julian's body. Her body is slightly shaking, and I know I need to calm her down before she makes herself pass out.

"He's going to be ok," I say to her.

Without warning, she drops to her knees and sobs so hard her body shakes, and in the same moment, Jocelyn is across the room throwing her arms around our daughter. I look over at them, unsure what to do.

I haven't known my daughter that long, but I know she is one of the strongest people I've come to know. Almost nothing affects her. So, for me to see her like this is killing me. I know it's a relieving kind of cry, but it's still hard to watch her like this. To see her body shaking and the tears running down her cheeks in a never-ending stream. I thank God that Jocelyn was awake because I don't know how I would have handled this. I've never been very good at the comforting thing, but now I should really try to get better at it having her around.

Her eyes find their way to Julian's body on the couch. Through the tears, I can see happiness in her eyes for the first time since she made it back home, and I couldn't be happier.

I Hope It's Not Too Late

TROY

"I don't think we can carry anymore," I say to the girls.

"Stop being a baby," Angela says to me.

"Hey, I'm not. I just want to get back."

She turns on me, and she looks pissed. "And you think I don't? He's my best friend, he's my brother. What you and Logan are to each other, well, that's Julian and me. And a few days ago, I lost him. He died, and now he's back, and you think I want to be here with you. Well, you're mistaken."

Amara slowly places a hand on Angela's shoulder. She looks over at it as calm washes over her. "Angela. Are you ok?"

"I'm so sorry." She looks in my direction, and I ready myself for another freakout. "I didn't mean that. I'm just so tired and seeing him like that. It just took a lot out of me. I'm sorry, Troy."

"Hey, it's fine. I get it. Plus, we all get out of character once in a while, but I would be lying if I said that was something I expected from you."

"What do you mean?"

"You're always so put together and composed. I've never seen you lash out like that. Honestly, never knew you had it in you."

She looks away as her cheeks turn pink. "Well, I'm sorry again."

Logan reaches for her free hand. "You don't need to apologize. This hasn't been an easy couple of days for any of us."

I smile. "You can say that again."

Amara smiles. "You can say that again."

I look over at her and frown. "I was being sarcastic."

Her smile reaches her eyes. "I know you were."

"See, this is why I like you."

Angela laughs. "Why because she reminds you of yourself?"

Amara and I scowl in her direction playfully.

She lifts her hands in a surrendering gesture. "Hey, I'm only stating the obvious."

Logan smiles. "The girl has a point."

We all look at each other and laugh.

Amara smiles at us as she says. "We should be getting these back to Aaron."

"Yea. Let's go." I say.

✳✳✳

AARON

I set up the drip and let the fluids go to work. Amberly is refusing to leave Julian's side until he wakes up. I expected nothing less. My daughter reminds me so much of myself. She has turned into a smart, beautiful young woman, and I have no doubt she will make a wonderful leader when the time comes.

Jocelyn leaves Amberly's side and walks over to me. "You're sure he's going to wake up after he gets these fluids in him?"

I take her lightly by the arm and move us further away from where Amberly sits with Julian. "I'm not entirely sure."

She looks back at Amberly. "How sure are you?"

"Not at all, actually." I can see the sadness starting to return to her features as I say, "He's been out there so long without simple human needs, and his body is still very cold. I'm afraid if we can't get his temperature to rise, that getting him the fluids he needs won't make a difference anyway."

She turns her attention back to me. "What else can we do?"

"Nothing."

"So, we just have to sit here and wait."

I nod.

"You know I've never been very good at that."

I smile. "It's one of the many things I've come to love about you."

"And that's because you're crazy."

"Why does that have to make me crazy?"

She gives me a small laugh. "Because no one in their right mind would want to be with someone as impatient as I am."

I grab her around the waist and pull her close to me. "Then I guess, call me crazy."

She laughs and throws her hand over her mouth as she looks back at Amberly. "We shouldn't be laughing like this."

"Why not?"

"Because it's inconsiderate of Amberly."

I look back at our daughter. "I think she would want us to be happy no matter what was going on in her world."

"Because that's who she is. But I still don't like doing it."

I let out a sigh. "Well, if you're asking me to be miserable around our daughter, that might take me some time to perfect." I smile at her playfully, and I pull her close and kiss her all over, and she starts to laugh quietly.

"Aaron, stop it."

"Make me," I growl.

She pushes me away playfully. "You're like a little kid, I swear."

I pout. "Only because you make me that way."

"What's that supposed to mean?" She says while placing her arms over her chest.

"It means my heart is so full, and I'm so happy that I get childlike tendencies around you."

She hits my shoulder lightly. "You're a geek, you know?"

"Yes. But you love it."

Chuckling, she replies. "Sometimes."

I shake my head. "Nope. All the time."

"Whatever you say, Romeo."

My grin leaves my face. "Speaking of Romeo."

She frowns. "What now?"

"I think Aidan was right."

"About?" She looks at me questioningly.

"We should get married."

Her eyes widen. "Aaron, are you kidding me?"

"Do you not want to?"

Taking my hand in hers, she says in her serious tone, "Of course I do, but right now, we have a lot on our plates."

"And that might never change. We've already lost enough time, and our family is all together for the first time in eighteen years. Now is the best time."

She sighs. "I'll make you a deal."

"Name it."

"When he wakes up and gets his strength back, we will talk to Amberly and see when a good time is."

I roll my eyes at her request. "Fine. But only because I know what she's going to say."

Her grin returns. "Oh, do you now?"

"Yup."

"Let me guess. You think she will say something like 'mommy and daddy are finally getting married. Let's do it now, please.' Does that about cover your thoughts?"

I chuckle. "I do not sound like that."

Dismissing me with her hand, she walks over to the bed.

I call after her in a whisper. "But I'm serious. I will marry you before the next thing arrives at our door."

She smiles over her shoulder at me, making my heart race. I can read everything in her eyes. I've always been able to. She wants to marry me just as badly as I want to marry her, and for the first time, it's confirmed when I look at her.

She will be my wife.

Having Faith

AIDAN

"Hey, Aaron, sorry to just walk in, but I knocked, and no one answered the door, and I really needed to." I stop dead when I look down and see Amberly asleep on the floor next to the couch and Julian's body next to her. I look over to the bed and see my parents asleep.

For the first time, I don't just feel like the outcast here, but I am. I turn to walk back out the way I came wondering what I missed.

"Aidan?" Amberly says, half asleep. "Is that you?"

I don't want to turn around, but I know I have to. "Hey."

"I was wondering where you went. I woke up, and you were gone."

I look at my feet. "I'm sorry. I didn't want to wake you, and I was hungry. Then I was feeling restless, so I went for a walk." I look over at her. "I went to your room, and you weren't there, so I came here to see Aaron."

She lifts her hand to cover her mouth as she yawns. "I'm sorry. I woke up and found Julian on my floor. After that, I couldn't think straight. I would have come and found you when I got up." She looks over at Julian. "I just don't want to leave his side until he wakes up."

"So, it worked," I ask.

"I guess. Angela and Aaron say he's going to be ok. But I don't know. Something feels off."

"Well, he was dead." I wish my mouth would stay closed until my mind had time to work.

"I know. But it took so long for it to work. I just feel like something's wrong."

I release a suppressed sigh. "Don't anticipate the negative. If you do, then that's all you'll get."

She looks up at me and smiles. "You're right. I'm sorry. It's just I lost him once already. I don't think my heart could take it a second time."

"I get it." I throw my thumb over my shoulder. "But I'm gonna get out of here. I'll catch you later."

"Hey, Aidan." I turn back to her. "I just wanted to say thank you."

Confused, I ask. "For what?"

"For earlier. For being there for me."

"You're my sister. What else was I supposed to do?"

She smiles at me. "I know, but you didn't have to stay, and you did. It meant a lot." She looks at her hands before she continues, "I never thought about what it would be like to have a sibling. I kind of thought it was overrated. Maybe because no one else in my village has one. I don't really know." When she looks back at me, I can see the light shining in her eyes. "But I never knew what I was missing. Not until a few days ago. I couldn't have been more wrong."

Unsure, I ask. "So, you're glad I'm here?"

"Yes. Why wouldn't I be?" She looks at me, confused.

"Well, I'm one of the bad guys, remember."

Her smile reaches her eyes. "Not anymore."

I lower my gaze and say in a whisper, "I wish it was that easy."

"It is. You chose to not kill me. You left to make sure I was safe, and you stayed because you wanted to know what it was like to have a family. Then when the time came, when I needed you, you were there."

"That doesn't make me a good guy. I've done," I hesitate. Not sure if I should continue, but I know she needs to hear this, "I've killed a lot of people, Amberly. That can't get washed away. Their blood stains my hands."

She looks at me sadly before slowly getting up, then making her way over to my side. "I know what you've done, just as you do." She takes my hands in hers, "But you need to let it go now. You need to stop living in your past. Stop reminding yourself of what you did. You need to start living, healing, and you can do that. You can remove their blood from your hands by doing what's right. There's still time. There's still hope. You're no longer with Vladimir. You can choose your own path now."

"I." I look away, not able to continue.

She places her hand on my cheek. "I have faith in you."

I look down at her. "How? How can you believe so much in me when you barely know me? All you know is all the evil I've done."

She smiles. "Because you're a part of me. Where there's darkness in you, it's in me too. And where there's light in me..." She trails off.

"Then there must be light in me as well." I smile down at her.

She nods her head. "Yes. And for that reason alone, I have faith in you."

"Well, I hope I don't let you down."

"With us in your corner, that won't be possible."

We smile at each other, and for the first time, I feel a warmth in my heart. Is this what love feels like? Is this what it means to love someone unconditionally? I wish I knew.

"Would you like some company?"

She smiles at me as she places her hand in mine. "I would love some, but I have to warn you it's not very comfortable."

I smile at her. "I'm used to being uncomfortable. So much so that I can barely sleep on the beds here."

She looks at me sadly.

"I'm sorry. I didn't say that to make you feel bad for me. I was trying to be funny." I pause and look down at my feet, "while also being serious."

"I know. I just feel horrible about what you had to go through the last eighteen years. I think about if I had to grow up the way you did, and I don't know how I would have turned out."

I look at her with panic, and I say. "I'm glad it was me."

She looks at me, confused. "Why?"

"Because I wouldn't have wanted that life for you."

She pulls me lightly with her over to the couch. "We should try to get some rest. I have a feeling tomorrow is going to be a long day for us."

I look around the room and see some pillows and blankets in the closet on the other side of the room. "Hold on a sec."

She reluctantly lets go of my hand. I go to the other side of the room, retrieve the things we need for a good night's sleep, and bring them over to Amberly.

She grins at me. "I didn't even see those."

"What would you do without me?" I ask playfully.

"Not get a good night's sleep, that's for sure."

We look at each other and release a low laugh. I place the pillows and blankets on the floor and make the area as comfortable as I can for her. "Here, come lay down. You will still be right next to him. But you need sleep just like I do."

She smiles and kisses Julian on the cheek and whispers. "I'll be right here." And then comes to lay down next to me. "Wow, this is really comfortable."

I look at her and smile. "Guess I've gotten pretty good at using what I can around me to make things more livable."

She smiles at me. "I guess so."

She puts her head down on the pillow, and I do the same. "Goodnight, sister."

"Goodnight, brother."

✳✳✳

AARON

I hear Aidan and Amberly talking, but I don't open my eyes. I can feel how important this conversation is for them to have. I try not to listen, but that's easier said than done when I'm only a few feet away from them. I didn't think it was possible to be prouder of my daughter than I already was, but I've never been more wrong. She has more wisdom than her years, and I can tell from the tone in Aidan's voice that she's saying all the right things. This is what he needed to hear from her. He needed to know that she would be in his corner and that she was as happy to have him in her life as he was her.

So, our little family grows from three to four.

A son.

Who would have thought?

Like Jocelyn said earlier, I always wanted a son. Someone to teach and to take over for me when I was gone. Someone to mold into my image like my father did me. Someone to hunt and goof off with. Someone to have in my corner like Jocelyn had Amberly. But I lost hope of that reality many years ago, and I never saw it becoming a possibility now because we are much older. Even though we live four lifespans, I don't know if Jocelyn could get pregnant again or if she would even want to. So, I had given up the dream of ever having a son. Then Aidan shows up. Not going to say I don't have my work cut out for me because I definitely do. He's already grown and already had all his formative years filled with a psychopath. It's going to take a long time to undo what Vladimir did. But I'm looking forward to the work.

***

LOGAN

I glance down to see Angela still sleeping, so I wrap my arm around her. *When did we fall asleep?* The last thing I remember is sitting with Amberly as she waited for Julian to wake up. Angela informed us that it would be hours, if not days, before that would happen, and so Amberly told us we should go get some rest, but she wouldn't leave. Finally, Angela and Amberly had convinced me to do just that. But I don't remember us going to the same room together or falling asleep in the same bed.

"Logan?" Angela says in a groggy voice.

"Yeah."

"Wasn't sure if you were awake."

I smile. "Yeah, I'm up."

She rolls over and lifts her arms above her head as she starts to stretch. When her body falls back to the bed, she looks at me from under her mess of hair and starts to laugh. "I'm sorry. I must be a sight." She says as she turns away, about to get up.

I lightly grab her by the wrist and pull her back to the bed. "No, you look perfect."

"Logan, don't lie." She says through a small laugh as she smiles at me shyly.

"I'm not." I reach up and move a strand of hair from her face. "You look as beautiful as always."

Her smile disappears and is replaced with uncertainty. "Logan?"

"Yeah."

"I don't think we should be doing this."

I sit up in the bed and look at her, confused. "Doing what?"

She gestures with her hand to her and me. "This. Us."

"What about it?"

"We shouldn't be doing it, this, whatever this is."

I look at her, confused. "And why shouldn't we?"

"You know very well why we shouldn't."

I roll my eyes. "I swear if you say because of Amberly, I might turn into a girl and scream."

She looks at me unamused. "I'm serious."

"So am I. She has Julian, so what does it matter if we feel something for each other?"

She releases a sigh. "She's one of my best friends, Logan."

"Mine too."

She looks up at me from behind sad eyes. "I don't want to hurt her."

"Neither do I." I reach over and place a hand on hers. "How about this? We wait for Julian to wake up, and then we talk to her. Have her give us her blessing or whatever. Would that make you feel better?"

"Logan, don't be mean."

"I'm not. I'm serious. If that's what you need in order not to feel wrong about what we are feeling for each other, then let's do it." I squeeze her hand. "I like you a lot. And I would like to see if there's something here."

"So would I."

I smile at her. "Then it's a plan. We wait."

She nods and smiles at me.

***

ANGELA

Julian couldn't wake up fast enough. I feel like an hour is a day, and every hour is getting longer and longer. Logan and I decided to keep our distance for now. So, I made up my mind that it was time to go check in on Julian.

I lift my hand and knock lightly on Aaron's door. He opens it and smiles.

"Good morning," I say.

"Mornin."

"I just wanted to come and see how everyone was doing."

His smile disappears. "No change, I'm afraid."

"That's what I was afraid of. Is Amberly still here?"

He nods.

"I figured she would be. Well, please let me know when there's any change and if anyone needs anything. And please make sure she eats something."

He smiles at me warmly. "I know Angela."

"I'm sorry. I didn't mean to imply."

He cuts me off, "I know. Now go and enjoy the sun. I have things handled here."

I turn around and head down the hall. Not too sure what I'm going to do with my time, but knowing I need to make the most of it. Lately, we haven't had much time to ourselves. It was always training, so today I would like to have a nice long run.

I smile at the thought of being on all fours and running for hours as the cool air caresses my fur coat. I haven't been able to do it much lately. Without a second thought, I run to the cave entrance without a care in the world.

Sight For Sore Eyes

JULIAN

It's hard to remember the last time I felt this weak. My body feels unbelievably stiff, and my skin feels so dry that if I move, it might crack. However, my tongue feels even worse. I need some water asap. I try to open my eyes. I need to figure out where I am, then get some water in me, and then I need to find Amberly.

Amberly.

I need to see her.

She needs to know I'm ok.

I need to know she's ok.

I peel my eyes open slowly so I can let the light leak in. Everything is a blurry mess, so I open and close them a few times,

and soon they adjust. I look over to my left to see Amberly. She's
asleep.

Did she stay by my side this whole time?

How long have I been unconscious?

The last thing I remember is stumbling into her room and passing
out in her lap. *How did she get me to Aaron's room?* Looking down
at her, I take in how peaceful she looks, and the thought of waking
her is unimaginable, so instead, I decide to sit here and watch her
sleep. Moments pass before I take notice of the very big person
lying on the floor next to her. I can tell it's a man, but I can't see his
face. Before I get the chance to think more about who it could be,
Amberly starts to roll over and stretch. She looks up at me in
surprise and jumps up.

"You're awake!"

I smile at her. "I guess I am."

She makes it to my side and takes my hand in hers gently. "How
are you feeling?"

I smile up at her. "Much better now."

Her smile disappears. "You must be hungry."

She turns away from me, about to take her hand away, but I hold
her in place. "I'm fine for now. I just want to look at you."

She smiles, and I see the tears starting to roll down her face.
"What's wrong?"

"I'm just so happy you're awake." She says as she begins to sob. She moves to lay her head on my chest.

I place my hand on the back of her head. "Please, don't cry."

She looks up at me with teary eyes. "You were dead, Julian. Dead."

"I know," I say sadly.

"I felt so lost. I didn't know what to do."

"I'm here now." I lay a hand on her cheek. "We are together, and we are both alive."

She looks at me and then leans down to kiss me softly on the lips. This is something I've waited so long for. Ever since I messed up with Amara, I've wanted to kiss her this way again. I've longed for it. To feel how much she wants, needs, and loves me all in one simple touch or kiss. Who thought it would take me dying to get here? I almost laugh at the thought. But I would do it all again if this is where we ended up.

I hesitantly pull back, just far enough to look at her. I lift my free hand to move the hair from her face and then place it against her wet cheek. "So, what's next?"

She smiles. "Well, let's get you back on your feet, and we can go from there."

"Piece of cake," I say sarcastically as I place my feet on the ground and try to stand, but I end up falling right back to the couch.

I look at her and let out a small chuckle. "Maybe I should try to eat something first?"

She smiles. "And maybe you should try pacing yourself. You were out there for four days and then laying here for another day. Your legs need to be broken in." She adds the last lines with a laugh.

"Whatever you think is best." I place my hand on hers. "I'll follow your lead."

"Smart man."

I smile at her. "Hey, I'm learning. Slowly," I laugh, "but that's better than nothing, right?"

She nods at me with a smile on her face as she leans down and kisses me again.

"Not that I'm not happy to be, you know, alive. But how is it possible? Serenity?"

I see worry creep into her eyes.

"What is it?"

"Serenity didn't bring you back."

"Oh."

She releases a sigh. "I did."

I bite down the urge to yell at her. How could she be so reckless? So careless with her own life? Then I think about what I would have done if our roles were reversed. How could I expect any different from her? Still, now I'll have to keep an eye on her. Seeing what's

happened to Serenity from this power, I don't want that fate for her.

✳✳✳

AMBERLY

I couldn't describe what I feel if someone asked me to. I have been living with this fear of losing someone I love for weeks, and then the day came when I lost one of the most important people in my life. Since that day, I've been living in a crippling fear that I would never see him again. Even as I was trying to bring him back from the dead, a part of me was trying to prepare myself in case I had to live the rest of my life without ever seeing his smile again, without his touch, his kiss, his laugh. The thought incapacitated me in more ways than I thought possible.

But now, looking down at his smiling face, feeling his hand on my skin, it's awakened a new part of me. This is something I will fight for, him, me, us, and my family and friends. I will fight for our future, to live in peace. I will fight until my last breath. I believe more now than ever that we can have a happy ending. We only need to get through these next few battles, and the world can live in peace.

"So, who's that?" Julian asks me as he nudges his head in the direction of Aidan's sleeping body on the floor.

I almost laugh. "Oh, um, well see, a lot happened while you were out of commission."

"So, fill me in."

I smile. "Well. Apparently, I have a brother."

Surprise is all over his face. "What? How is that possible?"

"I'm not too sure on the details yet."

He looks at me, unsure. "So, how do you know it's the truth?"

"I can feel it. We're twins."

He's looking at me like I have two heads, and his face looks so funny that I have to suppress a laugh. "Twins?"

"Yup."

"So, Aaron and your mom."

I smile. "Yeah. They had twins. But for some reason, no one remembered him."

"But when Aaron heard your heartbeat and sensed you, how come he didn't pick up on two heartbeats?"

I look down at the floor to see Aidan still asleep. "That's still a mystery. It's the only part of the puzzle we still need to fill in."

He follows my gaze to the floor. "So, what's his name?"

"That's the thing. You kind of already know him."

He looks at me, confused. "What do you mean?"

I put my hands up. "Don't freak out, ok?"

"Now you're scaring me, and I have a feeling that's a promise I'm going to have trouble keeping."

I close my eyes and let out a sigh. I have to just say it. I open my eyes and look at him, "It's Aidan."

"What's Aidan?"

"Aidan is my brother."

He sits up straight, "Wait, what?"

"It's a very long story."

He looks down at Aidan, still asleep on the floor. "What is he doing here?" He moves over in front of me in a protective way.

"It's ok. He won't hurt anyone. He saved me from Vladimir. He left him."

"Amberly, please don't tell me you're that naïve."

I feel the lines form on my forehead in frustration, "What's that supposed to mean?"

"This could all be part of Vladimir's plan."

I shake my head, annoyed that everyone keeps saying that. "It's not."

"You don't know that."

I smile at him. "I do. It's hard to explain, but I just need you to trust me."

He rubs his face in a furious motion. "You know I do, but this."

I cut him off. "Just meet him, and you'll see. Trust me."

He closes his eyes and sighs. "Fine." He looks at me, "but if I have even the smallest feeling that he is a danger to you, I'm going to."

I raise my hand, silencing him. "If you think I'm wrong, then we will talk about it. Ok?"

He smiles. "Deal."

"Just promise me you'll give him a chance."

He nods, but I see the uncertainty in his eyes.

"Don't think about what you know about him. Clear it from your mind and go in like you've never met."

His sigh holds a lot of emotion. "I'll do my best, but no promises."

"That's all I ask."

He turns his attention back to Aidan. "Your brother, huh?"

I grin. "Yeah. Who would have thought the emptiness I've been feeling would have been because I had a twin out there somewhere?"

"Not me." He mumbles.

We both look down at Aidan as he begins to stir.

Where Am I

AIDAN

I wake up to find myself on the floor, like always, but when I glance around at my surroundings, confusion takes over. *Where am I?* Sleep still lingering. It takes me a second to remember where I am and everything that happened yesterday. Now it seems like a lifetime ago.

I left the only home I've ever known. It's hard not to feel uneasy about my decision, but I wouldn't change it even if I could because now, I have my sister. And I've finally met my parents. Why would I ever want to go back?

Maybe because it's the only life you've ever known.

It was comfortable.

And now.

Now, I'm living in the unknown.

I hear Amberly's voice. "Yeah. Who would have thought the emptiness I've been feeling would have been because I had a twin out there somewhere?"

I wonder who she's talking to.

I'm about to sit up and turn around when I hear a voice I don't recognize, answer her.

"Not me."

I throw the blanket off of me and go right into an unexpected stretch. When I'm done, I roll over to see her on the couch next to a now very awake Julian.

Amberly smiles down at me. "Good morning."

I yawn. "Morning."

I feel Julian staring at me, and when I turn to look in his direction, he's scowling. Amberly looks from me to him and says. "Julian, I'd like you to meet my brother, Aidan. Aidan, I'd like you to officially meet Julian."

He smiles, but I can tell it's forced. "Hi."

"What's up?"

Amberly pouts. "Really? That's it?"

"What?" I ask.

"You two are the most important men in my life, and it's the first time you're meeting. You only say one word to each other?"

"Hey, I said two." I grin and point a finger at Julian, "He only said one."

Rolling her eyes, she growls, "that's not what I meant, and you know it."

I look over at Julian, speaking without thinking. "I'm glad to see you're not dead."

Julian laughs. "Yeah. It's good not to be dead."

Staring at each other, we laugh, but when I look at Amberly, she is anything but amused.

I sigh. "What now?"

She folds her arms over her chest. "Oh, nothing."

Julian smiles at her. "We are nice to each other. What else do you want?"

She scowls at him. "You call this being nice? I'm afraid to see what being mean is."

Julian raises his hands in a surrendering gesture. "Hey. I'm only doing what you asked."

"No, you're not." The annoyance is clear in her voice.

"What do you want from me? I just came back from the dead. Can't a man get a minute to breathe?" He smiles.

"Not funny." I can hear the tears coming in her voice.

She gets up and walks out the door without another word to either of us. Once the door closes behind her, we look at each other in shock.

"I guess I wasn't funny." He says.

"No, I don't think you were." I rub my eyes. "She went through a lot when she thought you died. I don't blame her for not thinking that was funny."

He lays back down on the pillow. "It's hard sometimes. Whenever I see something is bothering her, it just comes naturally for me to try to be funny. Most of the time, she laughs, but this time," he looks at the door, "I didn't mean to be an ass. I don't like seeing her cry."

"Neither do I."

Seeing Amberly in pain is hard for me. I don't know how to react to it, and I sure don't understand it, like many things nowadays, it seems. I never cared about anyone's feelings or emotions, but when it comes to her, it's a different story. I would do anything to always keep a smile on her face.

"You barely know her." His tone is a bit malicious.

I look at him, trying not to react to his tone. "You're correct, but I've seen her cry a lot these last few days, so my statement still stands."

Normally I would kill someone for talking to me the way he is. Being a changed man is hard. Fear was something I craved from everyone around me because with fear came respect. This man has no respect, and part of me wishes I could teach him some. However, that would go against keeping a smile on my sister's face, and it would also be going in the opposite direction of being a better person.

He glares at me. "So, how did you convince her?"

"Convince her of what?" I ask, confused.

"How did you get her to bring you back here, after everything you did? From what I know about her, she never would have risked it."

Needing something to occupy my hands, I begin to fold up my blanket. "I told her the truth. That she was my sister, and I took her to protect her from Vladimir and,"

He cuts me off with more than a hint of distrust in his tone. "You took her to Vladimir to protect her. Explain to me how that works?"

"He wanted to kill her, wanted her out of the way so he could take over. So I thought if I brought her to him, maybe I could find a way to save her and make him happy at the same time."

"You mean you wanted to turn her." He says angrily.

"That was the original plan. If I couldn't get her to come willingly."

"You got a lot of nerve." He says through bared teeth.

I almost yell back. "I was trying to save her. There was no choice."

"There's always a choice. You took the easy way out because you wanted your sister around. Who cares if it was right for her or not?"

"Of course, I wanted her around, but you know nothing about me. I did what I did because I thought it was the only way to protect her."

"Whatever. We will continue to disagree on that. But you still haven't answered my question."

I sigh. "Which one?"

"How did you convince her to bring you back here?"

"I didn't try to convince her of anything. Once I spoke with Vladimir, I knew nothing mattered. She wasn't safe, and she never would be. I knew I had to get her out of there. So, I did. However, she wouldn't come until I promised I would come with her."

"How convenient for you." He looks at me, annoyed. "How did she make you?"

"I knew she wouldn't leave without me. She knew Vladimir would kill me if I was there, and she was gone."

"Well, that would have been a real shame." He says sarcastically.

"Hey, if you think I want to be here, you're sadly mistaken. I came for her and her alone. If you think I'm comfortable here, think again."

His tone is sarcastic in nature when he says. "I'm sorry you're uncomfortable here." He looks over to where my parents are still sleeping. "I mean, you were the cause of my death and all of the hurt your sister went through because of it, but you know you being uncomfortable is more important than any of that."

Annoyed, I say. "That's not what I meant, and you know it."

"Well, it's how it sounded."

I sigh. "You're not going to make this easy for me, are you?"

"Would you expect any different?" He scowls.

"Honestly, no, but I was hoping for Amberly's sake we could at least try."

He looks at the door as he sighs. "You're right." Looking back at me, he continues, "For her, I can try. But it's going to take a lot for me to trust you, so know that until then, I have my eyes on you."

I grin. "I wouldn't want it any other way."

"Good because I can be a real hardass when it comes to protecting the people I care about."

"I guess we have something in common then."

His face tightens around the edges, and I can tell having something in common with me bothers him. I grin.

"So, being dead?" I ask.

His eyes stare at me intensely. "What about it?"

In genuine curiosity, I ask, "What was it like?"

His eyes grow dark. "I don't remember much."

He shifts uneasily on the couch, and I can tell something is bugging him. Something more than me.

"It was dark. I don't remember anything else other than being in the dark." His eyes go distant for a moment then a smile creeps onto his face. "Then I heard her calling for me."

"Amberly?"

He nods.

He tries to get up, but I can tell he's still too weak. Hesitantly, I ask. "What do you need?"

"Nothing."

He looks at me, closing his eyes as he releases a breath. He opens them to slits looking in my direction. "I was going to go check on Amberly, but," he pauses as he settles back into the couch, "I'm still too weak. Would you," he pauses, uncertainty clear in his expression, "would you go check on her for me?"

"You trust me to do that?"

He smiles. "When it comes to her safety and wellbeing, I guess I do."

I smile. "Well, it's a good place to start." I head over to the door, "I'll let her know you wanted to check on her yourself, but you weren't strong enough yet."

Panic sets on his face. "No! I don't want her worrying about me. Just tell her we were talking, and you said you were going to check in on her."

"Ok. If you say so."

As I'm walking out the door, I hear him say in a whisper, "Thank you."

Getting along with him isn't going to be easy, but there is nothing I wouldn't do for my sister, and I know she loves him. So, I need to find a way to get along with him, and more than that, I need to find a way to get him to trust me. Honestly, I don't know which is going to be harder.

Feeling Nostalgic

AIDAN

"Hey, you."

Amberly turns around, and a small smile creeps up on her face. "Hey, Aidan."

I reach her side and sit down next to her. "What are you doing out here?"

She sighs. "I just needed some fresh air."

"You know he didn't mean anything by it, right?"

She looks up at the early morning sky. "Yeah."

"He was only trying to make light of the situation."

She looks over at me. "I know that. But the problem is it wasn't a situation to be made light of. He died. He was gone."

"I know."

She looks at the ground as she kicks a small pebble with her foot. "He can just make me so mad sometimes."

"Isn't that normal?"

She looks at me, confused.

"I mean in relationships. Isn't it normal to be annoyed with each other? Or to fight? I thought that was always a good thing."

She smiles. "Yes, fighting is normal in any relationship, sadly." She laughs lightly, "And yes, it is good to fight because then you have to work it out later. I always thought fighting was a healthy part of being in a relationship because it shows how strong you are as a couple to get past them."

"Well then, maybe you should go and make up with him."

She looks back at the cave entrance. "I want to, but..."

I say in the softest way I can, "He was dead Amberly, but now he's back. Don't waste that."

She smiles. "I know you don't like him."

"I never said."

She cuts me off. "So, thank you. It means a lot."

I grin. "No need to thank me. I just want to see you happy." I shrug. "I mean, what are brothers for anyway?"

Her words are soft when she says, "You know for not growing up in normal circumstances, you're not doing a bad job at the brotherly advice thing."

I sit up straight. "Really?"

She giggles. "Yes, really. I'm glad you came back with me."

"Not like you gave me a choice."

Laughing, she nudges her shoulder against mine as she stands up. "I'll see you later then?"

"Count on it."

She smiles at me before she turns and walks into the cave. I hear footsteps coming from my right, and I look over to see Angela coming out of the forest.

AMBERLY

I slowly push the door open and find Julian sitting up on the couch. I look around the rest of the room to see my parents are no longer in bed.

"They went to grab something to eat." He says to me as I enter the room.

"Oh."

He glances at the ground. "I'm sorry. I wasn't thinking. I was insensitive."

"No. I overreacted."

"No, you didn't."

I reach his side, and he offers me his hand. I take it as I say, "Losing you was the hardest thing I've ever had to go through. When I thought healing you didn't work, and it started to sink in that I might never see you again, it broke me."

He lightly pulls me to the couch. "I'm so sorry, Amberly. I can only imagine what you went through."

"Just promise next time I go first," I say with a smile.

"Now, who's being insensitive?" He grins back.

"Hey, I owed you."

"You sure did." He says as he lifts my hand to his lips.

"How are you feeling?"

"Slowly getting my strength back."

I look at the door. "You ready for something to eat?"

"Your parents said they would bring something back for me after they ate."

I smile. "Ok, good."

"But there is something else I need."

I smile at him excitedly. "Anything."

He smiles as he places his hand on my cheek and pulls me in close. He kisses my forehead, then my cheek, and then my lips. The electricity is roaming through my whole body as his free hand takes up residence on my thigh. For the first time, I'm very aware of the shorts I'm wearing. They are way too big and very easy to get into. I feel him sending an electric trail up my thigh as he moves his hand closer to the hem of my shorts. A light moan escapes my mouth. His lips move from mine as they find a spot on my neck and my head falls back. How I have longed for his touch, his lips, this moment. And just like that, I'm suddenly very aware that we are in my parents' room, and they could walk in the door at any moment. I'm not one of those teenagers who wants her parents to walk in on her doing anything with her boyfriend, even if it's only a passionate kiss.

Reluctantly I pull away from him, gasping for air.

"What's wrong? Did I do something?" He pants.

I smile at him. "No, it's not you. You're," I touch his lips with my finger and bite on my lower lip, "amazing. I just became very aware that we are in my parents' room."

He laughs. "Right. I forgot."

"Yeah." I laugh. "And they could come back any minute."

"And the last thing you want is for them to see us in a passionate make-out session." He grins sinisterly.

I can feel the blood rushing to my cheek. "Can you blame me?"

"No, I don't want that either. So, let's go to your room."

He tries to stand, but I stop him with my hand. "We have plenty of time for that, Julian," I smile at him, "you need to rest first."

"That's all I've been doing."

I laugh at him. "I know, but you need your strength."

He closes his eyes, letting his head drop back on the couch, and releases a sigh. "Fine." He looks up at me. "But I want to move to your room by the end of the day." He smiles, "After all, you take better care of me than they can."

I giggle nervously. "Oh, so you're making me your nurse now?"

He nods with a huge grin on his face.

"Fine. I'll have Aidan help me move you if you're not strong enough. But not until later tonight, ok?"

"Deal."

I guess I didn't realize how much I really missed the little things with him. The banter back and forth and his goofy jokes that sometimes pisses me off. I missed it all. I couldn't tell you how happy I am to finally have him back, to have this back.

✳✳✳

ANGELA

"Julian's awake," Aidan says as he reaches my side.

I can barely hide my excitement. "What? When?"

"Just a little bit ago. Amberly is with him now."

I release a breath filled with relief. "Thank you for telling me."

"No problem. I knew you would want to know." He looks into the forest. "So, where were you just now?"

I can't help but smile. "I went for a run."

He looks at me questionably. "A run?"

"Yeah. You know, in my wolf form. It feels so freeing."

He looks at me sadly. "I wouldn't know."

"Wait. You haven't shifted yet?"

He shakes his head.

Without thinking, I reach out and take his hand. I can see the surprise on his face, as I know it matches my own. "We should get on that. I can teach you."

His nervousness is clear in his voice. "But didn't you want to go see Julian?"

"I will. He and Amberly need some time first." I say with a smile.

"I don't know."

"What are you, scared?" I grin playfully.

I understand why everyone is so nervous around him, but I've always gone by my instincts, and they tell me he's a good, kind soul deep down. I plan on finding that version of him and bringing it out for everyone else to see. After all, he's a part of Amberly, so I know there's good in him.

His life hasn't been a fair one, like most of us here. If I can help make things a little easier on him and Amberly, then I plan on doing just that.

Never Felt Freer

AIDAN

The pain is like nothing I've ever experienced before, and I've been through some pain. I can feel every muscle under my skin stretching. All my bones are cracking and moving into new places. I try not to wince, but it's hard to show no signs of pain when it's taking over every cell of my body.

Why would anyone in their right mind ever want to go through this on purpose?

"Just breathe through it. It's almost over, I promise." Angela's voice reaches out to me from far away.

I take in a slow breath through my bared teeth, and then I look down at my feet as they turn to paws right before my eyes. The next thing I know, I'm on all fours, and the pain is gone. I look over to see Angela smiling at me.

"See, I told you."

As I look at her, she shifts into her wolf form. It takes her no time at all. If I blinked, I would have missed it. I can't help but stare at her in awe. Her wolf form is beautiful. Her fur coat is shiny and light grey in color. I would have loved to share this moment with Amberly, but I understand what she needs right now, and I'm lucky enough to have people like Angela here who are nice enough to give me a chance.

She didn't need to offer me this moment, but she did, and I'm grateful to her for it. She wasn't lying about this experience. My mind feels free – quiet – as the noises of the forest make their way to my ears. My eyes scan over the landscape, seeing a chipmunk over twenty yards away.

How did I hear him?

I hear Angela's voice in my mind. *It's one of your many gifts.*

Wait, I can hear you.

She laughs. *I forgot to mention that's part of being a wolf. When we shift, we can communicate with the others in our pack. Sometimes even those who aren't in the pack.*

Like me.

She nods her muzzle.

I think it's time to stretch those legs of yours, Angela says.

I look down at my raven-colored paws and grin, placing one in front of the other.

That's it. Nice and slow.

Her words make me want to run, run fast as my fur coat moves against the breeze. I want to feel what she was talking about. I grin over my shoulder at her before I take off into a sprint. The forest blurs around me as the wind stings my eyes. I feel the morning air like a caress along my flank as I lift my muzzle and howl into the sky.

She was right. There's nothing like this feeling. Nothing in the world.

Angela

Running with Aidan was different but nice. I enjoyed being able to see him that way. Carefree and happy even. I started getting hungry, but he wanted to keep running. Can't say I blame him. I remember my first run. I didn't want to shift back for days, but my parents made me.

Making my way into the dining area, I see Amberly, and my heart stops. *Get it over with. Just talk to her.*

I approach her slowly, "Hey, Amberly, can we talk for a minute, please? There is something I need to talk to you about."

I feel bad taking her away from Julian, but I'm not ready to face him, talk to him, and this conversation with Amberly needs to be had as soon as possible.

She turns to him and says. "I'll be right back, ok?"

He nods and watches us as we leave the room. It's hard leaving. I haven't had a real moment to check in on him and see how he's doing. But I'm not ready to show him how bad I was when he was gone. More importantly, I'm not ready to deal with it.

"What's up? Everything ok?" Amberly's words ring through my ears.

Nervously I say, "It depends on how you look at it, I guess."

"Angela, you're making me nervous. What's wrong?"

I close my eyes. "Something kind of happened that I feel I should talk to you about."

"Angela, spit it out, please."

Don't think, just say it. "Logan and I kissed."

She looks at me for a moment and then starts to laugh. "Is that all?"

I look at her, confused. "Why are you laughing?"

"Because you had me thinking someone else died. Girl, you can't do that to me."

I look at her shyly. "I'm sorry, I just didn't know how to get it out."

She finally stops laughing and wipes away the tears that escaped her eyes. "Is that all?"

"Um. Yeah."

She smiles. "Why were you so worried about telling me?"

"Because you're one of my best friends, and well, you and he just broke up, and the girl code." I sigh, "I could go on and on."

She takes my hand in hers. "I just want you both to be happy."

"Really?" I ask, amazed.

I knew Amberly was selfless, but this is kind of amazing. I've never met anyone like her. I'm so lucky to have her as a friend, and I don't ever want to do anything to jeopardize that. Friends like her don't come around every day.

Appreciate the people and things that matter.

She nods. "Yes." She looks around us and then back at me, "Can I tell you something, and you promise never to tell Logan?"

Confused, I nod.

"I knew you were going to end up together."

Shocked, I almost scream, "What?"

She grins at me. "I saw it in a vision the night I broke up with him."

Afraid to ask, but I do anyway. "Is that why you left him?"

She nods.

"Why would you leave him because of a dream?"

"Because it became clear to me that night that you were always meant to be together, just like Julian and I were always meant to be together, and Amara and Troy."

I blink fast, "Wait, what?"

She laughs. "We are all meant to pair off with someone from the seven. We are stronger that way. We all have someone who we are meant to be with, and you were meant to be with Logan."

Mouth hanging open, I whisper, "Well, mind blown."

"I know it's a lot, trust me. I still don't completely have my head wrapped around the whole thing."

I look at my feet before I ask. "So, does that mean you're ok with Logan and me then?"

"Yes. You shouldn't even feel like you need to ask me that."

I look up at her. "I can't help it. You were in love with him, and you just ended things. The last thing I want to do is hurt you or mess up our friendship over a guy."

She smiles at me. "We both know he's not just 'some guy'." She uses figure quotes when she says the words *some guy*, and I can't help but start to laugh before she continues. "Plus, nothing could ever mess up what we have."

I stop laughing. "You promise?"

She nods. "I promise."

"Because I consider you more than just a friend. You're like a sister to me, Amberly."

"I know what you mean. I feel the same way. But I promise I'm ok. So, go find Logan and let him know, please, before you both go crazy."

I can't help but pull her in for a tight hug before I turn away with a smile on my face and a destination in mind. I turn to Amberly one more time before I make my full exit.

"There's still something that doesn't quite make sense to me, though."

"What's that?"

"You were both so in love. How did that just change so fast?"

"Johnathan told me we were holding each other back. That once I released him and removed myself that it would become clear to him who he is meant to be with. Kind of like being struck by lightning. Clean and fast, you wouldn't see it coming."

"I guess that explains a lot. Before you broke up, I never looked at him the way I do now. I thought he was a good guy, but that was as far as it went."

She waves goodbye as she says, "I'll see you later, Angela."

Finding The Truth

AIDAN

Running as a wolf was the best, most exhilarating feeling in the world. I never wanted to stop, but I knew if we wanted answers, I had to make my way back inside and find my mother. It took me no time at all to locate her. She was in the dining hall having breakfast. We exchanged pleasantries with everyone before making our escape.

Now we are back in their bedroom, and sitting in front of my mother, I'm having a hard time breathing. I can't remember the last time I was this nervous. I push the feeling down as deep as I can. Praying it won't resurface. This is something we need to do now.

She places her hands on mine as she looks me in the eyes with a small grin on her face, trying to calm my nerves. I close my eyes and take in a slow, shallow breath. Then I feel it.

JOCELYN

I look down at a pair of hands. They are mine but much younger. I glance around the room, taking in my surroundings. I'm home, back in my hut in the village. In the distance, I hear a baby crying. I round the corner slowly until two cribs come into view. I reach the side of the first and peer down inside to see Amberly. I would recognize her little face anywhere.

When her eyes come to rest on me, she stops crying and lifts her arms as high as she can, reaching for me. Begging me with her little tear-filled eyes to pick her up.

How can I resist?

I bend over and take her in my arms. I nestle her close to my chest and look down at her in awe as she smiles lightly in response. Then I hear it.

The other crib.

Something's moving.

I make my way slowly over to the object in question, unsure of what I will find. As I peer inside, I see a small baby boy, the same age as Amberly, and that's when it hits me.

"Aidan?"

How could I have forgotten this?

Forgotten him?

I reach down to place my finger in his outstretched hand. Longing to feel the touch of a son I have long since forgotten. His warm little hand closes around my finger tightly as a coo of happiness erupts from between his little lips.

How old are you now?

Has to be a few months.

How could I have forgotten?

I hear a loud commotion coming from outside my hut. I turn my attention elsewhere, momentarily forgetting my son as I remove my finger from his pleading grasp. I make it to the front of my home and peer outside to find the village in chaos, and I know something isn't right. I turn back to Aidan, still quiet in his crib. Amberly, sensing what must be happening outside, begins to cry softly in my arms.

"Oh, no, baby girl, it's alright," I say in the calmest tone I can muster up.

Rocking her back and forth, I begin to hum the only melody I can remember to her as I make my way into my room to see if she needs a fast change. Knowing a fight will soon be at my doorstep.

Not even a moment after I enter my room, the front of my house blows in. I cover Amberly with my body as I turn away from the debris flying everywhere.

I lift my arm and run it down the length of the wall. "Enchant, I have need of you."

The wall turns into a cabinet big enough for Amberly and her brother to rest in.

"It's ok, my love, don't you worry. Everything will be alright. I'll be right back with your brother."

I close the cabinet and run my hand over it once more. "Enchant, as you were."

The wall slowly returns to normal.

I enter the room, running to the crib. As I reach my arms in, an inch from grabbing my son, I'm weightless and thrown along the furthest wall. I hit with a loud thud and sink to the floor.

"Jocelyn, how are you? Sorry it took us too long. We had to find a way to enter the shields you placed around your village. Took us a little longer than I would like to admit."

Without looking up, I know it's Vladimir.

My need to protect my son is burning inside me.

"You can't have my son."

"I'm sorry. What was that?"

I look up at him with a fire in my eyes and a fury in my soul. I reply in a scream. "I said, you can't have my son!!"

I stand up, ready to charge.

Vladimir raises his hand with a sneer on his face. "My darling, I will take whatever I wish."

I'm frozen.

I try to move my legs, my hand, anything, but I'm stuck. I look at him in terror as he walks towards the cribs. He reaches my son's first, reaches inside, and picks him up.

"You will make a fine soldier for my cause."

"Put him down!"

He turns his sinister smile on me. "I don't think I will." He takes slow steps in my direction until we are only inches from one another. "I'm sure by now you've heard of me. Your parents have told you my story, I'm sure. I'm what goes bump in the night. Something every child should come to fear. I'm what they told you to be afraid of. Am I wrong?"

"You're a monster."

His grin widens across his young face. "That I am."

"Why are you doing this?" I ask pleadingly.

"Don't you already know?" He asks matter of factly.

But he says no more as he places my son in the arms of the man closest to him. "Take him home. I will be with you shortly."

"No!" I yell as all the anger boils up from my stomach to take hold of every cell of my being. "You will not take my son."

I feel my arm begin to move as all the anger reaches it and turns to fire in my hand. Before Vladimir can turn to see what I'm doing, the fireball is heading in his direction. For the first time, I see the surprise in his eyes as he deflects my effort at the last moment before it reaches its target.

A devilish smile finds its home on his face as he glances at me in awe. "You are as strong as they say. No one has ever been able to break from my enchantments."

He traces a finger down my face removing it just before my teeth sink themselves into his skin. "Interesting."

He turns around to another man who accompanied him. "I want her alive. Bring her."

"But sir."

He glances at the man in question with tornadoes in his eyes. "Are you questioning me?"

"No, sir. It's only. Enchanting one person," he gestures with his hand in my direction, "is fine, even those surrounding the children who would remember them, but doing it to a whole village. Making them forget not only the children who are only a few weeks old but their mother? The village's leader of all people. That will be a hard one to make stick. Even for you sir."

The realization is clear in his eyes as they soften. "You are right. Now isn't the time. My plan isn't ready yet." He turns his attention towards me, and I can feel the lust in his eyes. Suddenly, I feel very exposed.

I avert my gaze.

"Grab the other from her crib and let us take our leave."

I turn to the crib and remember at the last moment that Amberly is safe. Hidden where no one but me can hear her cries.

The man looks down to find an empty crib and turns back to his master. "Sir, the baby. She's not here."

Vladimir's hate-filled gaze rests on me. "Where is she?"

I can hear the sarcasm in my voice when I reply, "Where is who?"

He raises his arm high and lands a rock-hard blow across my cheek. I see stars.

"You know very well who. Where is the child?"

I peer up at him through blurred vision as a smile creeps across my face. "You'll never find her."

"I wouldn't be so sure of that." He smiles at me devilishly. Turning to his men, he canters, "Find the girl. Search everywhere."

"But sir-"

"I don't want to hear any excuses. Go!"

"The sun is setting, sir."

Fear creeps into his eyes for the first time, and I have to ask myself why nightfall would scare a man such as him.

"Gather the men. We are leaving."

He turns around to find me still on the ground staring up at him. "We will find her. It may not be today, but she will be mine. You can count on it." He turns for the door but stops as he looks at me over his shoulder. "Mark my words, if I find her too late to control, then she will die at my hand, and you will only have yourself to blame for not handing her over at this moment."

My fear cripples me as he raises his hand once more. As I close my eyes waiting for him to strike me, he whispers, "You will remember nothing of this encounter. However, I will. Know that I make good on my threats. I will be back."

Then nothing.

It's gone.

"Why am I laying on the floor?" I ask aloud.

Glancing at my front door, I see it's gone along with half my wall. I stand and make my way over to the opening to look out to my village. People passing by are beaten and bloody. Some I see trying to put out fires.

"What happened?"

Placing my hand on my cheek, I wonder why it hurts. My neighbor, Ruby, hurries over to me.

"Are you alright?"

I stare at her in confusion. Trying to find an answer. "I think so. What happened?"

She turns around to look at the destruction behind her. "No one's sure."

"Odd."

"It is. One minute we are sitting around talking about the next hunting trip, and then it's a fog. The moments between our conversation and now, they are just gone. No one can remember what happened."

I place a reassuring hand on her trembling shoulder. "Whatever took place here, it's nothing we can't overcome."

She smiles up at me with glistening eyes as she nods her head in agreement and takes off to continue helping the others.

"Odd indeed."

I turn back to my home, walk inside, and face the hole in my wall. With a lift of my arms, the scattered pieces lying on the floor around me rise into the air, making their way back to their rightful home. Every piece sewing itself back together in order until it's like nothing ever happened. I place my hands back at my sides and head for the kitchen.

Then I hear it.

A baby crying.

It sounds like it's coming from my room. Unsure, I follow the noise until I come to a wall in my room. Looking at it in confusion, I run my hand down the length of the wall.

"Enchant, reveal."

It turns into a cabinet. I reach in and open it, revealing a tiny baby girl.

"Now, how did you get in there?" I ask, reaching in to grab her.

I pull her close to me. As I rock her back and forth, in a calming motion, I begin to feel lightheaded. I sit down slowly on the edge of my bed and look down into the beautiful chubby face of a little girl I've never seen before. Her hand reaches out for mine, and as our skin touches…

Snap.

My memory of her comes rushing in.

"Amberly?" I sob. "What?"

Trying to recall the moments leading me to this one only makes my head throb more. I glance down into her happy face smiling up at me, and all I can do is smile back.

"It's ok now, my love. You're safe. Mommy has you, and I promise as long as my heart still beats, no one will ever hurt you."

I suddenly feel weightless.

I'm being pulled in another direction.

I fight it. Not wanting to leave. I won't leave my child.

"Mom."

I look up to see Aidan looking down at me with a concerned look on his face. I place a hand on his needing a moment to register everything that just happened.

"Are you ok?" Aidan asks.

"I. I don't know."

I turn my attention to the doorway as Aaron and Amberly walk through it. They look at me as their faces fall.

Aaron speaks first. "I take it from the look on your face we got the answers we were looking for?"

I nod.

"And it doesn't seem to be good news."

I look over at Amberly as the memories from that long-forgotten moment come flooding back to me.

I speak before I can stop the words from escaping between my trembling lips. "I'm so sorry."

Amberly moves to my side and drops to the space on the floor next to me. "Sorry for what, mom?"

"It's all my fault."

Aidan's pleading voice rings in my ears. "What is?"

I look up and glance at them both. "Vladimir. He came for you." I look at Amberly, "both of you. I heard a noise outside our hut, and at that moment, I had you in my arms. I hid you somewhere no one but myself would hear your cries." I turn to Aidan. "I went to grab you from your crib to put you with your sister, but Vladimir came in and attacked me before I could reach you."

He places a reassuring hand on mine, trying to comfort me.

"Vladimir and his men took you. I tried to fight them off, but he was too strong. He took you, and there was nothing I could do to stop it."

I throw my hands over my face as tears escape. I don't need to open my eyes to know that Aaron is standing next to me now. He places a hand on my shoulder as I open my eyes.

"He was looking for you," I say to Amberly. "I wouldn't give up your location. He told his men to search, but the sun was setting, and for some reason, that made him nervous. As he left." I pause, not wanting to remember the look in his eyes when he spoke. "He promised me he would find you and when he did if you didn't come to his side willingly that he would kill you."

"Mom, this isn't your fault," Amberly says sadly. "You tried to fight him off. You did your best for Aidan and for me, and we are together now. He can't take us all on at once."

I stare into her hazel eyes to find them filled with sheer determination. "He's stronger now. As all of our powers grew, so have his. I don't know if we can win this fight." I say defeated.

"Don't talk like that." I can hear the anger in her tone. "He's afraid of me for a reason, remember? He wanted Aidan and me together because we were a threat to him, and now he doesn't have either of us." She turns to look at her brother. "I know we can win this fight." She reaches out, taking his hand in hers and squeezing it lightly. "Together."

"When did you become so optimistic?"

"I learned it from you." She says with a small smile.

Aaron's voice settles the uneasiness in my stomach. "She's right. We are all strong individually, but together, united, no one can stop us." He looks from me to our daughter and lastly to our son. "Now that we are together again. I won't let anything separate us. Even if it is death."

"Dad." Amberly cries.

"We have to face the very real reality that not all of us are going to make it out of this fight. With that being said, I wouldn't hesitate to lay down my life for any one of you. When that day comes, I want you all to know how happy you have made me and how this time has been the best of my life."

"I couldn't agree more," I reply.

Suddenly my heart is filled with great sadness at his words. The thought of losing him, any of them, isn't something I want to entertain. I'll do anything to make sure that reality never comes to pass.

Will The Nightmare Ever End?

AMBERLY

The conversation with my parents took everything from me. All I want to do is lay with Julian and, for once, not think about the impending doom coming our way. I push open my bedroom door to see him still asleep, mouth wide open, snoring lightly.

The sight brings a smile to my face. I get in the bed as quietly as I can, not wanting to disturb him. His coffee-colored hair is a mess as I run my fingers through it lightly before placing a kiss on his cheek and settling into bed myself. Hoping, praying for a peaceful sleep.

"You can't run from me, girl. I will find you. There is no one left to protect you from me."

There is no mistaking that voice.

Vladimir is here, and he's coming for me.

I'm running faster than I ever have on human feet before. I try to shift, but my body is too worn down, leaving me no choice but to continue on my bloody, beat-up feet. Every step is agony.

Glancing behind me, looking for my pursuer, I don't see where I'm going until it's too late. My foot catches on something, and I trip. Face meeting the blood-stained earth. I turn to see what I fell over, only to find it's not a what but a who.

"Angela."

I bite back a sob, get up with a cry and keep running. Smoke lingers in the air all around me. Making it both hard to see and breathe. My eyes and throat sting. I call on my wolf eyesight, hoping it will help me see where I'm going. Maybe I can find a place to hide and wait him out.

It's not ten seconds before I regret my decision. All around me, on the ground, are bodies. I don't stop to see who they are. No time for that. I fight back the tears once more until my eyes come to rest on the place where I once hid.

It feels so long ago.

That day I first met Julian.

I crawl over to the hole in the base of the tree. Remembering the day I hid here while playing with Logan and Troy in the woods. Not knowing that day, my whole life would change. Given a chance, I wouldn't have changed a thing.

That day didn't only lead me to find out who I really am, but it led me to Julian, my father, my brother, and my family being reunited.

"Come out, little wolf. It's only a matter of time before I find you, anyway, so why drag it out?"

I place a hand over my mouth, trying to cover my sobs.

"I passed your loved ones back there. Did you see them?" *He taunts.* "Maybe not. You were too busy running from me. So let me fill you in. Your mommy, daddy, and brother. They're all dead."

I silence the cry and let it die in my throat as new tears make their way down my dirt and blood-covered cheeks.

"Oh, don't let me forget about, what were their names again? Logan, Troy, and Angela, I believe. Well, you can count them as dead too."

I close my eyes, not wanting to hear anymore. I want to wake up. This can't be happening. He's lying. He got in my head somehow, and he's trying to scare me.

"And your traitor brother. I made sure I prolonged his suffering. Gutted him like a fish."

I push myself back as far as I can until my body hits the bark of the tree. I don't want to hear this. It isn't true. They aren't dead. They aren't.

I hear his voice getting closer, but I refuse to open my eyes. Begging myself to wake up.

"Then there's Julian. He already died once because of you. But it seems bringing him back didn't matter much, did it?"

No. No. No. He's lying. You need to wake up.

His voice is right on me now. I can feel his hot breath on my skin. "You didn't save anyone, my dear, and you sure aren't going to save yourself."

I feel a hand close around my arm and yank me forward. I gasp as I open my eyes to see Vladimir's smiling face. The spot where his hand still holds me begins to burn.

"I told you I would find you."

I shoot up into a sitting position panting hard.

"Not again."

I lift my hands and run my fingers through my hair as I release a sigh of relief.

I can't keep living like this.

My arm stings, and I glance down at it to see a crimson hand mark on my bare skin, almost like someone on fire grabbed me.

"Not possible."

"What's not possible?" Julian's groggy voice asks from next to me.

"Nothing," I say while trying to cover my arm.

He wraps his arm around me and places a kiss on my shoulder.

"I know you better than that, Amberly. What's going on?"

"Promise not to freak?"

He looks at me with a concerned expression. "I'll do my best."

I sigh as I place my arm out in front of him, and his mouth opens wide.

"What happened?"

"I'm not too sure. I was dreaming and then woke up with it."

He looks at me skeptically. "What were you dreaming about?"

I stay silent.

"Was it Vladimir again?"

I nod.

"What happened this time?"

"I was running, like always. Apparently, I'm a coward." I look at him with sad eyes.

He places a kiss on my hand. "Never."

I smile. "Anyway, I was running and hid in the hollow of the tree where we first met. You remember the one?"

His smile is huge across his face. "How could I ever forget?"

"Somehow, I made it all the way there. I hid, and Vladimir kept taunting me. Trying to get me to come out."

He trails his fingers up and down my undamaged arm. "What was he saying?"

My heart skips a beat. Or two.

His fingers come to a stop. "Amberly?"

"He was telling me how everyone was dead. Again."

He sighs. "It was only a dream."

I throw my arm up in view. "Does this happen in dreams? I don't think so."

"He's strong. That's all that proves. He wanted to scare you, and it's working. You can't let him get to you."

"But what if it comes true?" I look at him with pleading eyes. "I can't lose you again, and I can't lose everyone else."

"Then we won't."

I look away from him. "He's strong, Julian."

"I don't doubt it. But you know what else I don't doubt?"

Still not looking at him, I ask. "What?"

He places his hand on my chin, turning my face until I'm looking at him once more. "You."

I smile, embarrassed.

"You're stronger than you know. You're brave, and you love fiercely. There is nothing you wouldn't do to protect the ones you love. That alone makes you stronger than him. You will come out on top of this, Amberly."

"How do you know?"

"Because I know you. You've been mauled by a wolf, stabbed, abducted," He smiles playfully, "lost the handsomely rugged man you're in love with."

"Stop playing." I hit him lightly on the shoulder.

He laughs. "And through it all, you still made it. There is nothing you can't overcome. You're the strongest woman, strongest person, I know."

I roll my eyes. "Alright, what do you want?"

He points at his chest playfully. "Who? Me?"

I laugh. "Yes, you."

"Oh, nothing. Well, maybe something." He looks at me with lust-filled eyes.

I cross my arms over my chest. "Well, out with it."

He leans over until I'm pressed flat against the bed, and he's over top of me. "I want the only thing I've ever wanted. You."

He leans down and places a gentle kiss on my lips before pulling back, looking serious. "I need you to remember you have something Vladimir doesn't."

I look up at him, unsure. "What's that?"

"You have all of us. People who love you and will protect you. He has followers who are afraid of him. There is a big difference."

He leans down to plant kisses on my cheeks, nose, and forehead. "There is nothing we wouldn't do for you, Amberly." He pulls back to look me dead in the eyes, and I can see all the seriousness in his. "There's nothing I wouldn't do for you."

Placing his lips on mine once more. At first, they are soft, gentle, and then I feel an urgency in them like never before. It feels like forever since we were alone like this. Longer than I care to admit.

No matter what's going on in my life, or head, in this case, being with Julian always takes me to the calmest place. I always knew he was different, and what we have is different, but at this moment, I feel the true importance of it.

We were made for each other.

I have no doubt in my mind about it. For the first time, I feel the truth behind Johnathan's words. I was always meant to be with Julian. I think a part of me always knew it. Even before we met. I felt empty. Not only because of the absence of my father or even my brother. I was empty for three reasons, and he was one of them.

Now having all of them back in my life, I find myself whole for the first time, and I'll be damned if I let anyone take that away from me. His lips pull me back to the moment from us. I won't let anyone take this from us.

My hands find the base of his shirt as my lips curl up in a smile as I begin to lift it off of his sweat-covered back. His lips leave mine as he pulls back to look down at me, unsure.

"What are you doing?"

"I'm taking off your shirt, silly."

He backs up slowly. "I don't think that's a good idea."

I feel the panic taking place in my heart. "Why not?"

"Because." He pauses. "If we start that." He looks me in the eyes. "I may not be able to stop."

He turns away, about to get off the bed, but I grab him by the arm lightly as I crawl up behind him, resting my knees on either side of his hips and resting my chin on his shoulder.

"Who said I would want you to stop?"

I feel his body stiffen under me in surprise as he turns slowly to face me once more. I see the desperate longing lingering in his emerald eyes.

"Amberly."

"What? I'm serious."

He places his hand lightly over mine. "Now isn't the time."

"I think it's a perfect time." I place my free hand upon his cheek. "I love you. I've loved you since the moment I met you, and I want to be with you."

"No one could ever love you more than I do, and for that reason, I have to say no." He turns away once more.

"Why are you being like this? Do you. Do you not want me?"

He swings towards me so fast I jump back in surprise.

"How could you think that?"

"What else am I supposed to think?"

He closes his eyes and releases a pent-up sigh. "Did it ever occur to you that I don't want to because I know we aren't ready?"

"And why aren't we?" I can hear the playfulness creeping up in my tone.

"Did you stop to think why you really want to do this?"

I sigh in annoyance. "Didn't I just tell you why?"

"That is part of it, I'm sure. But it's not the most important part."

I look at him, confused. "What are you talking about?"

"You're scared."

"Well, duh."

Julian looks to the far end of the room. "You're rushing because you know what's coming."

I quickly take his hand once more and make him turn to face me. "Yes. I'm afraid, and I don't know what's going to happen. All I do know is I want to be with you. I'm happy. For the first time in my life I feel whole and not alone, and I want to share it with you."

"That doesn't mean we need to have sex."

I throw my hands up in a defeated manner. "You are the first teenage boy to ever turn down sex."

He laughs playfully. "I doubt that."

"I don't."

"If they care about the person they are with, then it's not so hard to say no. Doesn't mean I don't want to or think about it every waking moment, trust me."

I smile happily. "Really?"

He grins sinfully. "Oh, yeah. You occupy my every thought. Awake or asleep. I think about you all the time."

"Do you undress me with your mind?" I say while leaning over seductively.

"Yes. And you're not helping right now."

I look down to see my cleavage popping out the top of my blouse, and when I look back at Julian, I see the hunger in his eyes growing. I reach over, grab his hand, and pull him back to the bed slowly.

"I want you, Julian."

"Will you please stop saying that?" He growls.

"No, I won't. Because I want you. For all the reasons we mentioned and so many more."

I reach down once more, pulling his shirt from his moist body. He lets me pull it over his head, and then I discard it to the floor below. I throw my arms around his neck, entwining my fingers in his hair and tugging him down lightly until his ear is to my lips.

I whisper seductively. "I need you, Julian."

I hear the growl deep in his chest. "Amberly."

I pull him down hard to my lips, sliding my tongue in his mouth. Needing him to feel what I'm feeling. Need what I'm needing. I want him to understand now is maybe the best time, the only time. He's right that I'm afraid. I don't know what tomorrow will bring or if we will still be alive to be with each other. I want to be with him in every way possible. To show him what he means to me.

He pulls back an inch, panting. "Are. You. Sure?"

I nod, smiling at him.

Without warning, he goes from a docile bunny rabbit to a bloodthirsty, very hungry lion. His lips slam into mine in such a force I wince, but he doesn't stop. I feel his hands roaming over my pants as he slides them off me in one fast motion. I feel his hands on my flaming skin as they crawl up higher and higher.

"This is your last chance." He growls in my ear before his lips move to my neck.

In response, I grab his head and move him down further. He kisses my navel softly as his hands find the hem of my underwear and pull them down slowly while his mouth follows in soft kisses. My head goes back as I release a moan.

He stops.

I look down to see him smiling up at me.

"Don't stop." I plead.

He pushes me back down until I'm flat on the bed and then lifts my shirt until it meets the bottom of my breast.

"I don't intend to."

I throw my head back as his lips meet the delicate skin at the base of my shirt. I close my eyes as my body grows almost too warm to bear. I throw my hands up around his head, urging him to move faster.

He takes my wrists in his hands and pins them down next to my head as he whispers in my ear. "Did I tell you that you could move?"

I laugh. "No."

He looks into my eyes, and I can see the wolf beating against them. Wanting to be free.

"Do. Not. Move."

I place my head back on my pillow and close my eyes with a smile on my lips. "Yes. Sir."

I can feel his grin as he kisses my neck all the way down to my panty line. All while running his hands over my aching body.

He's taking too long. I'm going to burst. One last thought occupies my mind before I get completely immersed at this moment.

Don't move.

Morning After Bliss

AMBERLY

I wake a few hours later to Julian still sleeping next to me, and my first thought is I've never seen him look so peaceful. A smile creeps onto my lips as I reach over and place my fingers in his hair as he groans in protest.

"Sorry," I say while starting to pull my hand away.

He growls into the pillow. "Don't you dare stop."

I laugh. "As you wish."

"And there you go."

"What?" I ask sarcastically.

"Taking my words and using them as your own." He peers at me through his hair. "Does that mean we are the same person?" He asks stupidly.

I laugh at his comment. "After last night, I think it's safe to say we are." I lean over to kiss him lightly.

He releases a content breath. "So, this is what it feels like."

"What?"

"Being truly happy."

I grin at him as I move to position myself next to his body. His arm automatically wraps around me, pulling me closer. "I guess so."

"Did you ever think we would end up here when we met?"

I think before I answer. "No."

"Really?" The surprise in his tone almost makes me jump.

"I never thought someone like you would go for someone like me."

"What's that supposed to mean?"

I place my hand on his bare chest. "Just that you were so smug."

"I was not." He laughs out.

"Really," I say matter of factly.

"Ok. Maybe a little."

I laugh. "A little. Julian, you would make comments. Very smug ones at that."

"Like?"

I smile, thinking about when we first met. "For example, when I fainted the first time I saw you. Do you remember what you said when I came to?"

"Something about my looks, I think." He says in almost a whisper. Not wanting to admit I'm right.

I smile. "If I remember correctly, you said something about your looks being too much for me. Meaning that's why I passed out."

He chuckles. "Oh, come on."

"So, what was I supposed to think? Someone like that could fall for me? I think not."

"That was just-"

"Your defense mechanism. Yes, I know."

He looks at me in surprise. "Hey, you're not supposed to know me that well yet."

"I think it's a good thing I do," I mumble into his chest, trying to get closer to him.

"Why?"

"Because now I know when you're lying."

He pauses for a moment. "I don't lie to you."

Stating the obvious, I reply. "No, normally you don't."

We are quiet for what feels like an eternity. Laying here enjoying each other's company. Completely in peace.

I'm almost asleep when I hear Julian whisper, "I love you, Amberly."

I smile. "I love you, Julian."

✳✳✳

AIDAN

The truth behind what happened all those years ago has my head spinning. To finally know the truth makes me feel liberated in many ways, but it's still life-shattering. My mother tried her best to keep me safe. To keep me, period. All these years, Vladimir lied to me. I'm not saying I'm naive. I knew deep down what he was telling me wasn't true, but I never pushed for answers. Partially out of fear of what he would do if I continued to ask him, I mainly didn't know if I would like the truth.

I thought many nights about what if he was telling me the truth. What if my parents didn't want me? I wouldn't have blamed them because I didn't want myself. I'm not a good person. I thought maybe my parents saw what I would become, and instead of finishing me off themselves, they threw me away. It wouldn't have surprised me in the least. However, to learn if it was true would have crippled me to my core, and that was something I wasn't quite ready to face.

To ease my conscience, I go back to the moments before I learned the truth. The feeling you get when you shift for the first time is hard to explain. There's nothing like it in the world. I would have loved it if my first shift had been with Amberly, but I understand, and Angela isn't so bad. I might honestly say I enjoyed her company.

It's a bitter pill to swallow, knowing not too long ago I was on the opposite side and that I'm the reason behind a lot of my father's pack's deaths. I wish things had been different, but this was the life I was cursed with, and there's nothing I can do to change that. All I can do now is learn from my past. Face it and try to be a better man. Atone for what I've done, and maybe I can find some sort of peace along the way.

Being abducted and beaten down is something no one here can understand, and I'm glad of the fact. What I had to endure, I wouldn't wish even on my enemy. I don't want anyone to pity me either. Pity is for the weak, and I'm anything but. After all the beatings over the years, I can gladly say they made me strong, and strong is what we need right now. I know Vladimir. I know how he thinks, and with that, we might have an advantage.

Moments In Time

TROY

"Amara, you have a sec?"

She turns away from the group of girls she was conversing with, and the way the light hits her eyes makes my stomach flip.

Why am I feeling like this?

"Hey, sure, what's up?"

I try not to sound nervous when I say. "I was hoping we could talk."

"What about?"

Oh, come on.

"You know what."

She begins to laugh, and I feel my heart land hard in my stomach. I've never felt this way about a girl before. I would mess around here and there but never long enough to catch any kind of feelings. There wasn't time for that. I had responsibilities, and a woman would come when the time was right. However, I don't think the time is now. I'm happy I never allowed myself to get close to women before because this feeling in my stomach is not happy.

She makes me crazy, and she doesn't even care.

Is this what it feels like to be a woman?

I shake my head violently. I am not a woman, damn it.

"You, ok?" She laughs.

"Yeah. I just – I would really like to talk."

"Troy, you're acting funny."

"Well, you bring it out in me. What can I say?"

I grab her lightly by the elbow and usher her outside.

"What's going on? What happened to the sarcastic Troy?"

"He left the building."

I release her arm, and she crosses them over her chest. "Has he now?"

"Yup."

"Well, I will only talk with him."

Lava begins to build in my veins.

God, this woman drives me wild.

"Damn it, I am the same person."

"No. You're. Not."

"What do you want from me?"

She looks at me with surprise in her eyes as her arms drop to her sides. "I thought it was obvious."

"Well, not to me it's not, and it's driving me crazy."

"I can see that."

I throw my hands up in the air. "It's not funny!" I yell as I turn away from her.

"I'm sorry. I didn't mean to make you. Whatever this is. I've never seen this side of you."

"Because it's not normal. You made me something. Different."

She smiles triumphantly.

"Don't do that."

"Do what?"

"Smile like it's a good thing."

She moves closer to me. "But I think it is."

"I guess you like seeing men go crazy then, huh."

She puts her arms around my neck, and my whole body responds. "Only the men I want to like me back."

"You like me?"

She giggles in response. "Duh."

I release a whoosh of air, relieved.

"Oh, Troy. Boys are so clueless."

"Hey. Hey."

She looks at me bewildered. "What?"

"I'm a man," I say while trying to make my face drawn out to look older.

She leans in so close that our lips almost touch. "Yes. Troy, you are a man."

She closes the distance between us then, and my world explodes.

$$* * *$$

Jocelyn

I can't believe I didn't remember. I'm the strongest witch in our village, maybe even alive, other than my children. How didn't I remember something so important? The glamour should have worn off me in time.

"You look a million miles away." I hear the pleading in Aaron's voice.

"I'm sorry."

He comes to sit on the bed next to me. "You never have to apologize. But I do wish you would put these thoughts to rest."

I look at the dirt-covered floor. "I can't. I don't understand how I didn't remember our son."

"He glamoured you. There's nothing you could have done to change it."

I feel the heat in my eyes when I turn my gaze on him. "I'm his mother. I should have sensed something wasn't right. Missing." I place my hand on his. "Just as I should have sensed you were still alive."

I see the sadness for me building in his tangerine eyes. "Then we are both at fault. I should have known as well."

"I'm his mother. I carried him. There is a bond there that shouldn't have been so easily broken."

He sighs. "Ok, fine. I'll let you take that one. However, I love you as much as you love me, and I should have known you were still alive. Searched harder. So that. That is my cross to bear, not yours. Deal?"

I look away from him. For the first time, I can't tell who I'm more furious with. Vladimir or I for what he's done to my family. We are equally to blame, are we not? What would my parents have done? If they were still alive and learned this information. It's hard to think of them after all these years. That night was the hardest of my life. Losing Aaron and my family all on the same night. I honestly don't know how I held it together for so long.

I may have lost them, but I have a family here. The pack is my home. Aaron, Amberly, and Aidan. This is the family I need to focus on. To protect.

"I will not fail again," I whisper.

"What did you say?" Aaron leans in closer.

"Nothing." I smile.

"It's been a long day for all of us, and we need our rest to face what's coming." He moves back further on the bed and offers me his hand. "Lay with me?"

Looking at him now, I feel the joy growing in my heart. To have him back after all this time makes me feel like a kid again. I feel complete with him by my side, and I never want to lose this again. I take my place by his side, resting my head on his shoulder and taking his hand in mine as they lay together on his chest. I can feel his heart beating at a slow, even pace.

He places a kiss lightly on my forehead. "This. This is all I need." He squeezes my hand before continuing. "And our children, of course."

I can hear the smile in his tone, and my heart skips a happy beat. I know the threat is right outside our door, and I don't know what will happen tomorrow, but this. This moment gives me hope that once we face it, our lives will be filled.

Taking Chances

Angela

LOGAN

"Hey there, stud."

I turn to see Angela walking down the hall towards me, and my face takes on a mind of its own as a grin takes hold.

"Hey, yourself."

She makes it to my side and takes my hand in hers. "Can we talk?"

I look over my shoulder at Troy. "It's cool man, go be with your chick." He smiles playfully as he throws a thumb over his shoulder. "I'm gonna go catch up with my fine lady myself." He looks at

Angela's shocked face. "Oh, yeah. Brother tells me everything." He winks, "and I mean everything." He slaps me on the shoulder. "See you later. Have fun."

I sigh as he walks away. Turning my attention back to Angela. "I'm sorry about that."

Her face turns from one of shock to something that looks almost like excitement. "You told him?"

I choke out. "Kind of. I hope that's ok."

She leans in and whispers. "I guess you're about to find out if you're in the doghouse or not." Taking my hand, she pulls me along with her.

I would be lying if I said I wasn't nervous. I'm still learning to read her. It's not like Amberly, who I've known my whole life and can read like an open book. I'm still trying to figure this girl out.

Curse you, Troy. Always have to open that big mouth of yours.

We make it outside the cave as she closes her eyes and lifts her head to the sky while taking in a deep breath.

"Beautiful night, isn't it?"

Looking only at her, I smile as I reply. "Very beautiful."

She cracks open her eyes to look over in my direction and sees me looking at her. She smiles. "Is it now?"

"Very much so."

Lowering her head, she positions herself in front of me. "I told her."

Confused, I ask. "Told who what?"

Glancing down at our hands, she says. "Amberly. I told her about us."

"You. What?"

"It's ok. She's fine with it."

I don't know whether I should feel hurt or angry. "Oh, is she now?"

I hear the hurt in her voice. "Why do you sound like that?"

"Like what?" I mumble.

"Like you're angry with me."

I sigh. "I'm not. I'm fine."

"Logan. I know you better than that. I thought this is what we wanted."

I pull her closer to me. "It is. I'm sorry."

"Then what's wrong?"

"I don't know. I knew she would be ok with it. She has Julian, and as my best friend, I know she wants me to be happy. But I thought maybe it would bother her. At least a little, you know."

Understanding is plain on her face. "I do."

"I don't know. I'm sorry, it's stupid."

She moves closer to look me deeper in the eyes. "No, it's not. You both spent most of your lives loving each other. Only to end up here." She gestures at the area around us. "I understand the feeling more than you know."

"Yes. But that doesn't make it ok. I don't want you to think I don't want you." I run my fingers over her cheek. "Want this. Because I do."

Her eyes close to my touch as she says. "I know you do."

I sigh in relief. "Oh, thank goodness."

She opens her eyes and laughs at me.

"So, she really seemed, ok?"

She nods, smiling.

"Well, then. Where were we?"

I place my arms around her back and dip her. A giggle erupts from between her lips as I look at her playfully.

"Logan." She laughs.

"Oh, you know you want this," I say in a seductive tone, making her laugh harder.

She throws her arms around my neck. "Just kiss me, you big dummy."

I smile. "Is that a request?"

She shakes her head. "It's a demand." Her seductive tone makes the heat rise in my body.

I lean down until our lips collide.

***

ANGELA

The feel of Logan's hands and lips is pure ecstasy. I never want it to end. In all my years, I've never taken someone seriously. It seems none of us have. I'm kind of like Troy and Julian when it comes to relationships. But with Logan. It's different somehow.

I remember how Amberly told me we are meant to be, but it doesn't feel forced like we have no choice. It's almost as if this feeling has always been inside me and was always meant for him.

I tangle my fingers in the hair at the base of his neck, making a moan escape from between his lips to vibrate on mine.

I could touch him like this forever.

I find myself wondering if this is what love feels like. I've never entertained anything long enough to gain any kind of real feelings for someone to really know the difference. However, I can safely say this feeling I have for him that burns deep inside me isn't normal. It can't be. However, from everything people have told me about love, it isn't a one, two, three you're there kind of deal. It takes time. So maybe this isn't love. But then what is it? Ever since we first kissed, all I wanted was to tell Amberly so that we could do it again. I caught myself thinking about him even in moments I shouldn't have been. My heart would skip a beat when I would enter a room to find him there as well.

I feel stupid.

How do I not know what it is I'm feeling?

And why do I feel I need to define it?

For now, we are together. We all are, and everyone is safe and happy. That's more than enough. Logan removes his lips from mine, moving them to my neck. Placing a soft kiss on my exposed skin in between each labored breath.

Each time his lips touch me, a new wave of warmth rushes over my body. Moving down every limb.

"Logan." I moan.

He mumbles against my flame-stricken skin.

"We. We should go."

Not removing himself from me, he pants. "Go. Where?"

The next words leave my lips before I know what I'm saying. "My. Room. Now! We need to go. Now!"

I feel it's hard for him to stop in his touch, and a huge part of me doesn't want him to. Is begging him to ignore my words and let his hands and lips continue to ravish my flame-kissed skin.

"Do. We. Have. To?" He pants harder.

"If you want to continue this, yes." My words come out in almost a moan.

With great effort, he removes his lips from my skin. They linger less than an inch from the flesh of my collarbone. I feel his warm breath making me shiver.

"Lets. Go."

And in one fast motion, he has me by the hand, making a beeline for the entrance to our home.

***

ANGELA

No sooner than the door clicks home Logan is behind me, pinning me up against the wall and moving my hair away from the back of my neck. He presses himself forward until every inch of him is touching some part of my backside.

I'm grateful for this position as my heat-stricken face rests against the cool wall lowering my body temperature. He grunts in my ear as his earnest lips kiss the back of my neck and his hands roam every inch of my body in a feverish frenzy.

I turn around quickly to face him. Not a moment passes before my lips meet the skin on his neck, and a loud, longing moan leaves his parted lips. I push him up against the wall I was inhabiting only a moment before.

My hands roam. Searching. Until I find the base of his shirt, tugging at it in a fast, swift motion until it's up over his head. Then my lips begin to trail themselves over and down his bare chest until I meet his pants line.

Before I can react, his firm hands grab my shoulders, pulling me back up to him as he smashes his lips against mine. I throw my arms around his sun-kissed neck as his hands cup my butt and lift me until my legs can wrap around his torso. He races across the room until we reach the edge of the bed, and he slams me down on the cool, welcoming surface.

I can see the pure desire burning in his eyes as he looks down at me.

"I. Need. A. Second." He pants.

Denied.

I reach out fast and grab his hands, pulling him forward. His eyes go wide as he falls to the bed, now on top of me.

"No break for you, Romeo."

"Angela. This is moving. Very. Fast. I don't want to rush this."

I place my lips to his ear. "I do," I whisper.

His body responds instantly to my call. I place his lips to mine once more, feeling his resolve disappear.

***

ANGELA

I wake to the feel of Logan's fingers running up and down my exposed spine.

"You awake?" He asks.

Smiling, I reply. "Yes."

He places a soft and tender kiss on my bare shoulder blade. I roll around to face him to see his face is a mirror image of my own. I reach up to run my fingers through his hair, and his eyes close at my touch.

"Last night," I whisper.

His eyes open. "Was amazing."

Planting a kiss on my lips, he smiles.

"You're happy?"

"Yes. You shouldn't even need to ask." He leans forward to kiss my forehead.

"Good," I say.

Pulling back, he looks me in the eyes. "I think it's time."

I look at him, confused. "For what?"

"You need to talk to him."

My eyes grow twice their size. "Julian?"

He nods.

"He's with Amberly. I don't want to bother them. They deserve this time together. Who knows when we will get it again?"

Taking my hand in his. "True, but you need to get off your chest what's been bothering you."

"How-"

He smiles. "I pay attention."

My face mirrors his. "Apparently, you do."

* * *

ANGELA

Walking to Amberly's room was nerve-racking. One moment I'm excited, and the next, I'm fighting not to turn around and go back to my room.

My knuckles cry in protest as they meet the door.

I hear laughing and then footsteps making their way towards me. The door swings open, revealing my brother. No longer dead. Very much alive. My heart jumps as my eyes take him in fully for the first time since he's been up and around. Without hesitation, I throw my arms around him.

"Hey, you." He whispers into my hair.

"Hey, yourself." I pull away slowly and look deeper in the room at Amberly, "You mind if I borrow him for a bit?"

"Go ahead. I was getting bored of him anyway." She says as she makes her way across the room to our side.

A playful look of hurt creeps on Julian's face. "You were?"

She nods. "Yup. Didn't know how to break the news to you." She slaps him on the back as she looks in my direction. "But thanks to Angela, now I don't have to."

"Wow. I guess this is what it feels like to be used." He says as he places his hand over his heart in a pain-stricken response.

"Better get used to it." She whispers as she plants a kiss on his cheek and makes her way past us to the hall.

"Where are you going?" He asks with a smile. "Off to your next conquest?"

Giggling she answers. "More like off to see the parents. Figured I'll spend some time with them while you two catch up."

"Sounds good. I'll meet you there later."

She nods and smiles in my direction, then continues on her way, leaving me confused and speechless.

"So I heard you and Logan are shacking up now. Guess I should thank you for that."

"Huh?"

"You know. Now that he has you, I don't have to worry about him." He says in his playful voice.

"Julian," I growl.

Throwing his hands in the air, he takes a step back. "I was only kidding." Placing them back down at his side, he continues, "Well, only a little."

I smile. "You're horrible. You know that?"

"But that's why you love me."

"Yeah, I guess."

We look at one another and erupt into uncontrollable laughter. After gasping for breath for I don't know how long, I slap him on the back before asking, "What was all of that about anyway?"

"What?"

"You and Amberly. I mean, you've always been weird, but I've never really seen that side of her."

Shrugging, he answers. "I don't know. She's different. More relaxed and happy."

"Happy I get, but relaxed? How can anyone be relaxed knowing what's coming?"

"We are trying to enjoy the moments we have now. We know what's coming, and we can't stop it, so might as well take what we can get."

Remembering only moments ago with Logan, I smile. "I guess I get that."

"I know that smile." He grins as he crosses his arms over his chest.

"I don't know what you're referring to." I turn around and head into the hall with him following on my heels.

"Don't play dumb. You did the nasty last night, didn't you?"

I stop dead as my cheeks burn. "Julian," I whisper. "Could you be any louder?"

"Oh. Don't play shy with me. You and Logan totally did it, didn't you?"

Now it's my turn to cross my arms. "And so what if we did?"

Julian erupts into enormous laughter, making my cheeks burn as the blood rushes to them.

"Stop."

"I'm sorry I can't. It's too good."

"Julian. Stop. Being. A. Dick. Or you won't like...." I stop dead, not sure where to take my threat.

"Won't like what?" He says as he wipes away the tears streaming down his face.

"Nothing," I say as I begin walking again.

"See, I knew you didn't have it in you."

"Julian, please."

Hearing the seriousness in my tone, Julian's face becomes slack. "Hey, I didn't mean..."

"I know. I just don't want to joke about it, ok? I already feel horrible enough as it is."

"Horrible? About what?"

I sigh. "They just broke up, Julian."

I feel horrible as I look at his pain-stricken face. "I didn't mean..."

"I know. I just don't like to think about it. Besides, they are both happy now, so why should you feel bad?"

"I love Amberly like a sister, and on some level, I just feel wrong."

He stares ahead. "Did you talk to her about it?"

"Yes."

"And?"

Looking at my feet, I reply, "She told me it was ok. That they weren't meant to be together, anyway."

"What's that supposed to mean?" He peers down at me in confusion.

"She said it was something Johnathan told her."

"Hmm."

I sigh. "Anyway. How are you feeling?"

"Great, honestly."

I smile. "Good."

"How about you?"

I try to look nothing other than happy, but I'm pretty sure I'm failing at it when I say, "I'm really good."

"You forget how well I know you."

He places his hand on my wrist, making me come to a stop. "What's up?"

Trying to ignore the real issue, I smile, saying. "Oh, you know. Impending doom coming our way. Pretty sure that would mess up anyone's day."

He doesn't smile. "Angela."

"Can we go outside?"

Without a word, he takes the lead for the exit. I follow slowly, not ready to have this conversation. Julian and I have always been there for everything and had each other's backs, but we just do a lot of joking around for the most part. You know him being a male, they aren't big on sharing real feelings. However, I think it's safe to say I'm the only one he's ever felt comfortable enough to confide in, and I feel the same way about him. But this. I'm not sure he's the best person to share this with. No matter how much everyone tells me I should.

We make it outside as my heart plummets into my stomach.

"What's going on with you? Spill."

And there it goes. Up into my throat. I try to form words, any words, but nothing wants to make its way out. Julian approaches me slowly and lifts a hand to lay on my shoulder.

"You should know by now that there's nothing you can't talk to me about. You know that, right?"

I nod. Not able to do much else.

"Talk to me. You won't feel any better until you do."

Silence.

I see the anger fuming in his eyes as he says through bared teeth. "Is it Logan? Did. He. Do. Something?"

And there's my voice. "God, no. Logan's been a godsend."

The fire is gone. "Good. But then what's wrong?"

"Well. I don't really want to talk about it, but everyone seems to think I should."

"Everyone?"

I look up to see hurt forming in his eyes.

"You spoke to other people about what's bothering you, but you won't speak to me about it?"

"It's not like that."

"You're like my sister Angela. If you can't talk to me about something, then I'm doing something wrong."

I place a reassuring hand on his forearm. "You did nothing wrong."

"Then bloody hell, what is it?"

"It's about you."

He throws his hands up in the air. "Didn't you just tell me it wasn't me?"

I sigh, feeling defeated, knowing I'm doing this wrong. Whatever this is. "I didn't mean it that way."

"Then please explain because you have this conversation going all over the place."

"I. It was..."

Seeing I'm having a hard time forming the words, Julian walks over to my side and pulls me in for an embrace. "Whatever it is, I can take it."

I throw my arms around his back, placing my chin on his shoulder as I whisper. "You died, Julian."

I feel his body stiffen under mine.

"You died, and it did something to me."

He squeezes me tighter, not saying a word.

"I felt lost. More lost than ever before in my life. When my village and family were slaughtered, it weighed me down for longer than I can remember, and that loss was heavy on my shoulders. But you. Losing you. I've never felt like that before in my entire life."

He releases me slowly. Trying to look me in the eyes, but I look to the dirt floor instead. He places his warm finger under my chin, forcing me to look up.

"Angela."

"I'm sorry. I don't mean to unload on you. But you were gone, Julian. You left me here all alone."

"You are never alone."

I know what he means, but it's not the same thing.

"You'll always have me. In the pack and in Amberly."

"Why are you talking like that?"

He's silent once more.

"Julian?"

He sighs as he looks deep into the forest. "We don't know what's going to happen, Angela. The only thing we do know is we aren't all going to make it out of this fight."

"Don't you dare talk like that. You just came back from the dead, and now you're talking almost as if you're ready to go back."

As he looks at me, I can see the light shining in his eyes like I never have before. "Ready?" He laughs. "Not even close. I want to spend my days growing old with Amberly. However, if it comes down to it, I will gladly lay down my life for her or anyone in my pack."

"Julian-"

He places his hand on mine. "I need to ask you for a favor."

I look at him, unable to move or breathe, as I see the seriousness of what he's about to say forming in his eyes.

"I need you to promise me if something does happen to me again that you will take care of Amberly."

"Don't talk like that. She can bring you back like before."

He looks to the cave entrance. "There's something she hasn't told everyone."

"What?"

"Healing anyone takes from her life. As much as I want to be here with her," he smiles, "with you, I don't want it at that cost to her."

I nod, understanding completely. I wouldn't want someone I love and care about putting themselves at risk for me if it was me. No matter what. But at the same time, it's hard for me to promise him that I won't let her not only for herself but for my own selfish reasons. I saw who I was becoming after only a few short days without him. I couldn't imagine going the rest of my life like that.

He's been my other half, my brother, for longer than I can remember. The only one I ever truly knew who, no matter what, I could turn to. We always have each other's backs, and I'm not ready to lose what we have. I can't lose my brother. Not again. Once is more than I can handle.

"So. You promise?"

"Julian, I..."

I stop dead. The pleading in his eyes is so intense that I can feel his need for me to agree to this, almost as if it's my own.

Defeated, I close my eyes. "I promise."

Family Bonds

JOCELYN

"You can't be serious?" Aidan erupts into laugher. Hand clinging to his chest, begging for breath.

"No lie. Ask mom if you don't believe me." Amberly smiles in my direction.

"It's true," I reply, grinning.

"Oh. My. God. You actually sent all the town's toddlers flying up into the air." He laughs harder. "I would have paid to see that."

"Hey, I was just starting to learn to use my magic. Not my fault they were the closest and lightest things around." I can see she's trying to stay serious, but it doesn't last long before she's slapping Aidan on the thigh, throwing her head back as laughter escapes her gaping mouth. "Oh man, you should have seen the look on their parents' faces when they thought I was going to drop their kids into the vegetable garden."

"Amberly," I say in the best scolding tone I can muster.

"Sorry, mom, but it was funny. I mean, come on, you were right there with me, and you're the strongest in the village. You never would have let anything happen to anyone."

"You're right. But thankfully, I didn't need to intervene."

She leans in to whisper to her brother. "Until it came to scolding me later that night."

"Amberly," I say in a shocked tone.

She smiles at me playfully as she straightens up. "What?"

"Seems we both missed a lot," Aaron says to our son.

"Seems so."

"Well, it's a good thing we have the rest of our lives to make up for lost time," I say to no one in particular.

Everyone's face falls.

I sigh. "Now, none of that."

"Sorry," they all reply in unison.

"This is meant to be a fun night," I state.

"And so it shall be, my love," Aaron says as he comes to sit next to me.

"So, what other crazy things did you do to get into trouble growing up?" Aidan asks his sister.

She laughs out. "A lot, actually."

"That doesn't surprise me."

"Hey, what's that supposed to mean?"

"Well, we are twins, aren't we?"

She crosses her arms over her chest. "So?"

"If you're anything like me, it means you got into loads of trouble."

Her smile returns. "When you put it that way..."

None of us can stop our bodies from convulsing as the laughter escapes. This feels better than I ever dreamt it would. To have my family together, whole, for the first time. Everyone smiling, laughing. It's how I always wanted it to be. The only thing missing is us being safe, and I'll do anything to make that a reality for my children.

"You ok?" Amberly asks with concern in her eyes.

"Yes. I'm sorry I went away for a moment. Where were we?"

Aidan perks up with a huge smile, "Amberly was filling me in on what a s'more was, and now I'm dying to have one."

I smile. "Oh, yes, they are divine."

"So, I've been told." He nudges Amberly's shoulder with his.

As she punches him playfully in the shoulder, it's almost like they were never separated. It pains me to know they lost all this time together. That they both felt alone all these years. Most of all, what my son had to endure at the hands of that monster. Remembering his threats all those years ago ignites a new desire deep in my being. He will never touch either of my children.

Not as long as I'm still breathing.

I look up at my family with newfound happiness. "I say we make them tonight. The whole pack."

Aidan brightens. "Really?"

I nod.

"Awesome!"

"Could you possibly sound any more like a child right now, Aidan?" Amberly says in her mocking tone.

"Hey, you've had them all your life, and you did such a good job explaining to them that my mouth is now watering for one."

She leans in close, taunting him with her eyes. "Oh, man, the ooey-gooey chocolate dripping over the side of the cracker is so messy but yummy. However, my favorite part is the melted and burnt marshmallow for sure."

I turn to see Aidan's mouth hanging open with his tongue out. "You're evil, you know?"

"Yup." She smirks as she straightens herself proudly.

"You two sure don't miss a beat, do you?" Aaron says.

Amberly looks at him, confused. "Meaning?"

"No one would doubt you're brother and sister. Not the way you two act with one another."

"That's a good thing, right?" Aidan asks, unsure.

"Of course, it is," I say, placing my hand lightly on his wrist.

He smiles up at me, and for the first time, I see hope shining in his eyes. A hope that I'm sure is a mirror of my own. When he first arrived, we learned the truth. I was worried he would never feel at home here or consider us a family. After all, how could I expect anything different after the way he grew up? Being told over and over how his family discarded him and how he was weak. Anyone would find themselves wondering and asking what was so wrong with them. I never wanted my children to ever feel unloved or unwanted, and here I am looking at my son. He was broken deep in his core when he arrived, so broken that I was worried we wouldn't be able to mend the pieces. But looking at him now, I can see them coming back together, and it sends a warmth rushing over me.

"So what about you, dad?" Amberly asks.

"What about me?"

"What's your favorite dessert?"

Aidan chimes in. "And why?"

Aaron smiles at our children while he thinks. "That's a hard one, guys."

"No, it's not." I voice.

"Ok, miss know it all. What's my favorite dessert?"

I grin. "Easy. Brownies."

"I thought that was your favorite?" He smiles.

I look at him smugly. "Nope. Always been yours."

"Damn. I was hoping I had changed your mind and made it your favorite as well after all this time."

"Nice try. I know you want it to be my favorite so that I would not only make them more often but also this way you could eat mine off my plate as well."

His cheeks turning red, he looks around the room shyly. "I guess the jig is up."

"I guess so." I laugh.

"So, why are they your favorite?" Aidan inquires.

"Why wouldn't they be?" He returns jokingly.

Aidan's smiling continues. "I don't know. I don't know what a brownie is."

Everyone's face drops except Aidan's until he sees our faces, of course.

"What? What did I say this time?" He sighs.

"Nothing son. I would have to say they are my favorite because of the chocolatey, gooey center."

"Hmm." I can see the wheels turning inside Aidan's head. "That does sound good. From what I've heard Amberly say, anything chocolate is something I would love to try."

"Then so you shall," I say before thinking.

Everyone looks in my direction, but Aaron is the first to speak. "Does that mean what I think it means?" He asks excitedly.

I nod, smiling.

Aaron jumps up off the bed, almost like a kid in the candy store. "Well, let's get to it, woman."

"What's he selling?" Aidan whispers to Amberly.

She starts to giggle. "I think it means mom is going to make both s'mores and brownies."

"Really?" He perks up. "Awesome!"

"Very." She replies.

Knock. Knock.

I turn my attention to the door. "Come in."

Troy pokes his head in slowly with a playful look on his face. "Hey, so this is where the party's at?"

He straightens himself up and enters the room, followed by Amara and Angela. I notice Amberly perk up and notice we are missing someone.

"Where's Julian?" She asks.

"He wanted to go for a run," Angela replies.

I see the worry forming in my daughter's eyes, and before I can speak to try to ease her worry, Angela beats me to it.

"He will be fine. He knows his way around the forest better than anyone. He promised not to go far."

Her words have no effect on my daughter. Aidan places his hand lightly on hers, and as their eyes meet, I see her shoulders relax a little.

"If he doesn't join us shortly, we can go looking for him. Deal?" He asks his sister.

She nods.

"So, where were we?" Aaron asks.

"Brownies and s'mores, I believe," Aidan replies with an eager smile while never removing his hand from his sister's.

"Someone say s'mores?" Troy asks enthusiastically. "Now we're talking."

Death Is Inevitable

JOHNATHAN

Aayda's hushed words reach my half-awake body. "I think we need to get Serenity out of here before it's too late."

With my eyes still closed, I whisper back. "You know she isn't going to leave."

"We need to find a way to make her."

I peel my eyes apart as I turn to look in her direction with a smile. "Make Serenity. Who are you kidding?"

"We need to do something."

"I think it's time, Aayda. She's tired."

Shaking her head forcefully, her voice cracks. "Don't say that."

"Would you rather I lie to you?"

"I didn't say that. I just. I'm not ready to let her go."

I look to the ceiling before I respond. "Neither am I, but that makes us selfish, does it not?"

"What do you mean?"

Looking back at her, I say. "She's done. She's held on so long for our sakes already, but she's hurting, Aayda."

I hear her sobs in the darkness. "We are all we have left of our family."

I reach out in the darkness until I find her hand and take it in mine. "We still have each other."

Between ragged breaths, she replies. "I know, and I'm so thankful, but we've already buried so many people we love. When is it enough?"

"I wish I had the answer. But taking her away, isn't it."

She expels a long breath. "I know. You're right."

"Plus, she would only make us come back."

"If it meant getting her somewhere safe, I would return to help them fight."

I pat her hand. "I know you would."

"Will you two stop that, please." Serenity's tired voice reaches us from across the room.

I feel Aayda's hand stiffen under mine as she says. "I'm sorry. I thought you were asleep."

"Even if I was, it doesn't make this conversation any better."

"You're right," I say.

"Enough talk of such sad things. What's meant to be will be. There is nothing we can do to change destiny."

"Then fight," Aayda says, defeated.

"I have. For many years and like Johnathan said, I'm tired."

"You're giving up."

"No, I will fight until there is nothing left in me, but you need to prepare yourself for the day I will no longer be here, for I have a feeling death is knocking at our doors."

I sit up slowly. "Our?"

She's quiet.

"Serenity. Do you know something?"

"No. It's more of a feeling." She says hesitantly.

"What kind of feeling?" I ask, more afraid of the answer than of anything else in my life before this moment.

"I fear many more will die in this fight than we thought."

"Meaning?" Aayda whispers from beside me.

"I fear this battle will take a bigger toll on Amberly and her friends than it did our family and us all those years ago."

"You mean...?" She doesn't let me finish my question.

"Yes." She states.

"We need to warn them." Aayda's voice shaking with fear. "We need to get everyone away from here. Train some more and then take the fight to him."

Even in the dark, I can see Serenity shaking her head in defeat. "It's too late for that."

"What do you mean?" She asks.

"He's already here."

"How long do we have?" I ask. Crippled with fear of the answer.

"Hours. If we are lucky."

***

VLADIMIR

"Sir, we are only a few hours away now."

"I know," I state, annoyed.

"What should I tell the soldiers to do?"

I turn around, anger fuming inside me. "Keep going. We will attack once the sun is set."

"Sir?"

"What?" I yell.

"Why do you wish to wait for the sun to set when we can take them hours before then?"

Annoyed at his question, I strike out mercilessly. He finds himself on the ground moments later in a daze. Standing slowly, he nods his head and takes his leave.

Why must they question my authority?

After all this time, why do they not follow my lead obediently?

I have kept the secret my whole life, and I will take it to my grave. I learned on my twenty-fifth birthday the truth about my powers. For us demons, we gain our power from the darkness.

Hell.

The depths of everything unholy.

The darkness is where my powers are at their highest, and so it is in the darkness I will fight my strongest enemy. These children will not be the end of me and my cause. I will put an end to them and anyone else who stands in my way. This world needs to be purified. Stripped down to its core.

No more mixed breeding.

No more humans.

No more weakness.

Only the strong will survive.

And I will be there to lead them.

I smile at the thought of ending them before the sun meets the sky in a day's time.

Do they know what awaits them?

"I don't think they do," I say to myself with a laugh.

$$* * *$$

Julian

I can't seem to shake this horrible feeling deep inside me. Last night was the best night of my life, and I wanted nothing more than to be there with Amberly, but I know we both needed this time. She needs to spend time with her family, and I need time too.

To...

Think.

Something isn't right. I can feel it. It's more than what we already know is coming, but I can't put my finger on it. I know Angela promised to take care of Amberly for me, but I could see the anger lingering in her fuming eyes as we spoke.

She thinks I've given up.

Only it's just the opposite.

More than ever, I want to live. I want to grow old with Amberly. I never in all my years thought I could meet someone to tame the beast inside me, but she has. She makes me happier than even my best dreams. Meeting her was a Godsend, and she freed me from my cage of turmoil. Since the day she returned home with me, my life has been shaken to the core but in the best way possible. She showed me what my life could look like, and I wanted it with her ever since. I never thought she would forgive me for my stupidity, and then she did. And then, well, I went and died.

I thought, well, this sucks, and the next thing I knew, I was on my way back to her. Back to the life I craved more than anything in my entire life. Only to find out it may be short-lived. I knew Vladimir was something we still had to deal with, but I had hoped we could have enjoyed life for at least a little while before fighting for our lives once more.

No such luck.

Then again, nothing good worth having ever came easy, right? I'll happily fight if it only means I can have her in my arms in the end.

But that's the problem.

The fear that lingers in the depths of my soul.

What if I don't make it out of this fight?

Worse, what if she doesn't?

I can't lose her. I won't.

She is my light in the darkness of this life I have lived. I fought to keep myself here and sane for Angela's benefit, and just when I was ready to give up, throw in the towel, Amberly came along. Life without her isn't an option for me. Not now.

As I round the corner, ready to exit the cave, laughter greets me. I step into the cool semi-dark night to a small fire not even ten feet from the opening. Circled around it is everyone I hold dear in this life.

"Having all the fun without me, I see."

Troy jumps up from his seat and runs to my side like a child about to receive a toy they have long since been without. "Hey, bro. Where you been?"

Surprised, all I say is, "Around."

"You made it just in time." He says, grinning ear to ear.

"For?"

"Amberly's mom is making," he turns around to the fire as his body begins to shake. It's not until he turns around to face me with a smile on his face that I realize it's from excitement. "S'mores, man. She be making the s'mores." He starts to rub his hands together in a greedy fashion, and I can't help but chuckle at him.

"Oh. Man, I guess I did make it at the right time, then."

He hits me in the chest. "Hey, if you don't like them, then move along, buddy."

As he turns his back to me, I yell, "What happened to 'brother'?"

He scoffs.

"So much for that, then."

"So much for what?" Amberly asks as she reaches my side.

"Troy. He's a hard one to figure out."

"Not really."

I peer down at her. "Well, then I think it's time you teach me, Troy One-oh-One, and while you're at it, maybe I should take the class for Logan and your brother too."

I glance back to the fire to see them both staring me down.

"If looks could kill."

She giggles. "Boys will be boys."

"I resent that."

She pokes me playfully in the chest. "I'm pretty sure, not too long ago, if I recall correctly, you were being the same exact way."

I place my hands on my chest. "Who? Surely not me?"

She nods, smiling.

I wave my hand in a dismissive gesture. "I think you have me confused with someone else."

"Nope."

"You sure?"

"Very."

I shrug. "Oh, well."

She smacks me across the arm, and I grab at it. "Ouch."

"That did not hurt."

I make the best pouting face I can muster up. "Yes. It. Did."

She sighs. "You're too much, you know."

I straighten up. "So I've been told. Heard your mom's making the s'mores."

"Yup. Her specialty."

"Any real occasion?"

"You mean other than the impending doom knocking on our door?"

I sigh, not wanting to think about it.

She shrugs off my reaction. "It's for my brother, mostly. He's never had much. But I never realized how bad it really was for him."

"We all knew it had to be bad. I mean, Vladimir is a psychopathic killer."

"It's more than that. Aidan doesn't know what the simplest things are."

"Like?" I ask, trying to act like I care about the man responsible for my death not that long ago.

"He doesn't know what chocolate is, for starters."

"You're telling me the kid has never had anything with chocolate in it?"

She shakes her head.

I glance in his direction to find him still staring me down. "Not possible."

"Like you said, Vladimir is evil. I don't think he cared about giving him the finer things in life, let alone feeding him."

I try to push the annoyance from my tone as I say. "We've all had it bad, Amberly. Not just him."

The look on her face is one I haven't seen in a long time and not one I ever wanted to see again. "Can't you at least try to be sympathetic?"

"Trust me, I'm trying."

"Not hard enough."

She begins to walk away as I grab her lightly by the wrist, and I can see Aidan rise from his seat out of the corner of my eye.

"I'm sorry."

"No, you're not."

I release a sigh. "I'm trying. But it's hard to feel bad for someone responsible for not only my death a few days ago," she flinches at the word, and I'm suddenly mentally kicking myself as I continue, "but also the death of thousands of people. Mine and Angela's tribe, for starters. He's the reason we were left alone. The reason we are so messed up. It's not something I can let go of so easily. Not even for you."

"You forget one main thing."

I rub my eyes feverishly. "And what's that?"

"He's a kid. He wasn't behind the attacks. He didn't plan them, and he sure as hell wasn't old enough to lead Vladimir's army into your camps when that happened. He's as much a victim as you are."

Final Talk

AMBERLY

I don't think I've ever been this livid with Julian before. Not even when I caught him kissing Amara did I feel this enraged. How could he act like that? I understand his worry and skepticism, but Aidan is my brother, and Julian should know me well enough by now to know that I would never jeopardize the ones I love. Not for nothing or no one. If I thought even for a moment that we couldn't help Aidan, I would never have brought him back here with me. As much as I wanted and needed him here with me, I wouldn't have.

Having Aidan around has made things easier and less scary somehow. Like a newfound hope igniting in my soul. I mean, if after all these years we found each other and he's here home, and we are all back together, if that would happen, maybe, just maybe we can win this battle and whatever comes next. As long as we have each other and stand behind one another, I believe we will come out victorious.

However, underneath all the joy and hope I've found in him and my family, there is still a deep darkness. I feel it just under the surface, threatening to swallow me whole. I find it hard to decipher what could be the cause. Is it the battle ahead with Vladimir that has all my nerves igniting? Or could it be something else?

I remember what I was told about letting the power overtake you and turning you evil, and I would be lying if I didn't say it was something that lingers on my mind at all times. I'm always trying to keep myself in check. So much so I barely use my powers unless I need to. In fear that they will take me over and I will lose myself entirely to the darkness I now know I have inside of me.

Like Aidan said, we are more alike than we realized. I would never talk about the darkness inside of him to his face, but I've seen it, and more than that, I feel it. Knowing he has it in him, the things he's done, I know that could have just as easily been me. That reality scares me more than anything coming over that hill and into our backyard.

Then there is another fear entirely.

One that rocks me to my core.

What if I can't save the ones I love from what's coming?

But worse, what if the only way to save them all is to let myself be taken over by this darkness?

What do I choose?

I know letting it in could do more destruction to the world and my loved ones than if I keep it at bay, but part of me knows I would sacrifice anything to protect those I love. Now that we are all finally together and happy, despite what's going on around us, I don't want anything to take that away from us.

Least of all, a madman like Vladimir.

But something feels off.

Something else.

I hear it in the dark.

Calling to me.

It's not the darkness within. It's more like someone is trying to warn me about something coming. Something other than Vladimir and the battle right around the corner. Something worse.

The more I try to listen, hear what it's trying to tell me, the further the voice seems.

"Amberly."

I jump a foot in the air.

"I'm sorry," Serenity giggles, "I didn't mean to startle you."

I take in a slow breath, trying to steady my heartbeat. "It's fine. How are you feeling?"

She waves her hand at me, brushing off the question. "I'm fine. No need to worry about me. However, I am worried about you, my dear."

"Me?"

She nods.

"Why?"

"You seemed somewhere far away just a moment ago."

"I was only thinking." I turn away, heading back towards the fire.

"Would you care to share what about?"

I hear her walking slowly behind me.

"Honestly, it makes no sense even in my own head. I don't know how I would form it into words."

"Try."

Unsure, I sigh. "I feel – off. Something's coming. Not Vladimir. Something else. I hear someone in the wind whispering to me about it, but I can't make out the words." I turn around to look at her, her expression blank. "I know it sounds crazy like I said."

"Maybe not."

I stop.

"One thing you never want to do is ignore your inner thoughts. Even if they make you think you're going crazy."

"So, what do I do about them if I can't hear them?"

She looks up to the sun, almost setting in the sky. "You find a quiet place. Empty your mind and listen."

I release a long breath. "You make it sound so easy."

"It's not. But from what you're telling me, it sounds like it's something important, and more than that, it's something you need to know."

I know she's right, but part of me is afraid of what I'm going to hear, and the other half of me is afraid that no matter what I do, I'll never hear what it's trying to tell me.

"There is another reason I came to find you."

I see something like fear in her eyes. An emotion I've never seen on her before. "What is it?"

"You aren't going to like what I'm about to tell you."

"That's never stopped you before." I laugh.

"True." She smiles.

"You want to sit down somewhere?"

She shakes her head no. "This will only take a moment."

I grab her hand lightly and lead us to a few rocks not far from where we are. I can see how tired and weak she is, and I don't want her standing longer than she needs to. I wish Aayda and Johnathan would have been able to convince her to leave by now, but I knew she never would. She's fearless and strong, and she would never run from a battle. Even if she knows it will be her last.

The thought of her not being here after this next battle brings tears to my eyes. Serenity is the best out of them, and they all know it. Her heart is so pure and kind. The world will be a darker place without her in it.

We sit, and she takes in a few slow breaths. "It's about the battle."

"Do you know something?"

She nods.

"What is it?"

"You can't do it again, Amberly."

Confused, I ask. "Do what?"

"You can't keep healing everyone. You remember what I told you?"

I nod.

"I need you not to forget it. This world needs you more than anyone else here. You will lead everyone back to a place of peace and happiness. They need you. They don't need us."

Before I can stop the words, they are flowing from my mouth. "But what if I need them?"

She smiles at me sadly, and I can see she understands the feeling. "You will be fine. No matter what happens, they will always be with you."

"You should know better than anyone. That isn't the same thing."

I regret the words as soon as they are spoken. Seconds later, Serenity's face falls to one of complete sadness.

"I'm sorry, I didn't mean..."

"It's fine, child. I understand. Like you said. But you can't make the same mistakes I did. This world, our world, will not make it without you. You need to lead them. No one else but you."

"I don't understand."

"It has always been your destiny. Vladimir wanted you for more than your powers. He knew you would be the one to stop him from the journals we told you about, but what we left out was that there is more in those books than you would think."

I ask her to continue with my eyes.

"The future of our worlds are in those books. There are always two paths. One was with you as the leader, and one was without. Vladimir saw that if you were to lead, he would fail, and that is why he wanted you."

"I don't understand what makes me so important."

"You are a born leader. Your family, friends, they look to you. People who just meet you feel the pull. They want to be led by you. Have you never noticed?"

I think back to all the times it was easy to meet someone new. Almost like we were always friends. How often had people told me things they might not tell someone else, but they told me, a complete stranger.

"The world needs you more, Amberly."

"I understand. I promise. But I need something first."

"Name it."

I place my hand on hers. "I need to know what you know. What aren't you telling me?"

She glances to the sun, now halfway in the earth as the night creeps in around us. "You will lose someone in this battle. Someone who means more to you than you know. You will want to save them, but you can't." She turns her attention back to me as my heart feels like it's beating out of my chest. "Do you understand?"

I can't speak.

I'm hoping I'm hearing her wrong.

Praying I'm hearing her wrong.

She squeezes my hand tightly, bringing me back to the present. "Amberly, I need to know if you understand what I'm saying. Time is short."

"I. You're asking me to let someone I love die?"

"You must."

I shake my head, trying to clear the noise ringing inside. "I don't understand. Why would it matter if I saved one person?"

"You bringing back Julian took more from you than I think you realize. He was dead Amberly, not dying. You brought him back. That is impossible for most healers, and you did it your first time. In doing so, you took a huge hit to your life essence. What you did was like saving over one hundred people on the edge of death at once."

"Ok. So I'll be more careful."

She releases my hand. "There is another battle on the horizon. Vladimir is only the beginning. You will need your strength, your power, for that battle. If you use it this time, you will be done, and you will fall in the battle ahead."

"Fall?" I choke on the word.

She nods.

"You mean..."

"You'll die."

A chill washes over my body as my palms begin to sweat.

"Do you understand now?" She asks in a sad tone.

"Yes," I whisper.

"As hard as it will be not to heal the person, you can't. You have to let them go. They wouldn't want your life traded for theirs, and more than that, this world is depending on you. Without you, we don't stand a chance."

"I understand."

I couldn't say another word. There was nothing to say. How are you supposed to react when you know someone you love is about to die, and you could save them, but you're being told not to? That saving them means you will die. I would easily trade my life for anyone I love, but I know Serenity is right. None of them would want that, and more than that, I have a responsibility to the rest of the forest. If there is a chance, even a small one, to reunite us all, then I can't risk it.

After so long in the dark, we all deserve peace, afraid, alone, and on the run. If I can give that to them, then I will. Even if it means losing someone I love. Continuing my life without that person in it.

Prepare For Battle

AIDAN

I've lost count of how many smores I've now eaten. My grin widens as I push another into its home in my salivating mouth. Nothing has ever tasted so good in all my life, and now I understand why it's my mother's favorite. Who wouldn't love this?

I glance around the fire to all the smiling faces, and for the first time, I feel at peace, at home. Something I've longed to feel for longer than I can remember. My mother, so beautiful and strong, just like my sister. My father, a warrior, a leader. And me, their son. A killer. Yet, they welcome me with open arms, never asking me why I did what I did. Never holding it against me. Even the rest of the pack welcomes me.

Logan, Troy, Angela, Julian, and even Amara have been kind to me. They may not trust me one hundred percent, but they are giving me the benefit of the doubt, which is more than I deserve. After the things I did to Amara alone, I don't know how she can be in the same room as me.

Sometime during my thoughts, my family had moved away from the safety of the fire and their friends that surround it.

My father looks at my mother before taking her hand in his. "We knew this moment was coming."

"Too soon." She whispers with tears in her eyes.

He takes her in his arms and mumbles into her hair. "No matter what happens, I'll always be with you. These last weeks have been the best of my life." He looks at me, placing his hand on my shoulder. "To be reunited with my family is a joy I cannot explain no matter how hard I try."

My mother begins to sob violently into my father's chest.

"Why are you talking like that?" I ask him.

"We don't know what's coming. The only thing we know for sure, son, is we aren't all going to make it through this battle."

"Maybe not, but I have faith we might make it out of this alive, so don't throw in the towel yet," I say in a growl.

"I'm not. But if it comes down to one of you or me, it will be me."

I glance down at my mother to see she now has a fistful of his shirt in her hands, and her knuckles are turning white. I find myself angry. Angry for finding them. For taking Amberly. For leaving Vladimir instead of taking him out myself, and angry at my father for giving up.

"It won't be any of us. It will be Vladimir."

My mother's red face peeks at me from my father's chest as a small smile takes place. "You are so much like your father." She chokes out.

I can't hide the surprise at her words.

"I think he's more like you, and Amberly is more like me, but that's just my opinion." My father says as he looks at me. I'm sure he sees the hurt in my eyes at his words, so he continues, "You have your mother's kind soul. I could see it in you the moment you came here. Scared and alone. You are the best part of her."

"I will accept that compliment," I reply with a smile.

He's right. In my short time here, getting to know them both has taught me a lot. My mother is the best woman I've come to know. She's strong and fearless. She doesn't take crap from anyone. They don't make women like her where I grew up. However, here in this place, I've come to know a lot of strong women. My sister being one of them.

I look up to see the sky turning red and the sun almost submerged into the earth, and my heart drops as my body starts to convulse where I now stand speechless.

"Aidan, what's wrong?" My mother asks.

"The sun. It's setting."

Troy, hearing my words from where he sits by the fire, laughs, "Like it does every day."

"You don't understand."

I feel my father's hand on my shoulder before I realize he's standing next to me. "Tell us."

"Vladimir."

"What about him?" My mother asks with concern in her tone.

"He's coming."

Troy, more serious now, says, "Yeah, we know. Tell us something we don't know."

I look at him with both annoyance and fear in my eyes. "It's almost night."

"And?" He asks.

"When the sun sets, he will be at his strongest." I look to my parents. "That is when he will attack."

"Are you sure?" My father asks me.

"Yes. I've felt him close for a while now, but it didn't dawn on me until this moment what he could be doing, or in this case, waiting for."

He goes into leader mode, "Alright everyone, it's time to head inside."

"And do what?" Troy asks with fear in his tone.

"Troy, shut up and do what he says." Logan grabs Angela by the hand.

I watch as they lead the way into the cave. My family and I stand back, waiting till everyone makes it inside.

✳✳✳

VLADIMIR

Sun's set.

The time has come.

I will end all of those who oppose me and my new world.

A pure world.

Approaching the cave, I see a group standing outside by a fire. From this distance, it's too hard to make out how many there are. I gesture to my warriors to flank on all sides as I take a select few up the middle with me.

As we get closer, I see Aidan standing with a man and woman embracing. I would know that woman anywhere. The only woman I've ever desired for myself.

Jocelyn Grayson.

The fearless warrior.

She would have made a wonderful queen at my side; had she not been tainted by that shifter. Still, she would make a nice trophy at the end of this.

Close enough now, I focus on Jocelyn and her lover, raise my hand, and throw them a distance away from my adopted son.

Now all alone and all mine for the taking.

The Beginning Of The End

AIDAN

I'm looking at my parents standing next to me one moment, and the next, they are flying through the air. My father, cradling my mother's head, protecting her from the impact when they hit the cave wall. They fall to the ground, and my father is limp. The blow has knocked him unconscious. My mother unsteadily removes his arm from around her and then checks for a pulse. Her tears of joy tell me my thoughts were correct.

I scan the forest around me until my eyes find him.

"Vladimir." I snarl.

I raise my hand, ready to launch my first attack. He deflects it.

I try again.

Nothing.

Again.

He laughs.

"You should know better than to try to take me on your own by now, my boy."

My lips lift into a snarl as I growl. "I'm not your boy."

"Aren't you? I made you what you are today. Did I not?"

"Yes. You did. You made me a killer."

I can see the anger rising inside of him even at this distance. "I made you strong. Feared."

He advances.

What am I going to do?

He's right. I'm not stronger than him. I never have been. I know I can't take him on my own, and right now, the rest of his clan will be flanking us, leaving no escape. My parents are powerless. My father is unconscious, and my sister is who knows where. Unprotected.

Pay attention.

I need to focus. What can I do to distract him until I figure out how to get my parents away from here? Every spell I try, he deflects. I glance over in my parents' direction to see my mother slowly getting to her feet.

I can't let her fight, not like this.

I turn my attention back to Vladimir, but it's too late. I see it in his hands at the last minute. No time to defend myself from his attack.

This is it.

Everything I fought so hard to have will be stripped away from me at this very moment.

I close my eyes and smile thinking, *it was worth it.*

***

AMBERLY

I see the fire and realize what it is too late. Vladimir and the fire are heading right towards my brother. THE FIRE HITS ITS TARGET before I can take one step, but Aidan continues standing as someone, a woman, begins to crumble in front of him. It's not until she hits the ground that I know who she is, and my heart sinks to my stomach.

"Mom!"

I run as fast as my feet will carry me. Forgetting all about Vladimir and his men that I'm sure are all around us. I see Aidan drop to his knees in a broken manner as he pulls our limp mother into his arms. I'm still too far away to know for sure, but something is screaming at me that this is it.

This is the person I am to lose.

This is the person I'm meant to let die, and as much as I promised, as much as I know, I should for the sake of everyone else in the forest, I don't think I can do what Serenity asked of me only minutes before. I can't let my mother die. Not when I only just found her. All my life, I tried to get inside the concrete bubble that formed around her heart. I wanted nothing more than to get to know my mother. To be her daughter. To feel her love, hear her laugh, feel how proud she was of me in a look. I wanted a mother, and now I finally have one, and I can't lose her.

Not now.

I'm a good forty feet away when a sharp pain runs through my shoulder. I turn around fast to see my attacker getting ready to land another blow with his now bloody knife. I throw my arm up, blocking the incoming weapon. I'm trying to focus on this moment and not what's happening behind me, but it's hard. I use my mind trying to enter his, and he laughs.

"That won't work on me, dearie."

I bare my teeth pushing him away from me as hard as I can.

"A matter of fact, none of your little witchy powers will."

"What?"

He looks amused. Almost proud, I should say. "I'm a warlock myself, and I've learned a few tricks along the way."

I lift my hands up and bring my fingers to meet my palms a few times. "Well, let's see what you have then."

"So eager to die."

"I have more important things to deal with than you."

He flashes his teeth. "If I were you, dearie, I would focus less on what's happening behind you and more about me."

"I think you're giving yourself too much credit."

He smirks. "We will see."

Suddenly I'm thrown off my feet and land hard on my stomach. The man behind me laughs triumphantly, only making my anger boil.

I stand in one swift motion. "Is that the best you got?"

"I'd watch your tone with me girly." He says in an angry tone.

"Bring it on."

My feet leave the ground as he sends me sailing through the air so fast that I don't have enough time to protect my face before I'm eating bark. I land on my back as the air is pushed from my lungs.

I flip over to my knees, gasping for air as the man leans down and puts his hand around my throat. Lifting me to my feet in one swift movement before pinning me hard against the tree.

"Maybe that will make you think twice before you mock someone you don't know."

My hands claw at his feverishly as he applies more pressure, and my vision becomes blurry.

I need air.

Now.

He places his knife over my left cheek while his hand around my neck loosens slightly.

"I don't want you passing out. Not before the fun starts." He says as he places the cool blade against my skin and pushes it inward.

I close my eyes, trying not to think about the pain but a way out of this situation. I feel the blade run down my cheek in one fast motion, and then thick warm liquid trails down my skin.

"Beautiful."

Think Amberly.

He moves the blade over my skin once more.

Then again.

And again.

My skin is burning as blood runs down it in thick lines. I open my eyes, lift my foot high and bring it down hard on his. He drops his blade to baby his foot jumping up and down in a funny manner.

I take in a few short breaths before bending down to retrieve his weapon. I'm three inches away from wrapping my hand around the hilt before I'm hit with an energy ball in the chest and sent flying once more.

"That's cheating, little lady."

On my knees, panting, I look at him through my sweat-infused hair.

I need to get to my family. Enough of this.

I charge him fast as he grins. "That's more like it. I like my women with some spirit."

I mumble. "I'll show you spirit."

He lifts the knife high, ready to drive it home. I drop low and under his extended arm, sliding along the ground until I'm behind him. I throw my arm around his neck, putting him in a chokehold.

I whisper in his ear. "My magic may not work against you, but this sure will."

He pulls at my arm desperately as his face begins to turn crimson. Knowing it won't work, he raises his knife and runs it down the flesh of my arm, pushing it deep inside. I wince in pain, but I do not release him.

A minute later, he falls to the ground unconscious. I stand over him, taking in air for a few moments before saying. "Who are you calling 'little lady' now?"

Then I turn away from him and run full on toward my family. I feel an intense warmth hit my body as I try to keep running towards my mother and brother. The invisible force is trying to push me away. Hold me in my place, but I continue to push.

I will reach my family.

Then I hear it.

A heart-wrenching scream.

My brother's head is back, his face looking at the sky. Mouth open.

"No!" He yells like a banshee.

A moment later, I'm thrown from my feet, sailing backward, past Serenity's concerned face. I'm about to hit the cave wall when I lift my arms at the last moment. I push all my energy to my hands, stopping my body in midair before I collide with the hard surface. I place myself lightly on the ground and make my way to Serenity's side.

"Are you ok?" I ask her,

She nods as she looks at my brother. "I fear it is not me you need to worry about."

"I have to reach him."

"If anyone can, it's you. You are each other's equal."

I nod and begin moving forward once more, using my power to ground my feet every step. I feel her hand on my wrist, stopping me in place.

"I need you to remember our conversation."

"I heard you. But right now, I can't promise I won't. If my mother is dying or dead. I won't lose her."

"Amberly, remember what I said. You will die in her place, not long from now if you do. I know your mother. As much as she wants to be here with all of you, she would not want you to trade your life for hers."

I rip my arm away, and she stumbles. Suddenly I feel angry with myself as I catch her before she hits the ground. "I'm sorry." She nods in understanding.

"Imagine how you feel right now. How you would feel without her. Now trade places. Would you want your mother here, without you, feeling the way you do now? Only her hurt would be much worse. Not only because you're her daughter and she failed as a parent to protect you but because you traded her life for yours."

Not wanting to admit I know she's right aloud, I only nod. "I need to get to my brother before Vladimir."

She nods in understanding with great sorrow in the depths of her eyes as she watches me go.

I push myself forward hard until I feel the invisible barrier break under my force. I run at full speed till I reach their side and drop to my knees next to them. My mother is unmoving. I can feel the anguish flowing off Aidan in waves. I place a hand on his shoulder as he lowers his head from the sky.

When he looks at me, I see a darkness in his eyes I've never seen in him before.

"Aidan?"

He's quiet.

"Aidan. Listen to my voice. Come back."

"Back to what?"

"To your sister. Your father. We are still here, and we need you."

He closes his black eyes. "No one needs me. I destroy everything I touch." He opens them and glances down at our stiff mother cradled in his long arms.

I take a moment to glance in Vladimir's direction. Hoping, praying he hasn't found a way through the shield like I have. Still far off in the distance, I see him banging on the invisible barrier, anger etched into his features as he takes a step back. Raising his hands, flames erupt from him in an inferno hitting the wall around us, but it doesn't shatter.

It's holding firm. For now, at least.

I place a comforting hand on Aidan's arm. "This isn't your doing. It's Vladimir's, and he will kill everyone here, everyone in this forest if we do not stop him."

He's silent.

I look down at our mother as tears form in my eyes. I push down the sadness and remember all the conversations with her and

Serenity that led us here. I peer up at Aidan. "What would she want us to do?"

I feel his body go limp under my hand. "She would want us to end him." He says the last two words with such conviction it gives me strength.

"Then let's do it. Let's fight." I say, standing, and as I look on at Vladimir, I feel my amulet against my skin, and I know it's time to give it my all.

$$* * *$$

JULIAN

"I don't understand why they sent us inside. We know he's coming." Troy says in an annoying voice.

Then again, he's always annoying to me. I find it hard to see what Amberly loves so much about him sometimes, but I try to tolerate his annoying behavior for her sake.

I sigh. "Because they want us to prepare."

"Prepare for what? All we've been doing is training. We should be out there waiting, not in here."

Logan turns to his friend with a stern look in his eyes. "Whatever Amberly's father tells us to do is what we do. He is the leader here."

Troy nods in understanding.

Angela takes Logan's hand in hers before adding. "I can't help but feel that Troy's right. We should be outside."

Amara, who is normally quiet around me, adds in her two cents. "What's taking them so long?"

Startled, I look at her.

"I mean, they sent us inside, but why didn't they follow?" She asks no one in particular.

"She's right." Angela glances at me. "Aaron would have followed right after with Jocelyn and his children. Something isn't right."

Without another word, I run for the cave entrance.

I hear their footsteps following.

I reach the entrance, and I'm welcomed with a swift punch in the face that sends me backward. Lifting my hand to cradle my jaw, I look up to see the woman I now know as Sage, and she's not alone.

"Hello, boys." She glances at Angela and then Amara. "And ladies. I have to say, Amara, I'm surprised you're still alive."

"I could say the same for you." She snarls in return.

Sage glances back at me. "And you. Didn't I kill you?"

I grin at her. "It didn't stick."

She sneers at me. "Well, maybe we should change that."

I see Angela trying to make her way to my side as Logan grabs her, holding her in her place. For once, I'm grateful for him. I turn my head in their direction while keeping Sage and her two friends in my view.

"You guys get going. I can handle this."

I can hear the worry in Angela's voice when she says. "Julian, no."

"Aaron and the others need you more than I do. I can handle three goons."

Troy walks over to my side. "I'll stay with him. You guys get going."

"This is going to be fun." Sage's sneer grows.

"You have no idea," Troy replies.

The others sneak around us and head for the exit. I look at Logan, "Watch out for her." I gesture towards Angela.

"Always." He smiles.

"And find Amberly."

He nods. "You know I will."

Troy

LOGAN

As much as I didn't want to leave Troy and Julian to fight alone, I know he was right. They can handle three of them, and Amberly and her family are going to need our help. Vladimir came here for them after all.

I feel my heart stop in my chest as I see Aidan on the ground holding their mother in his arms. She's not moving. Amberly is standing next to them, and I can tell from her body language she's ready to rain fire down on whoever is responsible.

I search the forest for Aaron until I see his unmoving body next to the cave wall, and my heart skips another beat.

Please don't let them both be dead.

I know Amberly couldn't survive if she lost them both. One would shatter her enough. I turn to Angela.

"Aaron's over there."

Her eyes locate him as she sucks in a breath. "I'm going to go check on him."

I nod. "Amara, go with her."

Without a word, they take off in his direction. My eyes continue to scan the dark, knowing there has to be more of his minions hiding, waiting to attack. To my right, I see a group of five men heading towards Amberly, whose focus is solely on Vladimir.

I lift my hands, sending the closest two hurtling into the trees. I hear a sickening crunch as they connect and drop to the ground below. The others take notice of me as they change direction.

"Now that I have your attention," I say with a smile.

The closest among the three raises his hands, sending a ball of flame in my direction. I deflect it without expelling any energy.

"Is that really the best you got?"

The man bares his teeth as his hands fly up, sending two more balls in my direction. He pulls his arms back and continues to launch more as I deflect each one like it's nothing. I can see the anger growing inside the man advancing on me.

Out of the corner of my eye, I see the other two beginning to flank me as a smile begins to creep upon his face. This was his plan. Keep me distracted long enough for one of them to take me out.

Nice try.

I deflect his next fireball then take his next two in my hands. The pain is excruciating. I feel my flesh burning underneath them as the smell of my burning flesh hits my nostrils, and I gag. Tears form in my eyes, making it hard to pinpoint where the other two are. Blinking a few times, I release the tears and find my targets.

Grinning through the pain, I whisper to myself. "Got ya."

I release the fire in my hands, sending one to my left and the other to my right. They find their targets seconds later. I watch them both as they fall to the earth.

"Now, where were we?" I ask the last man standing.

He pulls a knife from his belt.

"I see. Guess you want to fight dirty then."

His smile grows as he lunges towards me, knife extended.

I whip my hand out, knocking him at the wrist and sending the knife to the ground. I grab hold of his arm, keeping him in place as my fist connects with his jaw. Then his chest, his gut, and a right uppercut. Sending him to the dirt floor. I lean over him with my hand out over his head. I concentrate as hard as I can. Willing him unconscious until it takes hold.

***

ANGELA

I fall to my knee next to Aaron, turning him to face me as gently as I can. The first thing I notice is the huge gash at the base of his hairline. I place my hand a few inches over his mouth, checking for breath. It's slow, but it's there.

I sigh in relief.

"Is he ok?"

I turn to look up at Amara's worried expression. "He will be."

"What should we do?"

"I'm going to try to wake him."

Her eyes linger over to where Aidan, Amberly, and Jocelyn are. "Do you think that's a good idea?"

"What do you mean?"

"If he wakes up, he will want to fight. If he fights in his current condition, he will die. Then the pack will be without an alpha."

Looking down at my leader, I'm torn. I know she's right. A pack can't be alphaless. But nothing is more important to him than his family, and that includes the pack. He deserves to be in this fight.

I'm torn between my thoughts, and I don't realize I'm shaking him until his eyes begin to open.

"What?" Aaron touches his head lightly and winces. "What happened?"

I close my eyes, taking in a calming breath before I look over at where the rest of his family sits. He tries to get up, but I keep him in place.

"You need to take a second."

"Forget that." He says, pushing me to the side.

He doesn't make it five steps before he hits the barrier and is brought to his knees.

"I was trying to tell you."

"What is that?" He asks, bewildered.

"I'm not sure. I think it's coming from Aidan."

Amara breaks her silence. "It's a force field. Among other things."

We look at her in surprise.

"I learned a lot about Aidan when I was held captive."

Aaron looks at her, and I can see the pain in the lines of his face. "How do I reach him?"

She shakes her head.

I say. "There has to be away."

"Not that I know of. Once he's like that, nothing has ever reached him."

"What else does it do?" I ask, afraid of the answer.

"From the conversations I would hear between Vladimir and his other warriors, he was hoping to get Aidan to achieve something no one else ever has."

"And that would be?"

"The force field would grow so strong that anything on the outside of it that touched it would incinerate."

My mouth drops open. "What?"

Aaron says from the ground. "Did he ever get to that stage?"

"As far as I know, no."

"Then we should be fine." I can hear the uncertainty in his voice.

"We shouldn't take the chance." Amara pleads.

"She's right, Aaron."

"I have to get to my family."

I place a hand on his shoulder. "I agree. But I might have another idea."

He looks at me with pleading eyes.

"Amberly," I whisper.

Amara looks confused. "What about her?"

"She's with him. She can calm him."

"Yeah, ok. But how do you intend to reach her? We can't get in, remember?"

I smirk. "We don't have to."

* * *

JULIAN

Panting.

Trying to slow my heart rate.

Concentrate.

Focus.

Sage's smile is sinister in nature as she throws up her hands, launching her next attack. I dodge the incoming knife a moment before it would connect with my shoulder. I whip my head around just in time to see two more daggers flying through the air in my direction. I jump high, turning my body sideways as they pass on both sides of my body and sink into the earth wall behind me. I land on my feet, turning to glare in Sage's direction.

Her face is anything but happy.

I notice her hand ascending, and I know she's readying her next attack. I glance down to the dagger now at my feet. Closing my hand around the hilt, I send it sailing through the air as I'm struck in the chest with an energy blast. The force behind it sends me flying through the air at top speed. As I sail over Troy and the other two warriors, I glance in Sage's direction to see the dagger sink deep into her stomach, sending her to her knees. I smile before landing hard against the cave wall.

I hit the hard earth.

Breathe in slowly.

Make my way to my feet.

"Hey, man, you alright?" Troy yells over his shoulder.

Half standing, I whisper. "Don't worry about me. Focus on the fight."

He turns around to the others just in time to knock back his opponent's hand, that's now holding a knife inches from Troy's chest. Sensing the other, he ducks out of the way as his assailant misses him and his fist collides with the other's jaw, sending him rocking on his heels.

I smile. "That's more like it."

Troy grins over his shoulder at me before dropping low, shooting out his leg and spinning it around until it connects with the man's ankle, and he ends up on his back. Troy shoots to his feet and delivers the last blow to his enemy's face, rendering him unconscious.

"One down." He says.

"One to go," I reply.

He smirks. "Technically two."

I shake my head at him as I make it firmly into a standing position. I glance over to see Sage's hand on the hilt of the dagger that is still penetrating her abdomen.

I turn my attention to the other assailant as he charges at Troy, his fist pulled back. Troy smiles as he drops low, and the man passes him. They turn around to face each other once more, and that's when I see what the man is doing.

Troy doesn't.

"Troy, watch out," I yell.

The man's hand stops above Troy's chest as ice shoots out from his fingers and imbeds into his fragile skin. Troy's hand flies to the injured area as his mouth and eyes open wide, and he crumbles to the ground.

The attacker, not paying attention to me, doesn't notice until I'm on top of him. I extend my hand, raking my now four-inch-long nails down the length of his face to his chest. He screams in agony as he backs away from me. I grab him by his mangled shirt before landing three hard punches to his face, and now he too drops to the floor unconscious.

I waste no time as I drop to my knees next to Troy. "You ok?" I pant.

"I've been better." He croaks.

"We need to get you out of here," I say as I take his arm and wrap it around my neck.

"Not so fast," Sage says as she blocks our only exit.

I gently place Troy into a sitting position.

"Move," I growl at her.

"Not gonna happen, wolf boy."

I throw my hands down on either side of my body as my nails extend into claws once more. I growl. "Let's end this."

"That's what I'm talking about."

I lunge for her, but she's fast. I turn around as her knife sinks its tip into the hot flesh of my shoulder. Baring my teeth against the pain, I push her away from me hard. She staggers, and as she's correcting herself, I remove the blade from my body in one fast motion.

I drop it to the earth floor, feeling the hot thick fluid running down my shoulder along my arm as Sage's grin widens.

"That's more like it. I did promise to make it permanent this time, right?"

Knowing she has more in her arsenal than me, I have to think before I act. Which, for me, is a hard thing to do. I'm not much for thinking. I look around the room, searching for anything I can use to render her unconscious like the others.

I need to get to Amberly.

I need to get Troy out of here.

"I don't have time for this," I say out loud.

"Oh, well, I'm sorry. Am I interrupting something important?"

I growl as I run at her full-on. Ready to take her out.

She moves at the last second, I pass her, and she brings her elbow down hard on my back. I stumble until I hit the cold cave wall once more.

"You don't seem to be putting up much of a fight this time around."

I look over to see Troy's eyes closing. Panic starts to set in. Amberly would kill me if anything happened to him. I'm already on thin ice with her after our last conversation. I grind my teeth in frustration.

"Hey, Troy, wake up, man."

His eyes drift open at a snail's pace.

"You good?"

He puts up a thumb and adds a weak smile, for effect, I'm sure.

I look back towards Sage as I whisper, "Great." Unenthusiastically I might add.

Things aren't going so well.

"Loverboy isn't looking so good," Sage says with a mocking tone.

"Don't worry about him. Let's finish this. That's what you want, right?"

"Bet your ass."

I grin, hoping to bait her. "You want Vladimir to be proud of his little warrior."

She flashes her teeth at me in annoyance. "Shut up."

"From what I heard, you already let down Aidan and then angered Vladimir when you lost Aidan to our side."

"You know nothing." She growls.

It's working.

"I hate to break it to you, but killing me won't make him happy." I laugh.

"One less annoying mouth standing in his way."

"True, but not the right 'annoying mouth,' as you call it."

She stares at me, confused.

"I'm not the threat he needs to worry about. I mean, I can barely handle you on my own, am I right?" The words are bitter in my mouth.

"Get to your point, mongrel."

"Aidan is the real threat. You're wasting your time here with me."

"My master can handle him and your bitch."

I push my rage at her words as far down as I can.

I must not react.

"I'm sure he can." I shrug. "But he would be in awe of you if you took him out yourself, don't you think?"

I can see the wheels beginning to turn in her head.

I've got her.

"You're only trying to save your own skin." The words come slowly through her gritted teeth.

"Well, I do prefer to live. But hey, only giving you advice. What you do with it is entirely up to you."

Her eyes glance behind her. I can see she's unsure of what to do next.

She's mine.

I lunge forward and drop low at the last second. Taking her out at the knees. I jump on top of her once she's down.

"Submit."

"Never." She growls while wiggling forcefully underneath me.

"So be it."

I never liked hitting a girl, but in this case, I really don't have much choice, and I don't have the heart to kill her. I'm not that kind of person. She might not have blinked twice when she took my life. However, for me, it would haunt me until my last day on this earth. Until now, I haven't taken one life, and I plan on keeping it that way.

"I'm sorry about this," I whisper as I raise my fist.

"Go to hell."

"I'm already there," I reply as I land my blow.

She's out cold.

I jump off her and run to Troy's side.

"Hey, man. How you holding up?"

"I'm a trooper."

I chuckle. "That you are. Now let's get you out of here."

"But the girls."

I wrap his arm around my neck. "I'll take care of them. I need to get you somewhere safe first."

"Man, don't worry about me." He says in a defeated tone.

For the first time, I really look him over. Blood is dripping from the corner of his mouth. Enough to trail off his chin and leave a puddle now on his white and bloodred shirt. I feel my heart jump.

"It's too late for me, man."

"Don't talk like that. Amberly can heal you."

He shakes his head lightly. "Not in time, brother."

"Then Serenity."

I see the sadness forming in his eyes. "I won't let her."

"The hell you won't," I say angrily.

"She's already dying, man, and I ain't gonna be able to live with myself if she heals me and dies after."

"Like you said, she's already dying."

He looks away from me. "Yes. But if she heals me, she will die now. Not later."

"Why don't you let her make that decision?"

He glances at me, and I can see the fire in his eyes. "Because it should be my choice, no one else's."

All cards are in now. "What about Logan, Amara, and Amberly? Don't you think they need you?"

He smiles. "No one needs me, man."

"You're kidding, right?"

"Hey, you know it's true. I'm the funny guy and the troublemaker. I have nothing more to offer than that."

"Dude. Stop talking like that. Amberly loves you like a brother. To her, you're one of the people she treasures most."

I see the tears forming in his eyes.

I place my arm firmly around his back, straightening us both. "I'm getting you help."

Help Is On The Way

SERENITY

I see Julian holding up Troy as his feet drag behind him, leaving a path in their wake. I take a few steps forward to meet them.

"What happened?"

Troy forces a smile, but I see the pain beneath it. "Someone caught me by surprise. Nothing big."

Julian rolls his eyes as he turns his attention to me. I can see the question he's afraid to ask lingering on the surface of his eyes. "Could you. Would you be able to?"

I nod. "I can heal him."

"No," Troy says the words with great effort.

"Young man, it is not your time."

"I won't let you trade your life for mine."

I smile at him and his courage. "I have lived more than one full life. Try not to think of it as trading one life for another. Think of Amberly. She's going to need you." I glance at Julian. "Both of you. The next battle is already at your front door, and it's nothing like this one. You will need each other if you're going to survive it."

"Another battle. Great. Just let me die in peace." Troy says sarcastically. He looks at my serious expression and frowns. "Sorry. I was trying to make light of the situation. The thought of another battle isn't something I relish."

"I understand. But the other seven are here, and there is no stopping the final battle."

"The other seven," Julian says in almost a whisper.

I nod.

"I thought that we would have time before." He goes silent.

"I wish I could say that was the case."

His eyes are cold as he stares me down. "How long do we have?"

I hesitate.

"How long?"

I sigh. "Days, I'm afraid. Maybe a week."

"Days!" Troy yells and regrets it moments after as he clenches his chest.

"As long as you stay together. Have each other's backs like I've seen, then you will win this battle. But if one of you falls or there is hostility between any in your group," I look at Julian until I know he understands what I'm trying to say to him silently. "You will fail. You must be united on all fronts."

Julian looks behind him, and I know he's searching for Amberly.

"Do you understand what I'm saying?"

Julian nods.

"What about you, young man? Do you wish to die or stay and help your friends survive the next threat?"

His smile is tight. "Where do I sign up?"

I chuckle. "You are an interesting young man if I do say so."

"Hey, I've been called worse."

"Hang on to that sarcasm. People need your humor more than you realize."

I can see the question in his eyes, but I ignore it as I lay my hands over his wound.

"Wait." I can hear the fear in Troy's voice.

Ignoring his concern, I focus all my strength and picture his wounds mending. The tips of the ice emerging from his open flesh, then his skin stitching itself back together. Troy moves under my hands, making me lose focus.

"Hold him still," I say to Julian.

I feel the ice move under my hands to the surface. I take it and throw it to the ground as the boys gape at me in wonder. I smile lightly as my hands go to work once more. Closing my eyes, I picture the tears in his chest, muscle, tendons being repaired. I know it's working as Troy gasps and moves slightly under my touch. I take in a slow breath as I move my efforts to close his wounds. My energy drains faster than I planned. My breathing is becoming labored, and I see the worry forming on their faces.

"Almost there," I whisper.

The last of his flesh closes as my hands drop to my sides.

"Done." I look at Troy. "How do you feel?"

Staring at me in awe, he places his hands at the opening in his shirt. Pulling them back to inspect.

"I. I feel great." He looks down at me as sadness forms in his eyes. "Thank you."

"No need."

"You saved my life. A thank you is the least I can do."

Julian knees down beside me. "What can we do?"

"There's nothing to be done. This day was coming one way or the other. At least this way, I can make a difference."

Julian nods before turning his attention to Troy. "I need to find Amberly. Stay with her."

Troy nods.

I grab Julian by the arm. "She will be fine. The battle is almost over. There is something we must talk about."

He settles on the ground next to me.

"There is something I need you to do."

"Anything." They say in unison.

"Amberly."

"What about her?" Julian's tone is full of worry.

"You must not let her bring anyone back from the dead today. Even if they are only close to death. Do you understand?"

"Why? She did it before with this lug head." Troy throws a thumb in Julian's direction, getting a scowl in return.

"Things are different now. But her healing you like she did it took more from her than she thinks."

Worry is clear on Julian's face. "What do you mean?"

"As I've mentioned, when we heal someone, we are taking their wounds on ourselves, and by bringing someone back from the dead, it's like healing over a hundred people on the brink of death."

Julian looks at his hands.

"If she heals anyone today, she will die in the battle ahead. And if she does, all will be lost. She is meant to lead this land and bring peace back to the forest." I look between the two of them. "Do you understand?"

They nod.

"The fate of our worlds lies with you kids. I know it isn't fair, but it's the cards we are dealt. Stick together, and you will have a better ending than my family, and I have."

My chest tightens dramatically, making breathing difficult. "It's almost time. Please tell my family my last thoughts were of them and that I am at peace now."

Another nod from them both.

I smile, knowing they will be alright. Knowing that what I did here today will make a difference and that I helped bring peace back to my homeland in some way. A peace that I wish I could see but know I won't. For the first time, I'm ok with it. I close my eyes as I struggle to take in one last breath. I feel someone take my hand, and I smile.

They give it a light squeeze, and at the same moment, I release what will be my last breath on this earth.

Amberly. Can you hear me? I look around frantically at Angela's voice.

My eyes lock with her's about thirty feet away. She smiles sadly.

"How?" I ask.

I'm in your head.

I forgot we could do that.

She pauses. *It's not a wolf thing. I used your own power. How's your mom?*

I freeze. *I. I don't know for sure. Aidan won't let her go.*

Listen, you need to calm him down.

I scoff. *I don't know if I can.*

Amberly, if you don't, we are all going to die.

What?

For the first time, I see my dad sitting up against the cave wall as Angela looks at him, and he nods his head. Tears begin to fill my eyes. *He's ok.*

Vladimir was teaching Aidan how to go nuclear.

At the mention of his name, I look in his direction once more to find him pacing in fury along the perimeter of the barrier.

Addressing Angela, I ask, *What do you mean?*

I can sense her hesitation as the words come out slowly. *His force field. The one he's sending out right now. You and he are safe inside, but anyone on the outside... If he reaches that level and it touches us, it won't only keep us out. It will incinerate everyone*

here. Do you understand?

My heart skips about four beats inside my chest. I whisper. *I*

understand. I will find a way to calm him down.

If anyone can, it's you.

Her voice disappears. I take in a slow deep breath before I find

my place on my knees next to my brother once more.

"Aidan."

Nothing.

"I need you to listen to me. I need you to calm down. Shut down

your force field."

"I can't."

I place a reassuring hand on his shoulder. "I'm right here with

you."

He looks at me with anger embedding in every feature of his

face. "Don't you get it? I let it down, and he kills us."

I shake my head. "He won't."

"How can you be so sure?"

I take his trembling hand in mine and bring it to my heart.

"Because we are finally together."

He closes his eyes and lets the tears run down his face. "I won't

let him take you from me. Not again."

I lift his chin with my finger until his eyes meet mine. "I'm not

going anywhere."

He looks down at our mother, still unmoving. "I couldn't stop this."

"This isn't your fault. It's his. Now it's time to end this."

He glances over at me as he sets his jaw in sheer determination nodding hard in agreement. He pulls our mother into an embrace one last time as I hear him whisper. "I will end this for you. You will always be my mother. Never enough time, but I will hold you in my heart forever."

I hold back the violent sobs scratching their way to the surface as he places our mother gently on the ground beside us. He stands in one fast motion, offering me his hand. I take it willingly as he pulls me to my feet.

"You ready, sister?"

I nod.

He looks at where Vladimir is standing, throws his head to the sky, and screams a heart-wrenching yell. I find myself shrinking into his side, holding on for dear life. The energy around us is intense and hot. In the next moment, he looks back in Vladimir's direction, and I swear I see the force field shrink in around us until it all forms around his head. Then with one last yell, it shoots out in the direction of Vladimir. Hitting him square in the chest and sending him flying through the air.

Without hesitation, I release my brother and throw my arms up high.

"This is for my mother."

I feel the heat rising in my left hand and the cool in my right. Moments later, I release a yell of my own as fire, and an energy stream escapes my hands and hits Vladimir in the chest. As he screams, I smile.

Aidan stands next to me, raising his hands now to form a glow I've never seen before. It's a mix of maroon and lavender. The most beautiful thing I've ever seen, but my nerves tell me instinctively that whatever it is, it's deadly.

He sends it flying in the same direction. As it hits home, Vladimir screams once more. Then a smile forms on his face as he yells.

"This isn't over. You think you've won." He laughs through his cry of pain. "I was only the beginning. Something bigger and much worse is coming."

A moment later, I see his body begin to disintegrate into the atmosphere around him, and I see my brother, out of the corner of my eye, drop to his knees.

Death Takes My Heart

Troy

"We should find Johnathan and Aayda," I say in a whisper.

This fearless woman I barely had time to know willingly saved my life, knowing it would cost her hers. I promise to make it count. If what she says is true, this battle may be won and over, but another is on the horizon. I will ensure we prevail in the coming battle and make my life and her sacrifice mean something.

"I need to find Amberly first," Julian says from somewhere far away.

I turn to find him walking in the direction the fight had been taking place. "Serenity said they would be fine. I think we owe it to her to find her family first."

He stops and turns to face me. "Amberly is my family. I need to know for myself she is safe. Once I do, I will find them. Do not leave her side."

I nod my head in agreement.

I wouldn't go anywhere even if I needed to. The least I could do is sit with her until someone else who deserved to was able. For the first time, I notice similarities between this woman and Amberly. At least what I know about her. Amberly wouldn't hesitate to sacrifice herself for someone she loved or if it was for the greater good. Suddenly I remember Serenity's last words. Someone must have died in the fight. But who?

I suddenly feel torn. I want to make sure everyone is safe. I know Amberly is since the warning was about her healing someone else. But what about Amara, Logan, Angela, or Amberly's family?

Someone is dead.

If not for Serenity's words, I would still know it.

I can feel it.

In my chest.

Something is terribly wrong.

I glance down at Serenity's serene face as my chest tightens. I can feel that this death isn't only going to affect Amberly but me as well.

I feel something shifting inside, and I can't understand why.

"Please, Logan. You better be ok, or I swear I'll be coming to the underworld myself to bring you back."

✳ ✳ ✳

ANGELA

I open my eyes as I feel the air around me change and calm. It takes them a moment to adjust, and when they do, Amberly is the first thing I see. Her and her brother. I turn to Aaron, his expression mute.

"Are you alright?"

He doesn't answer.

"Angela, why don't you go check on things?" Amara gestures in Amberly's direction, and then I remember. "I'll stay with Aaron."

"I'm fine. I want to go check on my family." He mutters.

"Amara's right. You're hurt. I'll go and come right back. Stay here."

He ignores my words as he tries to stand and lands right back on the dirt floor moments later with a grunt in annoyance.

"Yeah. Fine." He says, defeated.

I haven't seen him look this bad since before he learned his family was alive, and for his sake, I hope they still are. I don't know how he can handle losing them again. I know if it was me, I wouldn't survive it. But Aaron isn't me. He's strong, and he has the pack. He will make it through this. I will make sure of that.

I walk slowly. Taking in Amberly's stone-like posture as she sits next to her brother on the ground. Jocelyn hasn't moved once. My heart skips a beat as I take my last step towards them.

"Amberly," I whisper.

She doesn't move.

"Is she?" I can't say the word.

Amberly moves slowly, turning her face in my direction. Her expression and the tears that now cover her face tell me all I need to know.

Jocelyn is dead.

Aaron's heart will be shattered.

I fear there is nothing anyone can do to make this alright for him. With her death so, comes his.

***

AMBERLY

I hear footsteps behind me, but I can't move. Fluid runs down my face in a waterfall, and part of me is unsure if it's blood or tears as my face begins to sting. I can't take my eyes off my mother. Her eyes haven't opened once, and her body has been unmoving. As I replay Serenity's words in my mind, anger pulls at my heart.

"You will lose someone in this battle. Someone who means more to you than you know. You will want to save them, but you can't. Do you understand?"

I can't speak. I'm hoping I'm hearing her wrong.

"Amberly, I need to know you understand what I'm saying. Time is short."

"I. You're asking me to let someone I love die?"

"You must."

"I don't understand. Why would it matter if I saved one person?"

"You bringing back Julian took more from you than I think you realize. He was dead Amberly, not dying. You brought him back. That is impossible for most healers, and you did it your first time.

And in doing so, you took a huge hit to your life essence. What you did was like saving over one hundred people on the edge of death at once."

"Ok. So I'll be more careful."

She releases my hand. "There is another battle on the horizon. Vladimir is only the beginning. You will need your strength, your power, for that battle. If you use it this time, you will be done, and you will fall in the battle ahead."

"Fall?" I choke on the word.

She nods.

"You mean..."

"You'll die."

A chill washes over my body as my palms begin to sweat.

"Do you understand now?" She asks in a sad tone.

"Yes," I whisper.

I know what I promised, but looking at my mother now, I don't think it's one I can keep.

"Amberly." Angela's voice calls to me from behind.

I don't answer. I can't. I know what she's going to ask, and I can't say it. Tears burn my cheeks as they run down my battered face in waves.

"Is she...?"

Still no words.

I turn my face slowly toward her, and I can see in her eyes she understands. I bow my head and move closer to my brother, placing one hand on his and another on my mother's.

"Aidan," I whisper. "I need you to give her to me. I can fix this."

His eyes have a river hiding in them when he turns to me. "I. I can't let her go."

"I can fix this. Trust me. It will be alright."

He nods his head forcefully as Angela's voice comes from behind me. "What are you going to do?"

"I'm going to save my mother."

"Are you sure that's a good idea? What if something goes wrong?"

I glare at her with more anger than I mean as she flinches away. "I did it with Julian, and he was dead for days."

"I know. But there were complications, remember, and we still don't know if he is really ok."

I scowl. "What's that supposed to mean?"

"I'm only saying you don't understand this power yet. None of us do. What if there is a consequence?"

I recall Serenity's warning again. "Consequences be damned. I'm getting my mother back. I dare you to try to stop me."

She looks hurt at my words. "I didn't mean it like that, Amberly. I love your mother."

"But she's not your mother. She's mine. You don't know what I'm feeling."

Shock takes over her features. "Don't I? Or have you forgotten I lost everyone when I was much younger than you are now?"

"I didn't forget."

"I've never seen you like this before."

I sigh. "Like what?"

She hesitates for a moment. "Cruel."

"I'm not cruel, Angela. I'm honest. There's nothing I can do about your family, but I can do something about mine. I'm sorry that's the way it is, but I can do nothing for your family. If I could, I would, so don't stop me from saving mine."

I can see the defeat as her body slumps forward. "Do what you want, Amberly. I'm not going to stop you."

"But I will." Julian's voice sounds behind Angela, and I don't see him until she moves to the side.

"What?" I ask in disbelief.

"You can't heal her, Amberly. But you already knew that."

I look at him in astonishment. *He couldn't possibly know.*

"Serenity is dead." His words are greeted with a gasp of surprise from Angela.

"How?" She asks.

"Troy was hurt really bad." He must see the worry forming in my eyes as his next words are, "he's fine now. She healed him."

Angela moves closer to him. "She traded her life for his?"

He nods. "But not before telling me something. Something you already know, Amberly."

"It doesn't matter," I say through bared teeth.

He kneels down next to me. "Yes. It. Does. Do you really think she would want you to bring her back if she knew the price?"

Aidan looks over at us for the first time. "What price?"

Julian's eyes never leave mine. "If Amberly saves her today, then she will die in the coming battle."

Aidan's eyes go wide as he looks from me to our mother. "You can't."

"I have to."

He looks at me with sheer determination in his features. "You can't, and you won't. That's final."

"Who are you? You're not my father."

He sighs. "No, but I'm sure he would agree with us. Should I go ask him?"

I look at the ground.

"I didn't think so."

"So you want me to just let her die?"

I hear Aidan suck in a breath. "She's already dead, Amberly."

"But I can save her."

"Not if it costs us you," Aidan says in a tone that lets me know his decision is final.

***

AMARA

With my arm around Aaron, I help him stand. "Let's get you inside."

"I don't want to go inside." He sounds defeated. "I want to see my family."

Knowing I won't win this argument, I mumble. "Ok," as we take our first steps in their direction.

I see a few shapes to my left. Looking over, I stop in my tracks.

"What is it?"

"I think we have a problem," I say in a whisper.

He follows my gaze as his eyes lock onto a group of Vladimir's soldiers walking towards us in a daze. "Stay behind me," he says as he puts his arm in front of me, moving me behind him.

The group approaches us slowly.

The man in the front stares at us in a puzzled fashion. "Do you know where we are?" He asks.

I look at Aaron, then the man, wondering if this is some kind of diversion. Aaron must be thinking the same thing as I see his eyes darting all around, looking for signs of an attack.

The man takes one step closer as he gestures to the people behind him. "We have no idea where we are. We've been trying to remember how we got here, but none of us can remember anything for the last few years." He glances to the back of the group as people continue to fall in behind them, "some of us even longer."

Aaron's voice is hoarse when he asks. "You don't remember coming here?"

The man shakes his head no.

"Do you remember Vladimir?"

The man looks terrified as he answers. "We've heard of him, yes. However, I get the feeling you mean something more than that."

"I do," Aaron says as he looks down at me. "Do you recognize this young lady?"

The man I recognize from my time being held captive looks me over. I can see in his eyes he's trying to recall a memory. "I'm sorry, I don't. Should I?"

Aaron looks dumbstruck. "I feel, my friends, that you were all under mind control."

The crowd begins to chat among themselves. I hear muffled conversations taking place.

"What did he say?" I hear a woman in the back ask.

Another, closer to the front, "What is he talking about?"

"My mind is too strong for that."

Lastly, "He's crazy."

Aaron raises his hands as he addresses the growing crowd gathering in front of us. "I know you are all lost and confused, and we will help however we can. For now, feel free to head inside. Get cleaned up and have something to eat. You can sleep here for the night, and tomorrow we can try to help you make sense of things. Or help you find your way back home."

The murmuring continues as the group makes its way past us into the cave. Some talking about how Aaron is generous, others asking how they can trust someone they don't know. Once the last person makes it inside, I turn to Aaron.

"What is going on?"

He tiredly rubs his eyes. "It seems our dear friend didn't get his recruits willingly."

"We knew he was brainwashing people."

"Yes. But as far as we thought, most of them joined of their own accord. However, as you can see, that isn't the case. These people are going to need a lot of help."

I smile at him. "It's a good thing they have you."

His face shows no expression. "I fear I can't help them. Not now."

"If anyone can, it's you."

His eyes soften as they look at me. "For now, let's just make them comfortable, and we can figure out the rest tomorrow."

I nod in agreement.

"Now. I would like to get to my family."

Aaron walks towards them, leaving me standing alone. For the first time since I've arrived here, I feel nothing can be done to piece this pack back together. I had hope in the battle, even believed we would win, but I never saw this coming. And I don't know how to help.

As I watch a broken man make his way to his family, I wish I was anywhere but here for the first time.

✳✳✳

JULIAN

The anger is clear in her body language as Amberly shifts away from her brother. Before I can say another word, I hear Aaron walking up behind me.

"Julian, Angela, we have guests who need some assistance inside the cave."

Confused, Angela asks, "Guests?"

"It seems Vladimir did more damage than we thought. Most of his so-called warriors have been brainwashed, and now that he's dead, his influence is gone. However, no one can remember anything."

"There was no end to that monster's doings."

Aaron sighs, looking defeated. "It appears not."

I place my hand on the back of his shoulder. "What do you need from us?"

"Can you get them comfortable? I don't feel like dealing with anything tonight. Just do what you can for them."

I nod before turning to Angela. "Let's go."

She looks down at Amberly sadly before walking towards the cave. I glance down at Amberly. "I'll be right inside if you need me."

"I don't need anything from you." She says without looking at me.

I turn away, taking my first step away from her. I feel the distance growing between us like a weight on my chest. Each step making it harder to breathe. I don't know how we are going to make it through this. I literally just told the love of my life to let her mother stay dead when we both know she could bring her back to life.

What can I say? I'm selfish. I love her mom, but I love Amberly more, and I need her. I can live without her mother but not her. The question is, will she be able to live without her? Will Aidan? Will Aaron?

I look back to see Aaron now on his knees next to his children and Jocelyn in his arms. He's bent over, holding her close to his chest, and even from this distance, I can see his body shaking from his sobs.

My heart is breaking for them. I don't know how Aaron will make it through this again. Once was enough. I saw the joy and the change in him since his family returned. Without them, he is a fraction of a man. I know I would be the same. The thought of continuing my life without Amberly in it doesn't bear thinking about.

I can handle her being mad at me, not talking to me. But not being here alive? That's something I couldn't live through. I can wait out the time before she speaks to me again. That's something I can handle. But if she was dead, that would be final. I would never see her again, talk to her, hold her. And that is an unbearable reality.

What am I going to do?

Serenity warned us. Not only was Amberly not to heal anyone, but we need to be a united front in order to win the battle ahead, and right now? Right now, we are more fractured than ever.

***

JOHNATHAN

Looking down at Aayda as she holds Serenity's limp body in her lap is a sight I prayed to never see. We have buried everyone we have ever loved. Now all that's left is each other. It's more than enough for me. But for Aayda? As much as I know she loves me, she needed Serenity.

She was something for us to hold onto from our life way back when. When things were peaceful and happy. Now that Vladimir is gone and we've won this war, it still feels like a loss. Serenity was the best of us, and we all knew it. The world is going to miss such a bright light, as we already do.

Whispers say that Serenity wasn't the only casualty in tonight's fight. People are saying Jocelyn fell taking a blast that was meant for her son. Knowing the kind of mother she was, I know it to be true, and my heart aches twice. Once for my family and me and our loss, and another for Jocelyn and her family.

I only pray that Amberly doesn't do something rash. She knows now that she has the power to bring someone back from the dead. However, Serenity told us what would happen if she was to do it again before the final battle.

She would fall.

And with her death, the light and hope for our world would dim once and for all. I only pray Amberly will listen. I know it's not a fair fate and one I wish I could spare her.

This world is a cruel place, and life is unfair, but we must take what we are given and make the most of it. We are stronger than we believe, and we can overcome any obstacle in our way. There will be bloodshed, pain, heartbreak, but we can and will rise above it. Once we do, we will be better for it.

I place my hand on Aayda's shoulder, praying it gives her some comfort. She squeezes my hand tight as she presses her tear-soaked cheek against it.

Things are forever changed.

The question is, will this future be the one we hoped and prayed for, or are we destined for a fate much worse than our past?

$$***$$

CELINE

Watching them from a distance makes me only want to act now. Why wait? They are broken, shattered, and separated. Now would be the best time to take them all out. Get justice for our fallen

leader. For the only father, we have ever known.

I look at my brother to see that his anger is a mirror image of my

own.

Cole grinds his teeth before he speaks. "What should we do, Mr.

and Mrs. Grayson?"

The older woman moves forward out of the shadows with a

sneer on her face. "How many times must I tell you, Cole? Call us

Annabeth, or Anne for short, and Henry. No need to be so formal.

Not between us."

Cole nods.

Annabeth steps next to us. "Fighting them now would be

pointless. We would lose."

My anger boils in my chest, and I'm speaking before I realize it.

"We can take them."

She turns in my direction with a smile. "My dear girl. We may

have taken out a few of theirs, but our leader is now gone. We

would be smart to regroup and gather the rest of the seven. Then

we can return and take our revenge."

Cole's tone sounds uncertain when he asks. "Do you really not

care?"

"About what, my son?"

"Your daughter. She was one of the fallen."

Anger, like I've never seen before, shines in her eyes. "That girl was not our daughter. She was tainted. Mixing with that mutt. She is no longer of pure blood." She shakes her head. "No. Our daughter died long ago."

"And what of your grandchildren? What of Aidan?" I ask.

She smiles in a sinister way as her husband mirrors her expression. "Let them burn. Let them all burn."

Thank You For Reading

I would like to personally thank all my readers and all of you who stood by me and continue to do so. I hope you have enjoyed the Dark Inheritance series so far. Keep an eye open for the release of the final in the series.

Please feel free to leave an honest review on my Goodreads, Amazon, and Instagram pages. Anywhere is appreciated as reviews in any form help authors know what worked and how to improve. They also help readers decide if it is a book they would be interested in reading for themselves. So I thank you for your time on reading and reviewing my work and for giving my books a chance. I hope you'll continue with me on this journey.

Below you can find the links for reviews or where to connect with me.

Amazon Author Page –

https://www.amazon.com/~/e/B09BPQQZ31

Amazon leave a review –

https://www.amazon.com/Moonlight-Legacy-Dark-Inheritance-3-ebook/dp/B09FFQ5YVP/ref=sr_1_3?crid=5SINGLSDAYWV&dchild=1&keywords=laura+lukasavage&qid=1631375741&sprefix=laura+lu%2Caps%2C158&sr=8-3

Goodreads Author Page–

https://www.goodreads.com/lauralukasavageauthor

Instagram – @Lauralukasavageauthor

Website –

https://lauralukasavageauthor.mailchimpsites.com/

Twitter – @LauraLukasavag1

About The Author

Laura Lukasavage started writing shortly after her mother's passing when she was only fourteen years old. She remembered how her mom would write poems and letters to her stepdad, and as a way to feel close to her mother, she took up writing. She started with poems in eighth grade and then short stories in high school. Once she started college in 2009 at Neumann University in Aston, PA, her interest only grew. By the time she would transfer from Neumann to Rowan University in Glassboro, NJ, in 2011, after her father's passing, is when she knew what her passions truly were. She majored in Radio, TV, and Film productions with a minor in creative writing. She found her love of film and writing meshed together, and this is where she felt at peace. Laura writes as a way to escape from reality but also to deal with life as a whole.

She writes hoping that one day her books will be an escape for someone needing them, just like the books she read in high school to escape the recent loss of her mother.